Praise ...

"A deliciously flavored duel of hearts. . . . Ms. Burrows concocts a heady romantic potion for Regency fans to savor."
—*Romantic Times*

"Maui magic and the enchantment of the islands are not to be underestimated, especially in matters of the heart. . . . You can almost feel the tradewinds." —*Booklist*

"Will entice the audience . . . simply fun."
—*Midwest Book Review*

"Burrows scores points." —*Publishers Weekly*

Miss Thornrose and the Rake

Geraldine Burrows

A SIGNET BOOK

SIGNET
Published by New American Library, a division of
Penguin Group (USA) Inc., 375 Hudson Street,
New York, New York 10014, USA
Penguin Group (Canada), 10 Alcorn Avenue, Toronto,
Ontario M4V 3B2, Canada (a division of Pearson Penguin Canada Inc.)
Penguin Books Ltd., 80 Strand, London WC2R 0RL, England
Penguin Ireland, 25 St. Stephen's Green, Dublin 2,
Ireland (a division of Penguin Books Ltd.)
Penguin Group (Australia), 250 Camberwell Road, Camberwell, Victoria 3124,
Australia (a division of Pearson Australia Group Pty. Ltd.)
Penguin Books India Pvt. Ltd., 11 Community Centre, Panchsheel Park,
New Delhi - 110 017, India
Penguin Group (NZ), Cnr Airborne and Rosedale Roads, Albany,
Auckland 1310, New Zealand (a division of Pearson New Zealand Ltd.)
Penguin Books (South Africa) (Pty.) Ltd., 24 Sturdee Avenue,
Rosebank, Johannesburg 2196, South Africa

Penguin Books Ltd., Registered Offices:
80 Strand, London WC2R 0RL, England

Published by Signet, an imprint of New American Library, a division of
Penguin Group (USA) Inc. Previously published in a Five Star Romance edition.

First Signet Printing, October 2004
10 9 8 7 6 5 4 3 2 1

For all my boys

Chapter One

In Which We Meet Our Heroine, Mistress Reform, Miss Verity Thornrose

*I*n the smoky purple twilight, the night haunts of the city
were beginning to come alive. The proprietors of the gaming hells lined up the ivory dice boxes and dusted off the green
baize tables. In the gin mills, the casks of Blue Ruin were set
up and tapped open while fresh straw was put down on the
floor for the benefit of those who became too drunk to stagger
home. The doors to the taverns, the cider cellars, the bagnios
and brothels were thrown open, and snatches of boisterous
laughter and bawdy song spilled out into the warren of side
streets that surrounded Covent Garden.

London's choice spirits were on the streets as well, traversing the district in search of an evening's lurid pleasure.
Young bucks, claret-cozy and ripe for any spree, mixed it up
with jolly workingmen made jolly by too much ale and looking for blokes to brawl with. Beggars keened their misfortunes while cutpurses and pickpockets sized up their marks.
And flitting among the Covent Garden crowds like so many
gaudy muslin moths were the women of the town, their
nightly promenade along the piazza already begun. Plying
their trade under names like Kitty Kitten, Betsy Careless, and
Brazen Belinda, they strolled along the marketplace's
columned portico, hoping to attract the attention of the rich
gents passing in their carriages.

In the midst of all the wanton, riotous gaiety, a young girl
stood shivering in the shadow of one of the piazza columns,

watching with wide, fearful eyes the nighttime panorama of sashaying cyprians, staggering drunks, and swaggering bucks. The shadows that surrounded the young girl were not quite deep enough to conceal the vivid tumble of red curls and the prettiness that somehow triumphed over the hunger that had gnawed her cruelly these past few weeks.

And now a carriage was slowing down before her, its door swinging open in licentious invitation . . .

But she could not. She just could not.

She turned to flee, only to be confronted by a worse menace. White Willie, the Arch Cove of Covent Garden, stood before her, his hair glowing white as a gravestone weird in the torchlight, his misshapen frame clad in mismatched finery filched from drunken gentlemen—or dead ones. He reached out and seized her by the hair, pulling her face frighteningly close to his strange pink-eyed countenance.

"And where d'ye think you're scuttling off to, you lazy Irish slut. Either you get in that carriage and earn some silver or it's back on the streets with you."

He gave her a shove that sent her stumbling to the door of the waiting carriage. But no lust-inflamed gentleman with unbuttoned breeches reached out to accost her. Instead, the carriage held two women: one, stout and middle-aged; the other, young and slender, with a face like an ivory cameo.

"Don't be afraid," said the beautiful young woman. "We want to help you. But you must come with us quietly."

"Aye, child," seconded the older woman in a rich brogue, "'tis helping you, we are."

They reached out their kid-gloved hands to her, and yanked her smartly off her feet and into the coach without so much as a by-your-leave. And then she saw the weighted baton lying on the carriage seat beside the stout woman, and the air rushed out of her lungs in a gasp of fear. She knew who had her now! The terrible Mrs. Peggy O'Grady who snatched Irish girls off the streets, knocked them unconscious with her baton, and took them away never to be seen again.

"She's spooked!" bawled out Peggy O'Grady. "Get a griphold on her, Miss Verity."

Miss Verity did, despite the unwilling prisoner's struggles. "I'm sorry if our methods seem a little rough and ready," she apologized as she knelt on the writhing girl's rib cage, "but we can't have all this screaming." And she cut her captive off in mid-screech by the simple expedient of thrusting a batiste handkerchief into her mouth. "It's a perfectly *clean* handkerchief, I assure you—"

"Miss Verity," cried out Peggy O'Grady, "it's trouble we've got."

A man's shaggy head pushed through the curtained coach window—one of White Willie's flash coves trying to prevent the loss of yet another doxy to the terrible Mrs. O'Grady. Miss Verity kept a wickedly long hatpin in her chip bonnet for just such emergencies, but she was unable to unsheathe it at the moment, being engaged with her flailing captive. Mrs. O'Grady was more than equal to the occasion, however. Snatching up her dear late husband's steel-weighted baton, she struck the flash cove squarely in the forehead. His eyes rolled back and he fell away from the coach with a thump.

"Drive on, Riley! Drive on!" shouted Mrs. O'Grady.

The coach gathered speed, but not before a grimy hand at the end of a sinewy arm snaked in through the window. Mrs. O'Grady's baton once again whizzed into action, thwacking the cove's hand with bone-crunching force. The unwanted passenger howled and hurriedly withdrew. The coach sped forward, leaving yet another of White Willie's men bunged up on the Covent Garden cobbles.

With a parade-ground flourish, Peggy O'Grady twirled her baton back onto the seat beside her. "I'm thinking there'll be no more trouble from those buckos tonight," she proclaimed with satisfaction. "We're out of the Arch Cove's bailiwick now. He'll never try anything west of Leicester Square."

Verity, meanwhile, had been noting with pity the skeletal prominence of the rib cage upon which she was perched. "If you promise not to scream, I'll take my handkerchief out of your mouth and let you up," she offered.

The captured Irish girl nodded in apparent agreement, but promptly let out a bloodcurdling shriek for help once the gag was out of her mouth.

Mrs. O'Grady winced. "Stopper her up again, Miss Verity. If she keeps up her noise, White Willie's men will follow us right back to Thornrose House, and no good would come of that white devil finding out it's the famous Mistress Reform that's diddled him tonight."

The distance between Thornrose House and Covent Garden where White Willie reigned over his flash house gang was less than three miles and scarcely more than two dozen city blocks. But in the course of that short drive, the surroundings changed dramatically, from the raffish theater district that served as the hunting ground for the city's harlots, to the wealth and respectability of London's best neighborhood.

Breathless and disordered from her ride across the city astride her squirming prisoner, Verity Thornrose greeted the sight of the mews that ran behind her family's elegant Bruton Street home with some relief. "Do you think we'll be able to get her inside without waking up the neighborhood?" she asked her fellow kidnapper.

"Never you fear," said Peggy O'Grady, regarding their flailing captive with a gimlet eye. "I didn't follow me dear late Paddy from pillar to post in the Provosts for twenty years without learning a trick or two about the handling of unruly prisoners. I'm well up to dealing with the likes of this one here."

This proved not an idle boast on Mrs. O'Grady's part. With brisk efficiency, she twisted the Irish girl's arm behind her and marched her into the Thornrose kitchen where they found Mrs. Allen, the Thornrose cook, wielding a bloody meat cleaver on a joint of some undetermined animal.

"You've had good hunting, I see," observed Mrs. Allen, wiping bloody hands on a white apron. "I've got the water on a good boil"—she eyed the grimy street doxy with distaste—"and the sooner we get her into it, the better."

The intended object of these ministrations blanched. Her old grannie had always warned her that the English liked boiled Irish children almost as much as they liked boiled beef, but she'd never really believed it until now. In mortal terror, she twisted free of Mrs. O'Grady, only to collide with a tall, young footman carrying a stack of starched table linen. Altering course, she darted up the corkscrew stairway that led to the main hall.

"Lord-a-mercy, she's got upstairs!" cried Mrs. Allen.

"Rafe—after her!" commanded Verity.

The young footman obeyed, taking the corkscrew stairs three at a time. There was no one in sight on the main floor, but a crash of crockery gave him an excellent indication of which way the girl had fled. He turned a corner and found Chester, the aged and venerable butler, sitting among the ruins of the second-best tea service.

Pausing only long enough to right the stunned and sputtering butler, Rafe began to methodically search the darkened rooms that led off the front hall. It didn't take long to flush out the fugitive. She flashed away like a frightened deer and skittered up the curving front stairway.

At the top of the stairs she was confronted by three strange-looking women clad in flapping green sacks. She gasped at the sight of them and they shrieked at the sight of her. She fled on, scrambling up another flight of stairs into what she recognized as the servants' quarters. But her pursuers were still after her, and there was no place to go except up a narrow ladder into the pitch-black attic.

"She's in the attic all right, Miss Verity," announced Rafe the footman, gesturing to the ceiling. "I can hear her thumping around up there."

"She must be frightened out of her wits, poor thing."

"Beggin' your pardon, miss, but those turn-outs your aunts are wearing didn't help to reassure her."

Verity smothered a smile at her aunts' expense. "They do look rather odd, don't they? But that poor girl frightened them as much as they frightened her. They're all having spasms, and Mrs. O'Grady has got palpitations from running up the stairs, and Chester says he has ruptured his hip. So before I do anything else, I must send a note to the doctor."

"But what about her?" Rafe raised his eyes ceilingward.

Verity followed his gaze, frowning thoughtfully. "We can't just let her sit up there in the dark forever. You'll have to try and coax her down."

Rafe looked dubious. "I doubt she'll come willingly. I may have to use force."

"Well, if you must. But be careful and don't hurt her."

Rafe thought privately that this cornered Irish hellcat was a lot more likely to hurt him than he was to hurt her. Nevertheless, he told Miss Verity resolutely, "You tend to Chester and the ladies. I'll get her down somehow."

Miss Verity gave him the smile that had bewitched him since he was ten years old. "Thank you, Rafe. Bring her downstairs once you get hold of her."

If I get hold of her, Rafe addressed his departing mistress silently.

Lantern in hand, he climbed up the ladder into the darkened, cobweb-festooned attic. He'd forgotten how crowded it was up here. For all their wealth, the Thornroses were thrifty, and it looked as if they hadn't thrown anything out since the Great Fire. The girl could lead him a merry chase up here if she chose, but maybe if he could talk to her, he could calm her down.

Setting his lantern on a handy trunk, he addressed the hidden girl in conversational tones. "You won't come to any harm in Thornrose House, miss. Miss Verity and Mrs. O'Grady are just trying to save you from the streets, just the way Miss Verity's aunts saved me from being a climbing boy. . . ." His eyes were becoming accustomed to the gloom, and he thought he saw a quiver of movement in the shadow of a tall clothespress. "You see," he went on, "I came here to do the chimneys when I was five years old, but I fell down and hit my head and the sweep ran off and left me for dead, and Miss Faith, Miss Hope, and Miss Charity—they're Miss Verity's aunts—nursed me back to health and I've been here ever—"

He pounced, almost getting a grip on a thin shoulder, but the girl dodged away, leaving him to be inundated by an avalanche of hatboxes that had been stored on top of the clothespress. Fighting his way clear, he charged after her. A mistake. In short order, he managed to bark his shin on a coal scuttle, trip over a crate, whack his head on a slanting roof beam, and put his foot in a brass chamber pot.

Profanity was not often heard in Thornrose House, but Rafe was indulging in it now. The Irish girl, meanwhile, was surreptitiously edging toward the trap door. In a blur of ragged dress she slipped down the ladder to the floor below.

Freeing his foot from the chamber pot, Rafe hurdled sundry obstacles and then dropped from the attic with a single catlike bound. The girl shot him a white-faced glance over her shoulder as she dashed into the hall. Rafe loped after her, grinning to himself. He had her now, by God.

He caught her on the floor below, his long legs easily out-distancing her. She struck at him like a trapped animal, but she was no real match for him, and he bundled her over his shoulder like a rag doll. He almost felt sorry for her. She weighed next to nothing, the frantic blows she rained down on the small of his back hurt him no more than the batting of an angry kitten, and beneath the Gaelic-accented aspersions she was casting upon his parentage, he perceived an undertone of pure childish terror.

The Thornrose House kitchen resembled a field hospital on the Peninsula. Mrs. Allen was fanning Peggy O'Grady's flushed and panting countenance with her bloody apron. Miss Verity was assisting Chester the butler in seating his wounded dignity on a cushion. Miss Verity's three aunts, still in their outlandish costumes, were providing commentary.

"A most alarming experience!" declared Aunt Faith.

"Extremely alarming!" seconded Aunt Hope.

"Most extremely alarming to everyone concerned!" elaborated Aunt Charity.

Rafe strode into the kitchen, his prisoner still fighting to the last ounce of her exhausted strength, her bright hair flaring about her panicked face.

"Really, Rafe," he was chided by his youngest mistress, "is it absolutely necessary to cart her about in such a manner? Put her down at once."

"Whatever you say, Miss Verity," replied Rafe dutifully. He dumped the girl into a chair with rather more force than was necessary, and placed a heavy hand on her shoulder to make sure she stayed there.

With a rustle of dove-grey skirts, Verity seated herself next to the shrinking girl and smiled her most encouraging smile. "I know you must be terribly frightened, but you have no reason to be. Would you care to tell me your name?"

After a long moment of hesitation, the Irish girl surrendered up her name—Deirdre Lanahan—in a barely audible voice.

"I'm very pleased to meet you, Deirdre. I am Verity Thornrose, recording secretary of the Society to Aid Distressed Irish Serving Girls. You are a distressed Irish serving girl, are you not?"

Deirdre had to admit that this summed up her situation nicely, and she gave Miss Verity Thornrose the recording secretary a wary nod.

"And this lady," Miss Thornrose continued, "is another of our members, Mrs. Margaret O'Grady. It was she who discovered your plight."

"You knew I was put on the streets by White Willie?" whispered Deirdre, amazed.

Verity's expression darkened. "We at the Society are quite familiar with White Willie and all his works."

"He's a devil, that one is," added Mrs. O'Grady, crossing herself.

Though her fears were receding somewhat, Deirdre still harbored deep misgivings about Peggy O'Grady and her baton. "They say terrible bad things about you in the flash house," she said, giving the stout Irishwoman a narrow look.

"Do they now?" asked Mrs. O'Grady, looking pleased.

But Verity Thornrose was looking worried. "It seems your fame has begun to precede you, Peggy. I hope you'll take due care in future excursions."

"Oh, pish and tish! I can handle that white devil and his scum well enough, never you fear."

Verity's violet eyes fastened thoughtfully on Deirdre's thin face. "It's no wonder you were terrified if that horrible man has been spreading lies about us."

Deirdre nodded. "And then seeing those ladies in those . . . sacks."

"Oh, they aren't sacks," said Verity with a smile. "They're dresses made of green baize. My aunts are sewing them for the female inmates at Newgate. Some of the unfortunate women confined there go about literally in rags. A splendid Quaker lady named Mrs. Fry is trying to improve conditions there, and we are contributing several garments to the cause. My aunts were fitting them on each other when you happened along."

Deirdre cast a sidewise glance at the three aunts in their odd attire and decided that the female inmates at Newgate might do better to continue in rags than to wear the garments these Thornrose ladies had turned out. Something of her feelings must have shown on her face, for suddenly Verity Thornrose burst into laughter. It was remarkably gay laughter for a young woman of such somber dress and apparent serious interests, and it had the effect of convincing Deirdre that perhaps things were going to be all right.

" 'Tis true we're not notable needlewomen and we could well afford to hire a seamstress to do the work for us," Miss Thornrose admitted in a voice that still held a note of mirth. "But, like Mrs. Fry, we believe it is ennobling to perform labor for others with our own hands."

Deirdre received this philosophical concept dubiously. She had been laboring for others since she was old enough to walk, and no one had ever invited her into the nobility on account of it. What an odd household this was.

"Where do you come from, child?" asked one of the aunts in a kindly tone.

"From Kilkenny Village in County Kilkenny, ma'am." Now that Deirdre had gotten a calmer look at the Thornrose aunts, they looked considerably less frightening.

"Should you like to return to your family, Deirdre?" asked another of the aunts—at least Deirdre thought it was another of the aunts. The family resemblance between the three ladies was so strong it was difficult to tell them apart.

Whichever aunt it was went on to explain, "Many of our rescued girls choose to return to their families in Ireland and we provide money for their passage."

Deirdre shook her head. "I've no family left to go back to."

The aunts responded with a trio of sympathetic clucks.

"Well," said Verity gently, "there'll be time enough to ponder your future after you've had some food."

"A bath won't hurt her none, either," put in Rafe unchivalrously, and then grinned at the murderous green glance that came his way.

"Oh, dear," exclaimed Mrs. Allen, "I forgot the bath water in all the excitement. I'll put some more on to boil."

A chagrined blush mounted Deirdre's thin cheeks, for she now realized that all the dire talk of boiling water had to do with preparing a bath for her, not a cook pot. But now the stew and the pickles, bread, cheese, and the milk were set before her and she forgot everything but the food, blessed food. It was the first real meal she had had in weeks, and by the time she had finished her second piece of Sally Lunn cake, her strength had come flooding back, and she felt bold enough to ask how the Society to Aid Distressed Irish Serving Girls had learned of her situation.

"Fortunately for us," said Miss Thornrose, "there's no honor among thieves, and Covent Garden thieves are no exception. Mrs. O'Grady has several paid informants among them who keep an eye out for girls in your situation. I don't wish to pry, Deirdre," she went on in a more serious tone, "but would you care to tell us how you lost your position?"

Deirdre studied her delftware plate intently. "It was Lady Eleanor Stanhope what turned me off, miss. You see," she went on in a barely audible voice, "her husband Sir Aubrey took a . . . particular interest in me and . . ."

"You needn't say any more," said Verity softly.

But Peggy O'Grady was less delicate. "Debauched by Sir Aubrey Stanhope! Why is it that men must be forever rutting with any female that crosses their path?"

"And Sir Aubrey's lady having just presented him with a son and heir, too!" put in Mrs. Allen indignantly. Mrs. Allen was a great reader of newspaper chitchat columns and was always *au courant* on the subject of births, deaths, and marriages among the Quality.

Deirdre, mindful suddenly of the interested attention of Rafe the footman, tried to explain. "But you see, Sir Aubrey said it was all right to . . . because it was the gander month and so it wasn't really wrong . . ."

Mrs. O'Grady was outraged. "The seducing blackguard! Filling an ignorant girl's head with such blather."

"It really is despicable," agreed Verity. Her voice was quiet, but there was a flash of steel in her violet eyes, the Thornrose steel that showed whenever she was confronted with injustice. This was not the first time she had heard this self-serving, male-invented excuse for adultery, husbands claiming that because they were denied access to their wives during the month after childbirth, they were therefore entitled to a month of dalliance with other women.

"You poor child," murmured Verity. "What you must have suffered at that dreadful man's hands."

Deirdre kept her eyes suitably downcast. In truth, she hadn't exactly been overwhelmed by Sir Aubrey's manly attentions,

Sir Aubrey having had difficulty in achieving manly vigor on the occasions he had tried to seduce her. She suspected that the gallons of claret Sir Aubrey habitually consumed in order to get up the courage to chase her around his canopied bed were probably to blame. If only he hadn't been so rich and grand, and so exactly the kind of man that had always figured in her girlish daydreams . . .

"You must put it all behind you," Miss Verity was saying, "and look to your future. As it happens, we are in need of an upstairs maid. Should you like to be employed here, do you think?"

It was more than Deirdre could have hoped for. One short hour in this amazing household had convinced her that this was a place like no other. She could only nod silently in answer to Miss Verity's wonderful offer, for suddenly her eyes had filled with tears, all the weak tears she told herself she mustn't cry when she was cold and hungry on the streets, or in the flash house watching White Willie take a salted rope to a girl who had displeased him.

Miss Verity smiled. "Well, then, it's a bath for you first and then off to bed. Tomorrow will be soon enough to learn your duties."

Still dazed by the sudden miraculous turn in her fortunes, Deirdre was led to a storage room where a copper bathtub was being filled. She was given a stack of wondrously white towels, a cake of lavender soap, and less pleasant but necessary, she realized, a jar of sulphur ointment to rid herself of any unwholesome little passengers she might have picked up.

A heady sense of well-being flooded through her as she watched Rafe the footman labor to bring in her hot water. It was the first time in her life she had been waited on in such a manner (although she had often dreamed of such luxury) and she couldn't resist commanding him to have a care about splashing the floor. Rafe ignored her, stoically hefting the heavy canisters one after the other into the tub. She watched his well-set frame with interest. It was obvious he hadn't missed many meals in his Thornrose House existence.

When the tub was filled and smelling deliciously of lavender steam, she grandly dismissed the first—but hopefully not the last—footman she had ever had at her beck and call. "And no peeking through the keyhole," she admonished him in parting.

This brought him up short in the doorway. He swung about and looked her up and down with cool, blue-eyed derision. "As if I'd bother to peek at a scrawny, carrot-haired snip like you. All I can say is that if Sir Aubrey Stanhope did have an eye for you, he must have been either blind as a bat or drunk as a wheelbarrow."

It was so humiliatingly close to the truth that for an instant Deirdre was bereft of speech altogether. By the time she had recovered her wits, Rafe had gone, and all she could do was stare after him, her eyes blazing emerald flame. She would show him. She would. She would get her looks and her health back, and then she would dazzle him with the flirtatious charm that had won her so many admirers in the past. And then, when he was thoroughly besotted, hopelessly enamored, worshipping the very ground she walked upon, then she would break his heart and cast him aside like a worn-out shoe.

The Thornrose ladies retired upstairs, blissfully unaware of the plot their new serving maid was hatching against their unsuspecting footman. In the serene confines of the Thornrose library, the ladies indulged themselves in an evening snack of warm milk and biscuits, and then took turns reading aloud from one of their favorite literary works, Mr. Bentham's *Introduction to the Principles of Morals and Legislation.*

By nine o'clock there was talk of retiring.

"But not before we make an entry into The Book," declared Aunt Faith, the oldest living Thornrose and warder of The Book. She went to the shelf and removed a large volume bound in red vellum and entitled *The Thornrose Book of Good Works: Volume the Third.*

Since the days of the First George, the Thornroses had been keeping a record of the family's numerous reforming endeavors and philanthropic deeds, and now in the Regency of the Fourth George, Verity Thornrose, the last of the Thornroses, was heiress to the family tradition. The Thornroses had long subscribed to the belief that with wealth came responsibility to the less fortunate, and over the course of a century, the entries in the three vellum volumes recorded their efforts to live up to this belief.

The Thornroses kept this record not as an exercise in self-congratulation, but rather so that each succeeding generation

would have an example to live up to. No entry was ever made
without first listening to a reading of some of the deeds set forth
in previous volumes. This office was always performed by Aunt
Hope, who was acknowledged to have the best forensic talents
among the ladies. In well-modulated tones, she treated her sisters
and her niece to a brief selection of earlier entries.

> *On this twelfth day of November, in the year of our*
> *Lord 1710, Phineas Thornrose hath donated monies*
> *to the Society of Ancient Britons to build a school for*
> *the Training of Vagrants . . . On this, the first day of*
> *Parliament, 1742, Godwin Thornrose spoke against*
> *the abomination of black slavery . . . Miss Patience*
> *Thornrose has this day in 1774 made an address to*
> *the Bluestocking Society supporting the proposition*
> *that Public Flogging of Misdemeanants be Abolished*
> *Forthwith . . . On this day in 1801, Valarian Thorn-*
> *rose, Esq. has submitted a Report on the Lamentable*
> *State of London Workhouses . . .*

Recording the beneficial exertions of the current generation of
Thornroses fell to the elegant hand of Miss Charity Thornrose,
acknowledged among the ladies to have the best penmanship.
On this particular evening she recorded that the Thornrose family had made a sizeable donation to the City of London Truss Society for the Ruptured Poor; that Miss Faith Thornrose had
addressed a gathering of ladies on the subject of the salutary
work being performed at the Spa-Bathing Infirmary for the Poor;
that Miss Hope Thornrose had passed the morning distributing
handbills for the National Smallpox Vaccine Society; that Miss
Verity Thornrose had passed the evening rescuing an Irish serving girl from an Unspeakable Fate.

When all the good works had been written down, the ladies,
as was their custom, bowed their heads, and prayed for the
wisdom to use their earthly riches wisely. Among the four
ladies it might be said that Miss Verity Thornrose stood most
in need of these prayers, for she, in particular, suffered from
an embarrassing surfeit of earthly riches. As the only surviving
granddaughter of the late merchant banker Jacobus Thornrose,
she was blessed with a handsome competence and would be

wealthier still in two years when she attained her twenty-fifth birthday. Nor could the opprobrious term "Cit" be affixed to Miss Thornrose, for the Thornrose family had turned to finance in Elizabethan times when it was not unusual for the younger sons of gentlemen to take up some profession in the City. The Thornroses had been making fortunes on Threadneedle Street long before many noble families had achieved their titles, and no one among the nobility would presume to scorn the Thornrose name, and certainly not their money.

In addition to worldly possessions, Verity Thornrose had riches of face and person as well, having been blessed with a light neat figure, hair the color of fine sable, and eyes that blue was too paltry a color to describe. Violet was the only word to do them justice. A young lady more blessed in face and form and fortune than Miss Verity Valora Mercy Patience Thornrose would be hard to imagine.

But there were many in London Society who felt that Miss Thornrose was stinting with her riches, for she had made it clear that she had no interest in gracing the Fashionable World with her wealthy and ornamental presence. And on those rare occasions that she did go about in Society, Miss Thornrose declined to simper, to flirt, or to cause her long lashes to play about coquettishly with her clear violet gaze. Moreover, Miss Thornrose was sometimes known to make remarks discomposing to male vanity. And worst of all, instead of marrying some eligible gentleman and delivering into his eager hands her lissome person and substantial fortune, she perversely insisted on remaining single and frittering away her money on indigent chimney sweeps, destitute war widows, and the unvaccinated of every class and condition.

It was this original behavior that had earned Verity Thornrose the not altogether complimentary tonnish sobriquet of "Mistress Reform." Not that she cared in the least. She knew her mission in life. She was born into the world to do good and be good, to reform those who could not help themselves, to chastise those who ought to know better, and to write a glorious conclusion to *The Book of Good Works* as befitted the last of the Thornroses.

Chapter Two

In Which We Meet a Notorious Rake

Alaric Tierney, eighth Earl of Brathmere, regarded himself in the silver-chased mirror that had been placed before his freshly shaved countenance. He nodded briefly in approval and bestowed a coin upon the dusky houri who held the mirror.

"You are most generous, my lord *sahib*," lisped the houri in an accent as exotic as her appearance. She slipped the coin into the plunging neckline of her Oriental bodice, *salaamed* prettily, and then glided away, her shimmering red harem pants clinging delightfully to her posterior.

The earl was unmoved, however. He leaned back in the brocaded barber chair, closed his eyes, and announced in world-weary tones, "God, I'm bored."

"How the devil you could be bored in a place like this, I'm sure I don't know," retorted his lordship's young cousin, the Honourable Laurence Mont. "You'd think you were in an Indian seraglio instead of a barbershop off the Strand."

The earl opened one dark eye. There was a glint in it. "Why don't you have a shave, Laurie, as long as you're here?"

The Honourable Laurie, a towheaded young man who had just attained his twentieth birthday and rarely shaved more than twice a week, quickly demurred. He was not at all eager to submit his callow cheeks to the tender mercies of the seductive ladies of color who made up the entire staff of Putnall's barbering establishment. "Where do you suppose Putnall finds these women, Alaric?"

"I wouldn't inquire too closely if I were you," was his cousin's worldly-wise recommendation.

And now Putnall himself approached, announcing that he would see to his lordship's ebony locks personally, for Putnall was well aware that where Brathmere led, a score of free-spending tonnish bucks were sure to follow. And in truth, the tall young earl could only be a credit to his barber, his lordship having been blessed with the kind of dark good looks that women liked to imagine were possessed by pirate corsairs.

As Putnall snipped artfully away, Alaric inquired of his cousin, "If you're not here for a shave, Laurie, then why are you here at this ungodly hour of the morning?"

Laurie grimaced. "It's my unpleasant duty to inform you, dear cuz, that our esteemed Uncle Ramsey is in town and demanding that we present ourselves posthaste. I'm sure we're both to be roundly chastised for our various sins."

Alaric raised a black brow. "Our sins, Laurie? You intrigue me. My sins, I've no doubt, are as numberless as the sands upon the seashore, but what the devil have you done to rouse the old boy's ire?"

Laurie sighed gustily. "Spent my entire quarter's allowance at Tatt's. Mother was beside herself, and promptly fired off a letter to Uncle Ramsey. Oh, I know I shouldn't have done it, but I just couldn't help myself. That mare, Alaric, was the sweetest little goer I've ever seen. Legs like stilts, and hind quarters that—"

"Spare me the ode to your new love's equine charms," Alaric interrupted dampeningly, "and tell me if you've any notion which of my transgressions has got the old boy in a lather now?"

"Well . . ." Laurie dropped his voice to a discreet whisper as he named the titled lady with whose ripe and luscious person the earl had been amusing himself of late. "I've got a strong notion Uncle Ramsey wants to see you on account of Lady Sherbourne."

"Does he now?" said Alaric in an ominously soft voice.

Laurie spread his hands in an apologetic gesture. "The thing of it is, Alaric, there's been a lot of talk. I mean, she is a married woman, even if old Sherbourne does have one foot in the grave. Not that I mean to criticize the way you conduct your affairs, but couldn't you have been a little more discreet, at least for the lady's sake."

"I've never been discreet in any of my affairs, Laurie. You should know that by now."

Laurie could only shake his head, prophesying a stormy meeting between Uncle Ramsey and his former ward.

Putnall removed the napkin and shook away his lordship's shorn locks. "Just a touch with a curling iron is all that's wanted, my lord."

"Well, I don't want it," said Alaric bluntly, "and I'll thank you not to come near me with that blasted contraption. Bring us some claret instead. My cousin and I face a tedious engagement and we need to fortify ourselves."

Laurie heard this with trepidation. Alaric in his altitudes and Uncle Ramsey incensed could only mean trouble.

Alaric saw the worried look his young cousin wore, and a softer expression briefly transformed his hard handsome features. "Stop looking so hangdog, Laurie. As it happens, I've broken it off with Fanny. That should please Uncle Ramsey."

Laurie's jaw dropped. "You've broken it off with Lady Sherbourne? What happened?"

Alaric shrugged. "She began to bore me."

"Lady Sherbourne bored you?" Laurie asked incredulously.

"Oh, I grant you she's as insatiable as a horse leech in the bedchamber," Alaric allowed with a conspicuous lack of gallantry, "but occasionally one does desire some conversation, and her acquisitiveness was getting to be altogether too much, so I wrote her a farewell note, and sent my groom round with it."

Laurie was awestruck at the savagery his audacious cousin dared to display to one of the most famous beauties of the day. "You broke off your affair with a *note* . . . delivered by your *groom!*"

"But how else should I deliver it, Laurie? The post takes forever these days."

"And did she reply?"

"Of course she did. Did you ever know a woman sporting enough to take herself off gracefully when an affair was over? I've got her reply here." He tapped his waistcoat pocket. "It's three pages of hysterical recriminations, *and* she demands the return of the lock of hair she bestowed on me. Of course, she makes no mention of returning any of the numerous expensive gifts I bestowed on her. Women!" he concluded, his mouth thinning with contempt. "Fortunately, there are enough around so that you don't have to put up with any particular one for very long."

A barbershop girl clad in diaphanous veils fluttered over, brush in hand, to whisk away the stray hairs from my lord's person. My lord ignored these charming ministrations, his attention suddenly fixed on the scattered locks of hair of every length and color that another girl was sweeping up from the shop floor. The Earl of Brathmere smiled, not at all nicely, and summoned Putnall with an imperative snap of his fingers. "Putnall, have that girl of yours tie up those sweepings in a packet for me."

The barber regarded him blankly. "Beg pardon, m'lord?"

"You heard me, man. And bring me pen and ink while you're about it."

"My lord?"

"I don't understand, Putnall, why you persist in standing there staring at me like an idiot. Go and do as I say."

Laurie, sensing mischief afoot, regarded his cousin worriedly. "What are you up to, Alaric?"

Alaric merely grinned. He took the tied-up packet from the barbershop girl and dipped a pen in the bottle of ink presented by Putnall. Balancing the packet on the arm of the barber chair, he wrote, *My dear Fanny. At your request, I am returning your lock of hair. Please sort through the enclosed and reclaim your property. Your obed. etc., etc.*

Laurie winced. "She'll not care for this little prank."

"I know," said Alaric silkily.

Laurie shook his head. "Word of it's bound to get around, Alaric. You'll look like a cad."

Alaric raised his brows in faint surprise. "But I am a cad, Laurie. Surely you knew."

A serving man in Brathmere livery made his way to Alaric's side. "You sent for me, my lord?"

Alaric tossed him the packet. "Take this round to Lady Sherbourne's house."

"Yes, my lord. Should I wait for a reply?"

"I wouldn't if I were you," advised Alaric.

"Very good, my lord." The servant bowed and departed.

"And now," said Alaric, elevating his long legs to a more comfortable angle in the barber chair and reaching for his claret, "I'm going to get drunk. I suggest you do the same, Laurie, for, by God, it's the only way to face Uncle Ramsey."

Sir Jasper Ramsey awaited the coming of his nephews with wrathful indignation. Laboring under a strong sense of ill-usage, he stomped about his suite in the Albany Hotel for Bachelors, meditating upon the injustice of his family situation.

Hadn't he already suffered twelve trying years as Alaric's legal guardian in the wake of the seventh Earl of Brathmere's violent demise in a gaming house brawl? And hadn't the eighth earl already made life miserable enough for his bachelor uncle, to say nothing of the unfortunate succession of nursery maids and tutors that Alaric had put to rout as a boy. At Harrow, he had behaved so outrageously that the put-upon masters had taken to calling him Earl Brat, an epithet that Sir Jasper was certain Alaric richly deserved. At Cambridge, Alaric's crowning educational achievement (which also got him expelled) was arranging for a village tart to be discovered stark naked in the narrow bed of a particularly stiff-rumped don. And now that Alaric was seven years into his majority, was his long-suffering uncle able to have done with him? Alas, no.

And as if coping with Alaric weren't enough, he was also expected to stand *in loco parentis* to his other nephew, Laurence Mont, while his father was off in Spain. Well, he had to admit there was no harm in young Laurie. He was biddable enough except when he fell under Alaric's influence . . .

And so it was back to Alaric again. Anticipation of the coming face-off with his elder nephew had already ruined his digestion for the entire day. Egad, but he needed a smoke, and neither the fancy Virginia snuff nor the newfangled Spanish cigars that the hotel stocked were to his taste. When it came to smoking, he preferred a stout English yeoman's pipe.

If only, he thought with regret, his younger sisters had preferred stout English yeomen when it came to husbands. But no. His twin sisters, Lavinia and Louisa, had, through some accident of nature, turned out to be beauties—"exquisite variations on the same theme" as one besotted admirer had described them. Both

girls contracted brilliant marriages to men who moved in circles far above their father's country squire existence. Louisa
made the more sensible match, marrying Lord Harry Mont, a
straightforward manly chap now doing his duty in Wellington's army. Lavinia, on the other hand, had married the Earl of
Brathmere, a dissolute young man who ran with the equally
dissolute Prince of Wales' set, and who had as his particular
cronies the three Barrymore brothers, known variously and notoriously as Hellgate, Newgate, and Cripplegate. Neither
Brathmere, nor Hellgate Barrymore, nor poor pretty Lavinia
had lived to see thirty, and neither would Alaric at this rate.

The sound of raised voices in the hall distracted him from
his musings.

"But, my lord," came the harassed voice of the landlord, "I
pray you to understand that this is a respectable gentlemen's
establishment."

Alaric! thought Sir Jasper in disgust. Who else could make
a respectable establishment notorious merely by crossing the
threshold? A sharp rap at the door confirmed his suspicions.
With some trepidation he swung the door open.

Alaric strolled in, wearing the characteristically cool, be-
damned-to-you expression that always made Sir Jasper want
to take a buggy whip to him. Displayed on each arm was a
gaudily costumed female, their burnished skin and great dark
eyes showing them to be of Eastern antecedents. Following in
attendance came Laurence Mont, looking pale and none too
steady on his pins. Lastly came the landlord, clucking like a
maddened rooster who had just discovered two vixens in his
very respectable henhouse.

"Good God, Alaric!" ejaculated Sir Jasper. "What have you
done—robbed a raree show?"

"Certainly not, Uncle. We brought them for you."

"*What?*" inquired Sir Jasper in a resounding bellow.

"We hired them from a barbershop. Laurie and I thought
you might want a shave."

"And when we're through here," Laurie volunteered, "we're
taking them to Gunther'ssh for ishesh."

Sir Jasper eyed his younger nephew grimly. Laurie was
drunk. Alaric was probably in a like state, but only the glitter
in his dark eyes betrayed him. Sir Jasper was forced to admit

that the young scoundrel could hold his liquor as well as his father ever did.

"Gentlemen," interjected the landlord pleadingly, "I cannot have these strange females standing about the premises—"

Alaric rounded on him. "Then why," he inquired in a soft voice that was all the more menacing for its lack of volume, "don't you go away and close the door, and no one will know they are on the premises."

Sir Jasper harrumphed dismissively. "Go on about your business, man." As furious as he was with Alaric, Sir Jasper had no intention of airing the family linen in front of an innkeeper. This worthy favored the two ladies with one more outraged look, and retired from the room muttering under his breath.

Alaric, meanwhile, had pulled out the chair to the dressing table. "Do come and sit down, Uncle Ramsey," he invited. "The ladies are most anxious to get their lovely hands upon your . . . physiognomy."

Sir Jasper's roar shook the ceiling. "You worthless young hound! Sit down and hold your tongue."

Alaric shrugged, sauntered to the settee, and arranged himself between the two exotic females.

Sir Jasper glared down at him, realizing that it was going to be deucedly hard to lecture Alaric while being stared at by his two doe-eyed companions. Alaric grinned up at him, perfectly aware of what he was thinking. Sir Jasper made a valiant effort at control. He had posted a hundred and fifty miles in abominable weather to lecture Alaric, and he would not be deprived of this irksome duty.

"I only wonder," he began trenchantly, "what your poor mother would think if she could see you now." Alaric's mother had died when he was five—before her beauty or her love for Alaric's wild father had had time to fade.

Sir Jasper's opening salvo caused Alaric to lose a little of his insolent manner. His black brows snapped together in a frown. "I'll thank you to leave my mother out of this, sir."

Sir Jasper snorted angrily. "I'll speak of Lavinia however I please, boy. She was my sister for twenty years before she had the doubtful felicity of whelping you. A sweeter gel there never was, but a judge of character she was not. She married your father when she could have had any number of more eligible fellows. And then there was the matter of having Hellgate Barrymore stand as godfather at your christening—"

"You mistake the matter, I think," Alaric interrupted, his faint insolent manner once more in place. "Hellgate Barrymore did not *stand* at my christening. From all accounts, he couldn't stand at all. He was so drunk he fell face first into the baptismal font, did he not?"

"I do apologize," grated Sir Jasper, "if merciful time has dimmed my memory of the sordid details of your christening. I warned Lavinia at the time that no good would come of it, but that's in the past now. It's the present that concerns me. Everywhere I go I hear talk of you, Alaric—and none of it's good."

"Well, what else would you expect, Uncle? What with my tainted Tierney blood and Hellgate Barrymore for a godfather, surely I've been condemned to vice from the very cradle."

"Is that your excuse for your outrageous behavior?"

"I make no excuses," said Alaric coolly, "not to you or anyone else."

Sir Jasper seemed on the verge of apoplexy. "A disgrace, that's what you are! A demmed disgrace. First you kill that Westcott fellow, and now this business with Fanny Sherbourne."

"Acquit me on that score, Uncle. I've put an end to my association with Lady Sherbourne."

"Well, that's something to be thankful for," grunted Sir Jasper, slightly mollified.

A noise that sounded suspiciously like a stifled giggle emerged from the tall wing chair where Laurie was sitting.

Sir Jasper rounded on his other undutiful nephew. "And what are you sniggering about, Laurence? And what in the name of heaven possessed you to throw down two hundred gold 'uns on that fool horse? There's not a horse alive that's worth that amount, you young nincompoop. And what do you think your mother will say when she hears about you making a spectacle of yourself at Gunther's with these . . . females? And what the devil do you mean by presenting yourself to me in a drunken state at this hour of the day?"

A sheepish shrug was all the defense Laurie could muster.

"Never mind," snapped Sir Jasper. "I can make a good

guess as to who your drinking companion was." He stomped back across the room to confront Alaric. "Blast it, man, if you want to debauch yourself into an early grave, I don't suppose I can stop you. It's in your blood to live hard and die young, but must you drag Laurie down with you? If anything happens to Harry Mont—and Lord knows, he's likely to get his head shot off by the French any day now—Laurie will have to be responsible for Louisa and that pack of daughters Harry sired on her. If nothing else, will you please consider the boy's family before you lure him any further down the road to ruin?"

Alaric rose to his feet. The harem girls rose too, pressing close to him as if fearing they might be left in the presence of this shouting, red-faced Englishman. "Your point is noted, Uncle," said Alaric lightly. "From now on, I shall do my utmost to direct Laurence upon the straight and narrow."

Sir Jasper gave vent to a sardonic snort. "Oh, will you now? Ha! That's rich. Mark my words: One of these days you'll get your comeuppance. I just hope I'm alive to see it. Now get out, the both of you, and take your heathen doxies with you. I've had enough of my scapegrace nephews for one day."

"Whew!" exclaimed Laurie, once they had escaped their uncle's sulphurous presence. "Peevish old fellow, ain't he! Talk about being chastised by scorpions. Well, at least it's over with and we can enjoy ourselves."

Alaric regarded him dispassionately. "I think not, Laurie. I believe the ladies and I will proceed on to Gunther's without you."

Laurie's face fell. "But you asked me to go with you not half an hour ago."

"I've reconsidered. It would be just the kind of thing to set your mama's back up, and she still controls your purse strings, does she not?"

Laurie was forced to admit that she did.

"And you are pinched of purse, are you not, after your little expenditure at Tatt's?"

Laurie was forced to admit that he was.

"Well, then, be politic. Go home and do the pretty with your mother this afternoon—only take my advice and put your head in a washbowl before you present yourself to her."

Laurie gave him a suspicious look. "You're not turning pious on me, are you, Alaric?"

"Good lord, no. I'm merely undergoing a temporary, mild reformation of character. It won't last. In fact," he went on, as one of the exotic females ran her hennaed fingertips along his thigh, "I feel myself backsliding already. By Saturday I'll be my old unregenerate self, and can be persuaded to take you to an illegal boxing match that's being arranged by the Pugilist Club—just the kind of event, I would imagine, upon which you'd like to wager the advance on your allowance that you're sure to wheedle out of your mama."

Laurie brightened visibly at the prospect of illegal adventure in Alaric's company, and threw his arm around his cousin in besotted affection. "You are a devilish fine fellow, Alaric."

"I know," said Alaric, Earl of Brathmere. "I know."

Chapter Three

The Temptress Tempted

*D*eirdre Lanahan sat laboring at the hardest task she had
been set to work at since her arrival at Thornrose House.
Carefully, carefully, so as not to drip, spill, blot, or splotch, she
applied her quill pen to the rough copybook paper and wrote *A
is for apple that brought us to sin . . .*

The discovery that she was entirely ignorant of the written
word had resulted in a daily summons to the Thornrose library
to receive reading and ciphering instruction from Miss Verity.
They were usually joined at lesson time by Prudence and
Comfort—not more Thornrose ladies as Deirdre had at first
supposed—but two outrageously spoiled lap dogs who were
now frisking about her skirts as she dutifully wrestled with the
next sentence: *With Adam's fall, so did we all.* Having produced a wavering facsimile of this cheerful admonition, she
presented it for Miss Verity's inspection.

"That looks very well, indeed, Deirdre. Now let me see,"
Miss Verity continued, consulting a small printed pamphlet,
"how Dr. Bell says you are to prepare for your next lesson."

"Begging your pardon, miss, but who is Dr. Bell?"

"Dr. Bell," explained Miss Verity, a reformist glow lighting
her eyes, "is the late director of the Madras Orphanage in
India and the man who devised the Monitorial System of
teaching. We, at the National Society for the Education of the
Poor in the Principles of the Established Church"—that Miss
Verity got this out in one breath was a tribute to her natural tal-

ent for elocution—"believe that Dr. Bell's methods will help to foster the spread of literacy among the unlettered."

Being unlettered, Deirdre had learned, was a state the Thornrose ladies could not abide, and all those in service at Thornrose House had got their letters (whether they wanted them or not) as per Dr. Bell's methods.

Her lesson for the day finished, Deirdre lingered in the library, preferring to daydream in one of the elegant brocade wing chairs rather than going downstairs to perform the dreary tasks that awaited her. The entry of Rafe through the library door brought her hastily out of the brocade wing chair, however.

In the six weeks that she had been at Thornrose House, Deirdre had learned that Rafe was a person of consequence in the household. He had a natural ability to lead, and the Thornrose ladies thought highly of him. It was generally understood that once Chester was pensioned off, Rafe would assume the exalted position of butler. This great expectation of Rafe's had, in Deirdre's opinion, made him full of himself and mighty anxious to lord it over her, as he did now with a curt inquiry as to why she hadn't presented herself downstairs to assist Mrs. Allen and Maria with the marketing.

"I've been practicing me letters if it's any of your concern," she replied loftily. "See for yourself."

Still looking suspicious, Rafe picked up her copybook and thumbed through it. He had nice hands, Deirdre decided, clean like a gentleman's hands, but strong and capable-looking too.

"Well," said Rafe, somewhat lamely, "since you've finished, Mrs. Allen and Maria are waiting."

He was standing very close to her now, his blue eyes focused on her, his expression intent. Deirdre wondered what particular attribute was serving to rivet his gaze upon her person: the primroses that good eating had put back into her cheeks, the scattering of curls she always contrived to have artfully escape from her mob cap, or the long lashes darkened with just the faintest touch of powdered charcoal.

Rafe's breathing seemed to quicken. The vivid blue eyes locked with hers, and it seemed so natural that her lashes would flutter down and that her mouth would soften, inviting his kiss. *Oh, he'll kiss me now, he will, he will,* she exulted, and he did, his mouth brushing tentatively across her waiting and wanting lips.

But suddenly he stepped away, and her languorously closed eyes flew open to find him glaring down at her.

"All right," he grated out, "I've had enough of your little games. I know well enough what you're about."

"Oh, and what would that be?"

"Playing the temptress with me, that's what. Well, it'll do you no good. I've seen your kind before. I know you were Sir Aubrey Stanhope's doxy once. But now that you're at Thornrose House, there's no upstairs gentlemen to practice your wiles on, so you mean to keep your claws sharp on me in the meantime."

"Why, I never would—"

"You may fool the ladies into thinking you're a poor little seduced and abandoned serving maid, but you don't fool me. I know a trollop when I see one."

"Trollop . . ." sputtered Deirdre.

"Aye, and no better than you should be. I wouldn't stoop to take the leavings of Sir Aubrey Stanhope."

"*Leavings!*"

"Just keep out of my way from now on or it'll be the worse for you. I promise you that."

Deirdre stared after him as he stalked away, his broad back stiff with disapproval. Her eyes filled with tears. As if she cared what a common footman thought of her. As if she cared in the least. Oh, but it wasn't fair.

Temptress . . . trollop . . . leavings . . .

Suddenly, more than anything else in the world, she wanted to call Rafe back and make him see that she wasn't any of those horrible things. She wasn't a temptress, not really. All she wanted was to be safe and warm and admired just a little. Was that so wrong? And what's a poor upstairs maid to do when the master gets his claret in him and tries to take liberties with you?

But Rafe Bowen would never understand that. He had made his low opinion of her clear enough. Not that she cared. Not that she cared in the least.

Having brushed away her couldn't-care-less tears, Deirdre soon found herself walking through Piccadilly, her market

basket brimming with treasures from such renowned shops as
Fortnam's Grocery and Berry Brothers Tea and Coffee. She
and Maria Orsini, the Thornrose ladies' maid, were kept in
close tow by Mrs. Allen, whose severe countenance served to
discourage the Bond Street Loungers from burdening them
with unwanted attentions. Deirdre thought that Maria, with her
black curls and sparkling dark eyes, was almost as pretty as
herself, but liked her anyway.

Maria Orsini's advent into service at Thornrose House bore
a striking similarity to her own. Maria had come to England in
the employ of an Italian couple. But the master had suffered
grievous losses in the English gaming hells, and he and his
wife had hurriedly decamped, leaving Maria stranded in a
strange country. Fortunately, the Society for the Relief of Destitute Foreigners learned of her plight and placed her in the
household of one of their members, Miss Verity Thornrose.

"And not a moment too soon," Maria had told Deirdre with
an expressive Milanese shudder. "Otherwise, I would have to
become the mistress of my landlord, Signor Fulwider, a most
ugly man with a red nose and a hairy mole. But instead, I
come to serve the Thornrose ladies, and I am saved."

(The Thornrose ladies, Deirdre had come to realize, did not
employ their servants so much as they rescued them from fates
worse than death.)

The morning shopping completed, the three women re-
paired to Gunther's Confectionary Shop on the east side of
Berkeley Square. This was the highlight of the shopping expedition as far as Maria was concerned, for she had a Romantic
Understanding with one of Gunther's pastry cooks, a young
man named Paolo Fabiani. As they entered the shop, the
white-aproned Paolo hurried toward them, his mobile countenance lit with a happy smile—the kind of smile, Deirdre
thought morosely, that she could never hope to inspire in Rafe.

While Mrs. Allen perused the glass counters filled with
Gunther's beautifully frosted creations, Maria and Paolo con-
versed in voluble Italian, Maria occasionally translating for
Deirdre's benefit: Such a stir was several days ago created
when a young gentleman brought in two exotic females of appearance that was not at all respectable . . . the scandalized
looks, the sweeping out in droves of affronted customers, the

loss of business to poor Monsieur Gunther, the young gentleman caring not a jot . . .

Feeling very much ignored, Deirdre announced that the aroma of pastry was making her faint and that she would wait outside. She was staring disconsolately at the passing traffic when a familiar voice hailed her.

"I say, Deirdre, is that really you?"

Deirdre spun about and found herself staring up at the floridly handsome countenance of Sir Aubrey Stanhope.

"S . . . Sir Aubrey," she stammered.

Her erstwhile employer was standing before her, a malacca cane swinging in his hand, a beaver hat perched on his blonde *en Cherubim* curls. He was dressed with his usual dash in a plum and ruby striped waistcoat that would have looked ridiculous on anyone without his high coloring.

Sir Aubrey, meanwhile, was staring back at her with a frankly admiring gaze. "I've been wondering what happened to you, Deirdre. Deuced shame about your being turned off. I hope you know I had no hand in it. I just came back from Epsom one day and found that Lady Stanhope had done the deed. But I must say you look as though you've landed on your feet. Got another position, have you?"

"Yes," said Deirdre coolly, "in a very fine establishment on Bruton Street. I consider myself quite lucky to be there." And she would cut out her tongue before she ever told Sir Aubrey how low she had sunk before her luck had turned.

"I'm glad to see you're well-settled," Sir Aubrey was saying. His china blue eyes, so different from Rafe's steely, disapproving ones, roamed appreciatively over her face. "You're looking well, I must say. It's nice to see a pretty face again. My good lady seems bent on filling our establishment with the most knockerfaced chits imaginable. Not one of them can hold a candle to you." A thought seemed to overtake him. "I say, you do get a half-day on Saturdays, don't you?"

Deirdre nodded. Once a month she got a whole Saturday off, as well as every Sunday morning for church, a very liberal arrangement compared with most London establishments.

"Why not come with me to a masquerade at the Pantheon?" Sir Aubrey proposed. " 'Twill be a grand romp, and you'll be the belle of the ball. I'll send a carriage for you."

Deirdre opened her mouth to say that this was madness, that she was a mere upstairs maid, but these sensible dissuasions never gained utterance. Her imagination ran riot instead. An evening at the Pantheon betokened all the gaiety and glamour that she longed for in her eighteen-year-old heart. But then her rioting imagination ran smack up against the cold reality of how romping at the Pantheon with her seducing blackguard of a former master would be perceived by the high-principled ladies at Thornrose House.

"Well?" prompted Sir Aubrey, his ruddy-complected face leaning very close to hers. "Shall you go with me, Deirdre, and make me the envy of every man there?"

Deirdre was on the verge of saying that her new mistress would certainly not approve, when an even more practical objection occurred to her. "I've no costume to wear, so there's an end to your scheme."

"I should say not!" protested Sir Aubrey. "I'll send my man over with one for you."

Deirdre bit her lip, unaware of how delicious she looked in her state of indecision. Sir Aubrey's ruddy complexion grew noticeably more flushed.

"Do say yes, Deirdre. We'll have supper and champagne. It'll be a grand time."

Deirdre gave him a significant look out of her emerald eyes. "If it's to be such an occasion, I wonder that you don't take your wife."

"Oh, my wife would never think of going to—" He broke off abruptly, aware that he was about to say something impolitic. "That is," he resumed, "she's out of town—taken the son and heir to visit her parents, so I'm at loose ends and in need of an evening's diversion."

"Well," prevaricated Deirdre, who in her imagination was seeing dozens of gentlemen toasting her beauty, inquiring of one another who the Irish rose on Aubrey Stanhope's arm might be, speculating among themselves that perhaps another Miss Gunning had come to town . . .

"Do say you'll come," coaxed Sir Aubrey. "A pretty girl like you deserves a few pleasures. I'll bring you straight back at a decent hour." To his surprise, Deirdre appeared to accept this statement at face value.

"It's only that I can't think how to arrange the costume," she said with a shake of her head. "I could never receive it without me mistress knowing, and she would never approve of any of this." Then, as if heaven-sent, an absolutely brilliant idea popped into her head. "Have your man wrap it up and address it to me from Mrs. O'Grady, and then leave it at the trades-man's entrance at 32 Bruton Street."

Sir Aubrey nodded eagerly. "All right. From Mrs. O'Grady. It's as good as done."

Deirdre cast an anxious glance in the direction of Gunther's shop. "And now I think you had better leave. I am not unac-companied."

"You've made me a happy man," declared Sir Aubrey. After surreptitiously looking around, he took her hand, kissed it very much in the grand manner, and then sauntered away, his cane swinging jauntily.

A few minutes later Maria and Mrs. Allen came out of the shop to discover that the fresh air had buoyed Deirdre's spirits considerably.

Intrigue became Deirdre. For the rest of the week she went about looking like a green-eyed cat purring over a cream dish. The occasional qualm of conscience was effectively squelched, particularly in view of the fact that circumstances seemed to increasingly favor her plans. Fate had expeditiously dealt with the problem of how to conceal her adventure from Maria, with whom she shared her attic quarters. The Thornrose aunts were going on a tour of rural workhouses and Maria was to go along to do for them. With Maria out of the way, Deirdre fan-cied that she would be able to slip out of the house, go to the Pantheon, create a sensation, and then, like Cinder-Ella, mys-teriously disappear, leaving behind hordes of heartsick men wondering where she had gone.

Even the matter of the costume passed off easily, everyone assuming that Mrs. O'Grady had left some of her daughter's old clothing for Deirdre's use. Tucked in with the costume was a note. Thanks to the good Dr. Bell, Deirdre was able to puzzle out the time and place of her rendezvous. She committed the instructions to memory and then, feeling deliciously conspira-torial, burned the note in her bedside candle.

On Saturday, as the hands of the clock crawled with tortur-
ous slowness toward the hour of her engagement with Sir
Aubrey, Deirdre began to fall prey to the notion that Rafe was
watching her. It seemed that whenever she looked up, his
steady blue gaze was fastened on her in a most disconcerting
manner, and she was hard-pressed not to fidget. At the end of
the day, she wanted nothing more than to escape him, and she
literally fled the kitchen.

But he came after her. "Deirdre, about this evening . . ."

Deirdre froze. She waited in agonized suspense as Rafe
went on speaking, his phrases emerging with a hemming and
hawing that was unlike the curt commands he habitually addressed to her.

"I thought . . . since we're both here tonight . . . that is, if
you would like it, I could help you with your penmanship."

"Oh, no . . . I mean, I can't," replied Deirdre, her syntax
quite as faltering as his. "That is, I must darn a stocking and
go to bed early. Yes, that's what I must do."

Rafe drew back. "As you please," he said coldly, and
stalked away, leaving her sagging limply against the railing.
Ordinarily she would have been thrilled with this sign of favor
from Rafe, but tonight she had grander plans.

In the safety of her attic room, she unwrapped her costume,
a frothy concoction of white draperies held together by a white
ribbon under the bosom. She hadn't the remotest idea who she
was supposed to be, she only knew that she had never before
put on anything so sheer, frilly, and frivolous.

At the stroke of ten, she stole, silent as a white wraith, down
the series of back staircases used by the servants. The kitchen
was empty as she had prayed it would be at this hour, and she
passed noiselessly into the foggy night. Giddy with triumph at
the ease of her escape, she flitted unobserved to the mews
where Sir Aubrey's carriage was waiting.

Unobserved by all save one.

Hackett the stableman had been making his evening rounds,
checking that his four-footed charges were tucked away for the
night, when an astonishing apparition flashed by the open stable door.

"All in fluttery white, it was," he told Rafe later. "I thought
it was a ghost, I did, until I realized it was Lanahan in some

sort of outlandish outfit. So I go outside, and what do you think I see?"

"Well, what the devil *did* you see?" demanded Rafe.

"I see her get into a hack, and I hear a gent inside direct the jehu to the Pantheon and then—"

"Yes, yes, go on."

"I hear the jehu say, 'Yes, Sir Aubrey.'"

Rafe's questioning expression darkened. It was perfectly and immediately obvious what had occurred. "Why didn't you tell me at once?" he demanded.

The stableman shrugged. "I needed to rub down Capability first, and then see to Temperance's shoe, and then muck out Amity's stall . . ."

Rafe lingered only long enough to growl something unkind about Hackett's mental prowess before striding away to inform Mrs. Allen of Deirdre's defection. The motherly cook was at first disbelieving—until she hastened upstairs to the maids' quarters. She returned, indignant.

"The deceitful little wretch stuffed her bed to make it look like she was asleep. Gave me a turn, I tell you, when I went to touch her and found it wasn't her at all. She's not taken her spare dress, though."

"Then she must mean to come back," hazarded Rafe.

Mrs. Allen harrumphed. "I wouldn't be too sure of that, my lad. Don't you know that when those fancy gents set girls up as their mistresses, they buy them everything to wear from the skin out. Likely our Miss Deirdre thought that brown poplin Mrs. O'Grady gave her wasn't worth taking."

The two servants exchanged glances. There was no help for it. Miss Verity would have to be told. Fortunately, their youngest mistress was still awake, laboring over a tract outlining the evils of child labor in Mr. Blake's dark satanic mills. Five minutes later, she was down in the kitchen to confer with the assembled staff which now included Chester, who had been awakened and informed of the crisis. The elderly butler did not mince words on the subject of Deirdre.

"I never liked that Irish baggage above half. I say let her go and good riddance to her."

"I'm sure you don't mean that," chided Verity.

Chester subsided, but his expression remained obstinate.

"What's to be done, miss?" asked Rafe quietly.

"I shall go to the Pantheon and fetch her back."

There was a concerted gasp from the assembled retainers.

"Miss Verity," protested Chester, "ladies should not enter the Pantheon. The things that go on there are . . ." Words failed poor Chester.

But not Mrs. Allen. "Miss Verity, I've read about those masquerades. All sorts of licentious, dissolute rakes congregate there, and some of the women who attend have their dressmakers sew them into their costumes with carpet thread so their clothes can't be ripped off."

"Mrs. Allen, I appreciate your concern, but I don't think you can credit everything you read in those chitchat pages."

"I don't like to think," Chester intoned direly, "what your aunts would say about this."

"My aunts," Verity informed him, "would doubtless tell me to follow my conscience, and at the moment my conscience directs me to the Pantheon Masquerade on Oxford Street."

The protests ceased. Once Miss Verity proclaimed something to be a matter of conscience, she would not be swayed from her course.

"I still say that Deirdre isn't worth the trouble," muttered Chester.

"We mustn't judge her too harshly," said Verity as Mrs. Allen helped her into her cloak. "Sir Aubrey must have had more influence over her than we realized if he was able to talk her round to this escapade. But it may be that by now she regrets her decision and would like to return to us."

Truer words were never spoken. From the instant Deirdre entered Sir Aubrey's hack, the evening had not gone auspiciously. After informing her that she was supposed to be dressed as Diana, Virgin Goddess of the Hunt, Sir Aubrey began pawing her person in a manner that showed he had very little respect for either Diana or her virginity. During a brief respite from her escort's fevered attentions, Deirdre learned that he was dressed as Lothario—whoever that was. Sir Aubrey's grappling left her little time for further inquiry. Fortunately, it was not a far drive to the Pantheon, and their arrival at this modern adaption of a circular Greek temple freed her temporarily from Sir Aubrey's heated advances.

Ordinarily, the Pantheon was used to mount theatrical productions, but tonight the stage and the pit had been cleared of scenery and benches, and given over to dancing. An amazing assortment of costumed people thronged the makeshift dance floor. There was a woman dressed as a page and a man dressed as a housemaid. There were continental peasant girls in short skirts, medieval knights and courtiers, Roman centurions, shepherds and shepherdesses, and nymphs and sylphs of all descriptions. Deirdre also noticed that the more sedately behaved ladies kept their masks and dominoes on, while women who were obviously part of the demi-monde went unmasked. She began to wish that Sir Aubrey had had the foresight to provide her with a mask and domino as well.

Sir Aubrey redeemed himself, however, in the matter of their seats and dinner. He had bespoken one of the red-curtained boxes in the gallery, from which they could have a good view of the dancers below. He also ordered a supper, complete with champagne and ices delivered by a liveried waiter. No sooner had they finished eating than the door to the box swung open and three gentlemen strolled in. Deirdre gave them her most coquettish smile. Here were the first of her legions of admirers, right on cue. She assumed an elegant pose on her lyre-backed chair and prepared to be introduced and adored.

Sir Aubrey, however, was looking pained, for one of the three visitors was Ratpit Revett, the owner of a ratting house where Sir Aubrey had recently lost a rather significant sum betting on how many rats a one-eared terrier named the Gorger could dispatch in ten minutes.

"Well, well," proclaimed Revett, a slight, pallid man in a bottle green coat, "fancy meeting you here, Sir Aubrey."

"Well, I don't fancy it in the least," growled Sir Aubrey. "Now if you don't mind, I'd like to be alone with the lady."

"Of course you do," agreed Revett, bestowing an unwholesome leer upon Deirdre. "I'd like to be alone with her myself. But first there's the little matter of this overdue note of yours."

Sir Aubrey's scowl deepened. "There's no use dunning me for the money tonight, Revett. I haven't got it."

"But you do have this delicious little Irish highflier here," pointed out Revett.

Deirdre gave him an affronted look, but no one seemed at all interested in her feelings. And how did the man in the green coat know she was Irish when she'd not had the chance to open her mouth? An uneasy feeling settled in the pit of her stomach, and her eyes strayed nervously to the doorway where Revett's two companions lounged, very much in the manner of watchdogs.

Sir Aubrey made a halfhearted attempt to defend his lady's honor. "She may look like a cyprian, but she's not really."

"No?" said Revett with a sneering laugh. "And what is she, pray? A duchess from Almack's? No matter. I like the look of her. Give her to me for the night and I'll tear up your note."

Deirdre gasped with outrage and turned to Sir Aubrey, expecting him to send this impertinent fellow packing. But Sir Aubrey seemed fascinated by a folded piece of paper that Revett was slowly turning about before his avid gaze.

"You'll tear it up, you say? Well, I must admit it's dashed tiresome owing blunt to you, Revett. You've no notion how debts between gentlemen are handled. And I suppose if the lady were willing . . ." He turned to the stunned Deirdre. "What do you say to five guineas to entertain Mr. Revett tonight?"

"I'll not!" cried Deirdre, leaping off her chair. "You'll not sell me to this swine."

She darted to the door, but one of Revett's men seized her and pushed her into the corner of the box where she fell in a heap. Revett stepped quickly to close the curtains at the front of the box against prying eyes.

A sheen of sweat had burst out upon Sir Aubrey's brow. He saw a loud and nasty scene in the making, word of which might reach his wife. "I s . . . say," he stammered, "steady on here. This is too much, by God. I'll have no more to do with this business. If you want the girl, make your own arrangements with her. I wash my hands of the lot of you."

"Wait," Deirdre implored desperately, "don't leave me."

But Sir Aubrey, making haste to gather his hat and cane, spared her not a glance, and Deirdre knew in an instant of bitter clarity that once again all her bright dreams were going to come down in smoke and ash.

Chapter Four

In Which Verity Goes to a Masquerade and Meets a Rake

*V*erity reached the Pantheon at the stroke of eleven, an hour she was rarely awake to witness. She had expected the festivities to be nearly over, but found to her surprise that the revels were at their height, and that traffic on Oxford Street had come to a standstill.

Rafe eyed the roiling crowd uneasily as Verity stepped out of the carriage. "I don't like the look of this, miss."

"I shall be perfectly fine, Rafe. Just bring the carriage in as close as you can and wait for me."

Clutching her cloak about her, Verity proceeded onward, undaunted. There was no denying, however, that the patrons loitering about the Pantheon seemed rather free of character. Still, she felt no real trepidation, and she approached the entrance door with the confidence of the righteous.

But here she suffered an abrupt check in her progress. The doorkeeper expected payment for admission. Verity was flummoxed. Like most wealthy people, she rarely carried money on her person.

The doorkeeper was growing impatient. "Yar 'olding up the line," he growled. "Yar got the price or not?"

"At the moment, I don't," Verity admitted. "But could you not let me in anyway, if I promise to send round the money first thing tomorrow?"

The doorkeeper gargled in disgust and waved her away.

"But I must get into the masquerade," declared Verity, standing her ground.

"Then go to the curb and ask one o' the gents to pay your way," advised the doorkeeper in the voice of one whose patience had been tried to the limit.

This struck Verity as a capital notion. She thanked the astonished doorkeeper for his suggestion, not realizing that it was common practice for cyprians to loiter outside the Pantheon importuning men to pay their way into the masquerade. Though she knew something of the amorous commerce of the streets from her expeditions with Mrs. O'Grady, of this particular practice she was entirely ignorant.

Taking up a station beneath one of the marble Greek goddesses that stared out from a niche in the front of the building, she scanned the crowd for sight of a Good Samaritan who would be willing to come to her aid. After surveying the crowd for some time, she still had not seen anyone she felt she could comfortably approach. Truth to tell, the costumed figures looming out of the fog looked a little frightening, and she could not help but condemn the masked men and women for moral hypocrisy. After all, did they not dress up and hide their faces so that they could come here, and act in a way they would never dare to act in their own drawing rooms?

But wait. Striding through the crowd was a dark-haired man who wore neither costume nor mask. His face was on display for all the world to see—and a handsome face it was too, although of course she, Verity Thornrose, would not be moved by such a consideration. Her appreciation of this tall, broad-shouldered gentleman stemmed solely from the fact that here was a man who disdained moral hypocrisy. Surely he was the Good Samaritan for her.

Bolstered by this certainty, she stepped from beneath her goddess and addressed him. "I beg your pardon, sir, but I am under the most urgent necessity of gaining entrance, and I would take it as a great kindness if you would pay my admission."

"Would you, by God?" drawled the gentleman. "Well, that's a novel approach, I'll have to admit." But then he took in the delicately cast details of the face that looked up into his. This was not your common painted harlot, that was certain. Her looks would have arrested his attention in whatever setting he had discovered her. "All right," he said on impulse. "I'll take you in."

"Oh, thank you, sir," breathed Verity. "I'm most grateful."

"Indeed, I'm counting on it," said the Earl of Brathmere.

He paid the two guineas required to hire a gallery box and took his lady of the evening into the shrieking revelry of the Pantheon. But now, instead of tripping along with clinging compliance, the lady suddenly became balkish.

"Sir, I must speak to you—"

"Not here," he commanded brusquely and herded her forward.

But the lady promptly set her heels against the marble floor and brought him to a dead stop. "Sir, I really must discuss with you the particulars of our arrangement."

Alaric frowned down at her, fully intending to manhandle her into compliance (he had paid two guineas for her after all) but suddenly he found himself all but drowning in a gaze of deepest twilight violet, and it took him a good three heartbeats to free himself from the spell. "I'm more than ready to talk terms," he said, collecting himself, "but not with half the city yammering in my ears. Now do you go with me or not?"

"Very well," said Verity stiffly—for though she could see the logic of his words, she was not used to being addressed in such a tone—"I shall accompany you to your box and then we shall talk."

"Mighty gracious of you, madam."

Verity strongly suspected him of being ironical at her expense, but decided it would not be prudent to call him to task. As they walked, she stole sidewise glances at him from beneath her lashes. He was undeniably a gentleman and undeniably handsome. Yet, he seemed dangerous. But it was too late for faintheartedness now. Wisely or unwisely, she had placed herself in his hands, and she would have to deal with whatever situation arose.

"Now . . ." said Alaric silkily, once they were in the box with the door closed behind them, "now, let's see what manner of bargain I've gotten for my guineas."

Before Verity could protest, his long fingers untied the cloak strings beneath her chin. She shivered a little when his fingertips brushed the pulse at her throat, but she found herself unable to voice a protest to this decidedly improper liberty. She

stood unmoving, half-thrilled, half-chilled and entirely fascinated by what was happening to her.

Alaric whisked the cloak from her shoulders, his face register-
ing surprise at the sight of the high-necked, dove-grey dress
completely devoid of jewelry and ornamentation. It was a dashed
dull costume in his opinion. Yet the matronly cut of the gown
could not completely conceal the high breasts and narrow waist.

"What the devil are you got up as?" he demanded. "A
Quaker maid gone to meeting?"

"Oh, no. This is my usual daily attire."

"Then I'd have a stern word with my dressmaker if I were
you."

"I believe you still fail to understand me, sir. I'm not here in
costume."

"Then why the devil are you trying to gain entrance to a
masquerade?" Alaric asked reasonably.

"I'm looking for someone."

"Are you indeed?" Alaric was suddenly on the alert. "Not a
gentleman, I trust?"

"Well . . . yes and no," she replied unhelpfully, and then flitted
away in a rustle of grey skirts, leaving him holding her cape like
a lackey. He tossed the wrap on the chair, thinking that if this female was indeed one of the muslin company, she had the most
diffident approach imaginable. She was now leaning over the
box railing, her eyes intently searching the ranks of the dancers
in the pit beneath them. Alaric watched her with equal intensity,
admiring her profile in the candlelight.

The masquerade had reached the point where all pretense of
being a polite entertainment had been done away with. The affair
had become a thoroughgoing romp with many of the embarrassing excesses that attended such affairs: gentlemen intent on en-
gaging each other in fisticuffs, ladies too inebriated to walk,
couples entwined in indecorous embraces in the gallery boxes.

"No sign of your 'someone'?" Alaric ventured finally.

She turned to him with a troubled expression. "It's hard to
tell in such a crowd." She shook her head. "I had no idea so
many people would come to such an affair."

"Masquerades don't interest you?"

"Not generally, and certainly not when they degenerate into
such a sad display of Saturnalian excess."

Alaric cocked an eyebrow at her, mildly astonished at hearing such language from the lips of a cyprian—if, in fact, that was what she was. "Don't tell me you think it wrong for the local citizenry to indulge in a little harmless pleasure? Or is it that you don't believe in pleasure?"

It was the perfect opening for the lady to declare herself to be a devotee of pleasure, but her pronouncement on the subject fell sadly short of what he would have liked to hear.

"Well, *this*," she gestured about her, "is hardly to my taste. But I would never go so far as to condemn pleasure out of hand."

"I confess I'm relieved to hear it," said Alaric dryly.

Her thoughtful expression deepened. "Certainly, pleasure has a place in human existence. It only becomes injurious when one descends to the level of the Sybarite and pursues pleasure to the exclusion of all else. Wouldn't you agree?"

Alaric, who had not listened to so much lofty philosophizing since he had been "let go" as it were from Cambridge, contented himself with a noncommittal murmur. He had captured a *rara avis,* this evening. No doubt about that.

"I don't wish to pry," he said mendaciously, "but why don't you tell me exactly who you are looking for and perhaps I can help you."

The violet eyes looked measuringly into his. "I don't think that would be . . . wise," she said after a moment. "I'll keep looking on my own. I've imposed upon your good nature long enough."

So that's the game, thought Alaric, comprehension dawning. *Well, you don't play it on me, my girl.*

Ever so mildly he pointed out, "You won't find me good-natured in the least if you take my guineas and then run out on me before keeping your part of the bargain."

The young lady regarded him with an expression of puzzled wonderment that would have done credit to Mrs. Siddons. Then, sudden scalding color rose in her face. "You can't mean to say . . . you can't actually think that *I* am an immoral woman?"

"Well, what else could you be," asked Alaric in a voice of cold reason, "except possibly an abbess? And you're much too young and pretty for that."

"An abbess?" repeated Verity, puzzled but at the same time fairly certain that neither she nor the Catholic religion was being complimented. Come to think of it, neither her dress nor the Quaker religion had come off too well either, and religious intolerance was something she could not abide.

"I must tell you, sir," she said in her most chilling voice, "that your derogatory references to various religions exceeds the bounds of propriety, and further—"

"Bounds of propriety!" interrupted Alaric with a jeering laugh. "By God, that's rich. As if you had a care for that, offering your-self for sale in front of the Pantheon like the lowest whore."

Verity saw now that she was in deep, deep trouble. Her escort was lounging against the closed door of the compartment, his arms folded across his chest in a manner that suggested he had no intention of allowing her to leave. He was looking her up and down, an alarming glint in his half-closed eyes, his very expression an insult. She felt as if those dark eyes were stripping her naked and that those long-fingered, sinewy hands would soon be following suit . . . and perhaps she ought to have listened to Mrs. Allen's advice about carpet thread, after all . . .

With trembling hands she picked up her cloak and draped it across her shoulders. "I don't deny," she said in a voice that quivered slightly, "that my manner in approaching you has given you good reason to think the worst of me. I have only myself to blame. But you must believe that the only reason I came to your box was to make arrangements to repay you. If you will kindly give me your name and direction, I will send you two guineas for your trouble."

"A gentleman," said Alaric in a low, deadly voice, "doesn't give his name to females he buys at the Pantheon."

Verity crimsoned, but went determinedly on. "Y . . . your point is well-taken, sir. If you would give me the name of your man of business, I will send the money to him."

Alaric laughed derisively. "I'd have to be a complete fool to give a woman of your character the name of my banker."

"I . . . I had thought you a gentleman, sir."

"That was foolish of you."

Verity drew herself up stiffly. "My only desire, I assure you, is to pay my just debts."

"Oh, you'll pay all right." He crossed the box in two swift strides.

Verity backed away, only to be brought up short by an inconvenient wall. Then he was upon her, his tall frame pinning hers to the wall, an iron hand on her shoulder, the other hand grasping her chin to turn her face upward to meet his dark-eyed countenance which she still found mesmerizingly handsome, even in this dire instant when she, Verity Thornrose, was about to be forcibly kissed against her will.

It would have taken a great deal to distract Verity and her would-be molester from their individual concerns at this moment, but a thud that shook the wall against which Verity was being pressed did the trick. They both paused for an instant, and then the words *Sir Aubrey* articulated at the level of a shriek could be clearly heard.

Verity was galvanized into action. She clutched at the shirt-front pressed against her bosom and said desperately, "Let me go, I beg you. The person I'm looking for is in the next box. You must let me help her, I beg you."

Her manner was so earnest, her eyes so imploring, that Alaric was assailed with doubts. Possibly matters weren't as they appeared.

"All right," he said softly, relaxing his grip. "But we're not finished yet, you and I."

She bolted away without a backward glance. He followed after her, wondering what would happen next in this diverting melodrama.

He was not disappointed.

His mysterious lady flung open the door to the next box to reveal an amazing tableau. A young girl clad in white draperies and possessing a head of red hair you could warm your hands over was struggling in the grasp of two unsavory fellows who looked like strolling gentlemen from *The Beggar's Opera*. Two other men were engaged in vehement conversation. And, by God, if he didn't recognize one of them. Surely, the man in green was the ratting house keeper, Ratpit Revett. The other larger, red-faced fellow also looked familiar, although no particular name came immediately to mind. All the aforementioned characters regarded his mysterious lady's dramatic entrance with varying degrees of surprise and chagrin.

Deirdre was first to recover her wits. Twisting away from the men who held her, she ran to Verity, gasping out in nearly incoherent Irish accents, "Oh, miss, thank the Blessed Mother you've come for me. Sir Aubrey was meaning to sell me, he was, to settle his gambling debts."

Verity put an arm around her. "No one is going to sell you, I promise you that." Surveying the assembled occupants of the box, she inquired of them in a Terrible Female Voice compounded of one part nursery maid, two parts governess, and one part Sunday school instructress, "Which of you is Sir Aubrey Stanhope?"

Three pairs of shifty eyes shifted toward that gentleman.

Verity turned to him, her eyes flashing like summer lightning. "You will allow me to tell you, sir, that your behavior towards this girl has been despicable. You took shameless advantage of your position as her master to make her the object of your advances."

"Young woman," huffed Sir Aubrey, attempting bluster, "I fail to see that this is any of your affair."

"On the contrary, it is very much my affair. This girl is now in my employ and you have sought to lure her away. I am fairly certain that I have the basis for legal action in the courts, should I choose to pursue it."

Sir Aubrey's perspiring hand went in search of his handkerchief. Being embroiled in a legal dispute with whoever lived at the grand house on 32 Bruton Street was the last thing he wanted. What had started out as a harmless little dalliance while his wife was out of town was rapidly turning into a nightmare.

"And now," Verity went on, angry and beautiful as an avenging angel, "I find that not only have you attempted to lure her from my employ, but that you intend to sell her to these creatures here."

"M . . . madam," stammered Sir Aubrey, "'pon my soul . . . 'pon my honor . . ."

"Have you any soul? Any honor?" inquired Verity awfully. "I doubt you do."

Alaric, who had been attending developments carefully, regarded Revett with narrowed dark eyes. "I didn't know you'd taken up peddling women along with your rats, Revett. What's this girl to you?"

Revett shrugged. "Can't remember at the moment. But a gold 'un or two might refresh my recollection."

Verity sighed inwardly and made a mental note to never

again venture out of doors without money on her person. It
was obvious that this Revett knew something, but she had no
money to bribe him with.

But once again her Good Samaritan came to the rescue.
With a look of contempt he flicked a coin at Revett, which the
ratting house keeper dexterously caught.

"I'll repeat myself, Revett," said Alaric in a hard voice.
"What's your interest in this girl?"

Revett shrugged. "There's a flash king named White Willie
who's looking for her. He's spread the word to be on the look-
out for a redheaded Irish doxy that used to belong to Sir
Aubrey Stanhope. Why he wants her, I don't know, but you're
wise to do Willie a favor whenever you can, if you understand
my meaning."

This revelation caused Verity and Deirdre to exchange mutual gasps of consternation while Sir Aubrey sputtered indignantly, "Is there not a rascal in London who does not know of
my personal affairs?"

Verity rounded on him. "If you behave in the manner of the
gutter, sir, you must not be surprised to find your affairs dis-
cussed there. And now your deplorable behavior tonight has
placed this child in the gravest danger."

"Madam, I swear by Almighty God—"

"I shouldn't if I were you," interrupted Verity. "You'll only
perjure yourself all the more—and before your maker at that."

Alaric could almost feel sorry for the hapless Sir Aubrey.
The lady's tempting mouth concealed the tongue of an adder,
it seemed.

Verity turned to Deirdre, who was looking more pale and
shaken than ever. "We must leave here at once. White Willie
has eyes and ears everywhere."

"We'll be going as well," said Revett, edging his henchmen
toward the door.

"I think not," said Alaric. He still maintained his languid
pose by the door, but his eyes were alert and watchful. "I
think, gentlemen, that we will all wait here together until the
ladies are safely away in their carriage. You do have a carriage
at your disposal, do you not, madam?"

Verity laid a hand on his sleeve. "Yes, but I don't like to leave
you alone with them." Her eyes flicked to Revett and company.

"Pray, don't distress yourself, madam. They'll not trouble me." His lean fingers fastened with sudden strength round her forearm and his dark eyes compelled hers. "You'll wait for me outside?"

Verity nodded. "We shan't drive away until we see you are safe."

"All right, take the girl and go. I'll be along directly."

He opened the door wide enough for them to slip through. Verity shepherded her strayed serving girl down the marble stairs, through the crowds of drunken masqueraders, and out into the midnight mist. Happily, Rafe had worked the carriage to a spot directly in front of the Pantheon and had managed to defend this enviable position against the crowd of competing vehicles. He hailed them with a wave, his eyes lingering on Deirdre in her scanty draperies.

"The sooner we're away from here the better," he called down to Verity, pointing his whip to what looked like the beginning of a street brawl between several groups of costumed men.

"No, wait!" cried Verity as she and Deirdre settled into their seats. "Don't leave yet."

A tall unmistakable figure was striding toward the carriage.

Hastily Verity flung back the coach's window curtains. "So," she said with a smile, "they did not trouble you after all."

"Hardly," he grinned, and suddenly Verity felt a piercing sadness that she could never see this man again.

"I am in your debt, sir, and for a great deal more than money."

He covered her hand where it rested on the window frame and carried it slowly to his lips, his dark eyes never leaving her face. "I ask only one thing in return."

"Y . . . yes?" said Verity, a little breathlessly.

"May I know your name?" he asked with a humbleness that would have astonished the ladies with whom he had had previous associations.

Verity's eyes sank down before his dark, intent gaze. "My name is not mine to give you, sir. Forgive me." Almost in a panic, she cried out for Rafe to drive on.

The carriage gathered speed and the Good Samaritan was left standing alone in the swirling fog.

Chapter Five

Enter the Alarming Octavian Smythe

To say that Verity pined after her Good Samaritan would be an exaggeration. She knew she had been right not to trust him with the Thornrose name, for he was certainly a rake and an *intrigant*. Still, she found herself thinking about him at the oddest times, wondering if that hard handsome mouth was capable of kissing a woman (but not her, of course) with tenderness and singleness of heart . . .

Seeking to rid herself of such dismaying thoughts, Verity threw herself into a dizzying round of meetings, good works, and beneficial exertions of every description. She was in the midst of penning a letter on behalf of the Society of Young Ladies to Sell Used Clothing to the Poor at Reduced Prices when Chester appeared to make a most unwelcome announcement.

"Master Octavian has called, miss."

"Damnation!" said Verity.

Chester, being half deaf, failed to notice this uncharacteristic utterance. "Do you wish Master Octavian shown into the library, miss?"

A slight shiver shook Verity's frame. "No," she said in a low voice, "I'll see him in the Blue Salon."

Chester bowed and departed, with Verity following slowly, struggling to compose herself so that she might present a tranquil countenance to her cousin, Octavian Thornrose Smythe.

That she should be afraid of Cousin Octavian was ridiculous. He was family, after all, and a worthy heir to the Thornrose tradition, which had come to him through his mother, Seraphine Thornrose. He was a banker of great financial acumen, and more importantly, a man of unquestioned virtue, a supporter of many charities, a stern-principled moralist of the highest order.

And now she was two doors away from the Blue Salon . . .

So unyieldingly upright was Cousin Octavian, in fact, that he sometimes made her feel as if he knew her to be guilty of some hidden secret sin of which she herself was not aware. Strange, she thought to herself, how a single childhood incident could make such an impression.

She was five years old and had been consigned to her cousin's care while the adults took tea. She had hoped Octavian would play droughts with her, but he took her off to the library instead, to read to her an improving tome that he had brought for the occasion.

Even at five, Verity knew her duty. Without protest she climbed up on the big library settee, and listened to Octavian read to her about a dreadful, iniquitous place called Babylon, which she assumed must be near that other dreadful, iniquitous place called France. In a voice that sounded very dire and booming for a fifteen-year-old, Octavian read about the Babylonians burning little babies alive in idols and beating drums to drown out their cries.

Oh, poor babies, thought Verity, tears prickling against her eyelids, *poor little Babylonian babies . . .*

Octavian was watching her. "Did I frighten you, Verity?"

She nodded, a tear trickling down her cheek.

"Good," said her Cousin Octavian. "You must always be frightened of me, Verity, and you must always do as I say or you will be punished, terribly punished."

And now there was only one door between her and the Blue Salon . . .

You are preposterous, Verity Thornrose, she told herself sternly, to let a few ill-judged remarks by a half-grown boy play upon your mind in such a manner. And doubtless your childish imagination has exaggerated the entire incident.

She squared her shoulders and went into the Blue Salon.

Octavian Smythe stood before the bow window that over-looked Bruton Street. He was a man of great size, and when he turned toward her, his huge frame seemed to cast a shadow across the whole of the room.

Octavian had once been described as very well looking for a bullock, and in truth there was nothing untoward about his features, except, perhaps, that he had no neck to speak of. He reputedly possessed great physical prowess, amazing even for a man of his size. It was whispered that once when a footpad dared to accost him, he had grasped the misguided felon's neck in his giant fists and slowly throttled the life out of him, pronouncing quite a nice funeral eulogy for the unfortunate fellow as he did so. Of course it was all nonsense, Verity told herself sternly.

"Good afternoon, little cousin," Octavian greeted her in the deep rumbling voice that always seemed to resound down on her from on high.

"Octavian," she managed, "what an unexpected . . . pleasure."

"I fear all my visits must of necessity be unexpected since I am never invited here."

Verity essayed an airy laugh, but feared she only succeeded in sounding shrill. "Why, what can you be thinking of? You know you are always welcome here. And I believe that you were bidden here to dine only last . . . that is . . . as I recall . . ." Unfortunately, after this promising start, no particular event at which Octavian Smythe had enjoyed the hospitality at Thornrose House came to mind.

Octavian took a step toward her, causing the china displayed on a nearby table to vibrate slightly. "I was particularly distressed, cousin, that I received no invitation to the affair marking the anniversary of your birth."

"Then you distress yourself for no good reason, sir," said Verity, rallying a little. "I made no great celebration of my recent birthday."

Octavian nodded wisely. "To be sure, Verity, a spinster at twenty-three would not greet with joy the passing of another year. But were you a married woman, the passage of the years would not dismay you, for you would be immersed in the contentment of your married state. You would know the quiet joy of living as the tender helpmate of a husband, the helping hand of his endeavors. But as it is, you can know only the restlessness of a woman unanchored by male strength, the confusion of a woman unguided by male wisdom."

Oh, merciful heavens, thought Verity, *not another marriage proposal!*

"I am sure, dear cousin, that you must know what I am leading up to," rumbled Octavian in the uncannily omniscient way he had of guessing her thoughts. "Once again, Verity, I renew my offer for your hand in marriage. It pains me to see you leading this unnatural existence of spinsterhood. Marriage is the preferred state for a woman of your age. Surely you can see that. I cannot understand why you continue to deny yourself the benefits of our union. Our marriage would bring together two truly like-minded people. Think of all that we might accomplish together."

"I *have* thought, Octavian, and I must tell you that I am still of the opinion—" It was as if she had not spoken.

"But perhaps," Octavian went on, "you feel that our familial connection is too close, that by marrying, we would trespass into the Forbidden—"

Verity sighed mentally. Trust Octavian to find some dark wicked sin lurking somewhere.

"—but you must recollect that we are a generation away from being first cousins, and there is no law of God or man that would gainsay our union—"

"Octavian, please!"

"I am not finished yet, Verity. Surely you will not be so rude as to interrupt me again."

"I beg your pardon," said Verity, and then was immediately disgusted by her own humbleness. She could feel perfectly comfortable lecturing government ministers three times her age about the appalling conditions in the workhouses, but the prospect of having Octavian annoyed with her left her completely unnerved.

"I beg you to consider, Verity, that it was your late parents' fondest desire that our two branches of the family be united. I cannot believe that you would be so willful as to thwart their wishes."

Feeling as though she was fighting in the last ditch, Verity tried to form a reply that would depress her cousin's aspirations once and for all. "My parents may have indeed spoken of our marriage when I was a child, but who is to know if they would have persisted in this opinion as I grew older? I do not contemplate marriage with any man, and I would fall sadly short of the tender helpmate that you imagine. I—I wish you would not speak of marriage to me again, Octavian."

Octavian regarded her with grim displeasure. "Once more you crush my fondest dreams, Verity. I can do no more than I have done to commend my suit to you, and still you refuse me. But understand this, little cousin, I will never abandon my pursuit of you. I will always be behind you, following after you in unhurrying chase until you tire of your youthful female fancies, and allow your soul to sound in harmony with mine."

Verity spread her hands in a helpless gesture. "I beg you to understand—"

Octavian cut her off. "Make no more foolish protestations, Verity. You will only repent of them in the end. I shall call again next week at the same hour and I will hope to find you at home and not upon some errand manufactured to take you out of the house. Until then, I remain your most loving cousin who lives for the day when you will submit to me as a loving wife."

He bowed and departed, the floor creaking protestingly under his weight. When his footsteps sounded no longer, Verity Thornrose, redoubtable rescuer of distressed serving maids, intrepid distributor of lye soap in the lowest slums, indefatigable campaigner against cruel sporting events, the very same Verity Thornrose sat down in the nearest chair and sobbed helplessly with dread at her cousin's promise to call upon her again.

Chapter Six

The Earl Makes Inquiries in Odd Places

To say that the Earl of Brathmere had been moonstruck by his mysterious lady of the masquerade would have been an exaggeration. Rather, his thoughts on her ran as follows: *Who is this woman who comes to the bawdiest, gaudiest masquerade in town wearing no ornament but the amethyst of her eyes? Who is this woman who has the face of an angel, the gall of an adventuress, and the conversation of an Oxford graduate? There is a mystery to this woman, who is like no other I have met before, and I am going to solve that mystery.*

But first he had to find her.

The logical point to begin, he decided, was with Sir Aubrey Stanhope. Calling at Sir Aubrey's club, he learned that the gentleman in question had developed a sudden uncharacteristic surge of family feeling and had hurried off to the country to reunite himself with his wife and infant for an indefinite period of time.

Though disappointed, Alaric did not remain at a standstill for long. He directed his energies toward proving that his mysterious lady was indeed the adventuress he had taken her for at first glance. And where better to inquire about a woman who was a high-class tart, than in the boudoir of the Queen of Tarts—the clever, beautiful Harriette Wilson.

The soiree was well advanced—as was the hour. The candle-lit, smoke-hazed salon was crowded with tonnish gentlemen in the company of fancy women they would never admit to knowing in the light of day. Harriette Wilson was the hostess, assisted by her sister Amy, also an elegant frail one. Both women wore fetching if rather insufficient frocks that made the most of their much-ballyhooed charms.

Alaric watched with interest as Harriette sailed gracefully among her guests, dispensing the wit and potent allure that had made her a favorite with the jaded men of the *ton*. But Alaric was here to do more than just admire Harriette for the highly finished piece of nature that she was. He wanted information about the demi-monde, and no one knew that world better than Harriette. She was a woman who kept her ear to the ground—not difficult, thought Alaric with an unseemly grin, when you spent as much time on your back as Harriette did.

But getting Harriette alone for a private chat was not easy. Beating out her other admirers and bringing the lady around to bestowing some private unguarded moments upon him required the exercise of all his charm and persistence. For three straight evenings he had been paying extravagant court to her at the charming little house she shared with her sister. He was hopeful that tonight his exertions would bear fruit, for it seemed that Harriette's cinnamon-brown eyes had been resting on him speculatively this evening. Perhaps she was ready to succumb—if not to his manly charms, at least to the heft of his purse.

The evening was winding down and the guests were bidding each other farewell in drunken good-fellowship. Amy was preparing to retire in the company of her current protector, Count Beckendorf, the brother of the Countess de Lieven. Harriette was wafting over toward the Earl of Brathmere (and about time, too, thought Alaric), a beckoning smile playing upon her lovely lips.

"Come, my lord," she said huskily, her voice as rich and full-bodied as her person. "It's time to retire."

A chorus of bawdy hoots and cheers arose at the naming of the lucky man for this evening. Alaric inclined his head gallantly to the lady who had so honored him—but not quite quickly enough to hide the cocky grin of triumph that showed on his face as Harriette drew him through the rollicking, back-slapping crowd and up the stairs.

*   *   *

Harriette Wilson in gauzy dishabille was a sight to delight a man's eyes, and she had no doubt delighted a fair number besides his, thought Alaric, as he poured claret from a decanter on the bedside table. He had been provided with a luxurious gentleman's dressing gown from Harriette's extensive collection, and he now disposed himself on the spacious damask-hung bed wherein so many gentlemen claimed to have caught a glimpse of paradise. The angel who had conducted them thither was at the moment brushing the auburn silk of her hair into a cloud about her half-bare shoulders.

The sight of Harriette in her negligee would inflame most men to unbridled passion, but Alaric had more finesse than that. At the tender age of nineteen, a wise woman had bestowed upon him some excellent advice along with her practiced embraces: to wit, treat whores like ladies and ladies like whores. He had seen the wisdom of this axiom born out many times during his notable career with the female sex. So he treated Harriette Wilson like a virgin bride, waiting with respectful forbearance as she retired coyly behind a brocade screen to slip into something less confining, not presuming to hurry her as she burnished her glorious head of hair.

Noting how engrossed Harriette was with her reflection in the gilt mirror, he decided now was the time to make some subtle inquiries. It was amazing the things women let slip while their minds were on their appearance. He was also aware that he would have to proceed carefully in quizzing Harriette about another cyprian, for Harriette never openly admitted to being a member of that frail sisterhood. Rather, she styled herself as a lady of extremely romantical leanings who was lucky enough to receive many generous gifts of money from her numerous admirers. So he spoke with seeming carelessness, yet intently watching her reflection.

"I've heard talk that a dazzling new incognita has arrived in town," was his opening gambit.

"Dazzling new incognitas are always coming to town," replied Harriette without missing a brush stroke. "And most of them sink like stones in the river never to be heard of again."

"Ah, but this one is not just in the common style," he countered. "My cousin, Laurence Mont, met her at the Pantheon Masquerade and she tipped him a leveler. The poor boy was so smitten he forgot to inquire her name." Alaric was not so foolish as to reveal himself as the party interested in the incognita under discussion. Harriette's professional vanity would never tolerate that. "You'd do him a great service if you put him on this woman's track. The lad's besotted."

Evidently he had captured Harriette's interest, for she put down her hairbrush and turned to face him. "And what is it, pray, that elevates this incognita so far above the common herd?" There was a distinct chill in her voice.

"Dashed if I know. According to Laurie, she dresses like a Quaker, for all she's young and remarkably pretty. She was with a red-haired Irish girl when Laurie met her."

No flicker of recognition showed on Harriette's lovely features. "What an odd pair, to be sure," she observed with a shrug of her white shoulders as she turned back to her reflection. "I've not heard of any such women."

"Ah, well, poor Laurie," said Alaric lightly. But inwardly he groaned. *Another dead end, and it's cost me fifty guineas for nothing. Well, almost for nothing,* he amended, eyeing the voluptuous splendor of Harriette.

Her roguish eyes met his in the mirror. "Why don't you bring your languishing cousin round some evening?" she suggested in a husky purr. "Perhaps we might offer the poor boy some . . . consolation."

Alaric gave a low laugh and rose to stand behind her. "Oh, no, my pet," he said silkily as he lifted the wine-colored curls off graceful shoulders. "I'm afraid, my dear, that I simply couldn't allow you to practice your ravishing wiles on Laurie. You're much too rich for his boyish blood . . . and for his purse." He leaned over and pressed a light kiss to the back of her scented neck.

A knowing smile curved Harriette's mouth. She rose gracefully and gave him her hand along with a sultry look that told him the rest of her would be forthcoming shortly. As she led him toward the paradisiacal bed, Alaric wondered if a night in the arms of the most famous courtesan in London would cause him to forget his mysterious lady of the Pantheon. It was going to be interesting to find out.

* * *

It was well past noon when Alaric finally made his way back to his Albemarle Street residence. Harriette had performed according to her talents and he had enjoyed her lustily, but in the clear light of day, the mystery of his masquerading lady seized him again, and he realized disgustedly that his nocturnal exertions had not brought him one whit closer to solving the mystery.

While breakfasting with Harriette, he had essayed further oblique inquiries, but she was having none of it and had advised him snappishly that if it was so very important to him, he had better take his inquiry to Bow Street.

It wasn't until his butler Robling reminded him of the affair he was scheduled to attend that evening that a possible solution appeared. He might not be able to go to Bow Street, but tonight's engagement would give him the opportunity to consult the next best thing.

So it was that at ten o'clock that evening, the Earl of Brathmere was seen entering a certain residence that the press was wont to label the "Vice Den of the First Rake of Europe"—a many-pillared mansion known to the less censorious as Carlton House, the residence of the Prince Regent.

The Prince and the previous Earl of Brathmere had been young and wild together in the days when the Prince was in the full flower of his youthful rebellion against his straight-laced father, George III. The Prince Regent was, in fact, practically the only person on the face of the earth who had a good word to say about Alaric's father, and Alaric would in turn regale Prinny with choice accounts of his own adventures, just to show that he was living up to the family name. So it was that Alaric was often invited to the gentlemen-only entertainments that the Prince held in the splendidly over-decorated salons of Carlton House.

Tonight's affair had been mounted in the Gothic Conservatory, so named because its elaborately carved ceiling had been fashioned—at appalling cost to the British taxpayer—to resemble the stained glass and flying buttresses of a medieval cathedral. The guests were already thick about the damask-draped table which held a huge bowl of the potent Regent's punch. Musicians played on a raised dais, accompanying a pretty operatic soprano who trilled arias.

Alaric cast a questing eye over the assemblage, searching for a certain distinctive profile which he finally espied next to the sideboard bearing the cold collation. Before he could approach that gentleman, he had to beat his way past Clive Hastings and the Honourable Freddy Marlowe, two gambling acquaintances who were engaged in their usual pastime of getting up a betting pool. The subject of the bet: Who would enjoy the affections of the pretty soprano at the end of the evening?

"Who's in?" inquired Alaric, mildly intrigued, for the competition involved two things he excelled at—gambling and seduction.

"Drury, of course. And Hughs, Devereaux, and Ashton-Emery."

"A dashing group, indeed," observed Alaric, over his punch cup. "What's to be the proof of the pudding, so to speak."

"The lady's garter," Hastings informed him.

"Ah, but what if she won't give it over?"

The Honourable Freddy waved away the objection with a manicured hand. "I've already thought of that, Alaric. I gave the maid who assists the performers a shilling to tell me what sort of stocking hanger our little songstress is wearing tonight. I'll be able to set the question to rest, one way or the other. So hand over your money and try your luck."

Alaric cast a quick glance toward the opera singer. She was undeniably pretty, but she stirred him not one iota. Another face danced in his mind's eye.

"Not tonight, Freddy. I've got more pressing matters to attend to."

His friends eyed him in frank astonishment. Where was their libertine Alaric, always game for a wager and willing to have a go at any pretty female in sight? Further persuasion failed to move him, and when he took himself off, he left behind two greatly confounded gentlemen.

The Honourable Freddy ventured an explanation. "Maybe he's in love."

"Not him!" retorted Clive Hastings.

The man Alaric sought was homely of visage and portly of build. He was dressed respectably enough, but with considerably less dash than the rest of the gentlemen. He was John

Townsend, the most famous of the Bow Street Runners, a man who had risen by wit and acumen and great good luck from the police office to become the pet of the royal court and high society. When the Prince Regent went to the races, it was John Townsend who held the royal betting purse. When a fashionable hostess desired to protect her garden party of four hundred against lowborn interlopers and crafty pickpockets, it was John Townsend she hired to police the affair. No man who stood on the right side of the law knew the London underworld better than John Townsend.

After greeting the famous thief taker, Alaric got quickly to the point. "Johnny, what do you know of this underworld fellow, White Willie? What's his particular game?"

"Ha!" ejaculated Townsend boomingly. "What's *not* his game? He poses as a humble tavern owner, but he's known to be in with half the criminals in London. Cracksmen, tea leafs, petermen, coiners, mackerels, kidsmen, thimbleriggers—they all tip their hats to White Willie."

"He sounds a formidable fellow," Alaric observed.

"Aye, he's a bad 'un all right—crafty, mean and slippery as a river eel." The ex-Runner fixed a pair of shrewd eyes on Alaric's face. "Might I be asking, m'lord, what you'd be wanting with the likes of White Willie?"

"I think," said Alaric blandly, "he might have something I want."

Seeing that his lordship was not inclined to be confiding, Townsend frowned and shook his head. "Make no mistake, m'lord. You cross White Willie and you're like to wind up in the gutter with your chin separated from your neck."

"I doubt he'd dare to raise his hand against an earl," said Alaric.

Townsend gave a short bark of laughter. "Oh, he'd never do the dirty deed himself. He'd pay someone to pay someone else to pay a footpad to do it and make it look like robbery. There'd be no trail back to our ghostly Willie."

"Ghostly?"

"Aye, that's what he looks like. His skin and hair are white as graveyard bone, and he's got a pair of eyes in him that are pink as rats' peepers. He's got no liking for the light of day either, for he's only seen out on the streets at night."

It was a description that would have given most prudent men pause, but not Alaric. His curiosity was only whetted all the more. What could this White Willie possibly have to do with his mysterious lady?

John Townsend, seeing the speculative gleam in his lordship's dark eyes, felt compelled to issue a stern warning. "I don't know what's between you and Willie, m'lord, but if you take my advice, you'll not press your luck with that wheyfaced cullion."

Alaric only laughed and commanded a waiter to bring another cup of Regent's punch to cure poor Mr. Townsend of his jellied nerves.

Still and all, Johnny Townsend's warning had born fruit in Alaric's mind, and he decided that for the next portion of his inquiry it might be prudent to have an extra pair of eyes watching his back. Laurie pronounced himself game for the adventure—if Alaric would grant him a favor in return.

"My mother is having a rout party—"

"God, no, Laurie! Anything but that."

"Well, I'm not looking forward to it, either," Laurie told him gloomily. "With my father gone, it's me who'll have to shake the hands and dance with Georgiana."

"Good God! Is Georgie out?"

"My mother shot her off last year—something you'd know if you ever attended any of the family parties. Anyway, she's been out for a year and not a whisper of a serious offer has come her way. Mother is getting desperate, I can tell you, and so she thought—"

Alaric regarded him in horror. "Your mother can't mean to promote a match between Georgie and me. Why, I can't even abide the sound of her name."

"Don't worry," said Laurie frankly, "my mother wouldn't have you as a son-in-law. She informs me, however, that there are dozens of other mothers who are not nearly so discriminating, and when they hear you've condescended to put in an appearance, the affair is sure to be a first-class squeeze."

Alaric groaned inarticulately and reached for his claret.

"Come on, Alaric," pressed his cousin. "I'll accompany you tonight, and you attend the rout party."

Alaric regarded him grimly over his glass. "All right, I'll

put in an appearance if I must, but I'll have you know that I much prefer Revett's bloody rat pit to your mother's rout party."

Revett's ratting house was situated behind a tavern in a part of town that might charitably be said to fringe upon the fashionable quarter. Alaric knew his way to the establishment so unerringly that Laurie immediately deduced that his cousin had been here before.

"A few times," Alaric admitted, "when I first came up to London. I've refined my taste in wickedness a great deal since those days."

He led Laurie down a rough-cobbled alley to a dilapidated shed, the door of which he pushed open with his cane. In the light of a swinging overhead lantern were three solid walls of rats, their eyes gleaming redly in the faint light. Cage upon cage of the captured rodents were stacked in the shed to await their turn in the pit.

"Ugh," muttered Laurie involuntarily.

"We'll have a private word with Revett when he comes to resupply the pit," said Alaric, pausing to listen to the sounds floating from the rat pit next door. "He should be along soon from the sound of it."

This was true, for strident yells urging Chomper to chomp, Mauler to maul, and Killer to kill, along with the occasional barking of an excited dog testified to the slaughter going on next door. There was also an announcement from Revett that each and every one of his rats had been brought in from country haystacks and barns by his expert purveyors who roamed the shires looking for select specimens.

"Why should it make any difference where the wretched rats come from?" muttered Laurie.

"Ah, but it does," countered Alaric. "London sewer rats smell to high heaven. Nobody wants to be in a closed room with a couple hundred of them."

"I take your point," said Laurie, eyeing the ranks of chittering rats, who were suddenly chittering at a greater rate than before, for they had heard the footfalls of their executioner well before Alaric and Laurie became aware of his approach.

Revett drew up short in the doorway of the shed; his eyes close on Alaric's face.

"I see you recognize me," said Alaric.

The ratting house owner shrugged, watching them with evasive eyes. "What do you want from me?"

"Information." Alaric took out a well-filled purse and hefted it suggestively in front of Revett's face. "I want information about a certain lady."

"I know a lot of ladies."

Alaric doubted that, but went on. "I want to know the name of the lady who took the Irish girl away from Stanhope."

Revett shrugged unhelpfully. "Don't know her. Never saw her before or since, nor the Irish girl neither."

Alaric tried another tack. "Why does White Willie want the Irish girl? Surely he has plenty of street doxies at his beck and call? What's so special about this one?"

Revett glanced nervously over his shoulder. People did that a lot when discussing White Willie, Alaric was beginning to realize.

"I don't know why Willie wants the girl. He don't confide his business in me. He just wants her back, that's all I know." Revett's voice was sullen.

"How did she get away from your friend Willie in the first place?"

Revett glanced nervously over his shoulder again at the mention of the Arch Cove's name, but this time there was a difference to the man's wariness that led Alaric to believe the rat purveyor might be willing to talk if the price was right. He took two guineas out of the purse and held them in front of Revett. The coins glinted in the lantern light. "How did the Irish girl get away from White Willie?" he repeated.

After a final look around, Revett leaned forward and muttered in a low voice, "An Irish lady with a truncheon snatched her off the street and took her away in a carriage."

Alaric eyed his informant with skeptical mistrust while Laurie scoffed, "You can't possibly expect us to believe that?"

"It's true, I tell you," insisted Revett. "This Irish woman sometimes comes in a carriage and snatches Irish girls away. Clouts anyone who gets in her way with a baton like the Runners carry. All the dollymops, even those that ain't Irish, are afraid of her."

Alaric shook his head inwardly. A club-wielding Irish woman who kidnaps her countrywomen off the streets! This was preposterous—another bizarre personage to add to the already unbelievably strange cast of characters that made up the drama of his masquerading lady.

"I don't suppose," he asked Revett, "you happen to know the name of this Irish woman."

"She don't exactly leave her card."

Alaric tossed him the coins. "There are a hundred more of these waiting for whoever finds the woman I'm looking for. A hundred guineas, Revett. You could buy a lot of rats with that. And one thing more," he went on in soft-voiced menace, "just remember that I can be a very bad enemy. If I ever find out you've played me false, I'll make you wish you were in the pit with your rats. Do you understand me, Revett?"

He turned away without waiting for an answer, Laurie on his heels. Driving back to Mayfair, Alaric brooded. His foray to the ratting house had benefitted him not at all. Instead, he had another mystery to add to the one he already had. He felt defeated. It was a new and distinctly unpleasant sensation.

Who was she? What was she? Where was she?
Why did he care?

Chapter Seven

※

Wherein Deirdre Has a Remarkable Staircase Encounter with Rafe the Footman

*D*eirdre was in disgrace. Not Upstairs with the Thornrose ladies, who still thought of her as a poor little led-astray serving maid, but Downstairs with the Thornrose servants, who knew her better.

At the long kitchen table where the servants took their meals, she was coldly ignored, even by Maria, her erstwhile friend. Worse still, she was favored with trenchant opinions as to how she should have been punished for her little escapade. Mrs. Allen advocated putting her on bread and water. Rafe said she ought to be thrashed and looked positively eager to perform this duty himself. Nell the parlor maid thought she should be given extra chores, all of which, as it happened, would contribute markedly to the upkeep of the parlor. Samuel the groundsman, a personage she hardly even knew, suggested that she be made to kneel on dried peas, a punishment often meted out in the workhouse that he had been placed in as a child, and from which, of course, the Thornrose aunts had rescued him.

But it was Chester who made the direst threat. "I shall tell the ladies that you are a Distraction to the Household and must leave."

For nearly a whole month Deirdre had been on tenterhooks, fearing that the ladies were engaged in finding another position for her, and once all was arranged, she would be hustled off to a new establishment. Now that she was facing the prospect of being cast out of Thornrose House, the place seemed unaccountably dear to her, and she realized that she would never find another situation to match it, not even if she worked at Carlton House itself. Other establishments crammed servants together in unheated attics, providing them with only a few hooks to hang their clothes on, and a straw pallet to sleep on. But at Thornrose House, each maidservant had a bed, a washstand and mirror, and a wardrobe box for her clothing. There was even a charcoal brazier to ward off the chill on cold winter nights.

Of course, the adored mistress of a handsome nobleman could expect a great deal more luxury Deirdre was certain. But as no nobleman seemed about to step forward to adore her, she now realized that she had bungled what was probably the very best situation a serving maid could hope for. As things stood now she couldn't even enjoy the luxury of a good cry over it, for she was too proud to show her distress to the other servants. Late one night, as Maria lay snoring prettily in the other narrow bed, she slipped from their shared quarters, curled up in a miserable knot under the stairs, and indulged in a tempest of muffled weeping.

So engrossed was she in her paroxysm of misery that she failed to notice the sound of stealthy footsteps until they were all but on top of her. A large hand reached in and pulled her from her sanctuary and a disgruntled male voice sounded from behind the glaring yellow light of a lamp.

"I might have known it," said Rafe, who had crept stealthily from the footman's quarters at the other end of the hall to investigate the strange snuffling noises he had supposed to be squirrels in the chimney. "What are you up to now? Do you mean to run off in your nightgown this time?"

Deirdre lifted a quivering chin. "I'm not running anywhere. I merely wished to be alone."

"Well, that's a good place for it, right enough," observed Rafe, setting the lamp on the newel post. "It's not likely to be crowded under there this time of night."

"For your information," said Deirdre, with all the dignity she could muster, which she suspected wasn't much at this point, "I happen to like it under staircases. It reminds me of me childhood in Ireland."

"Oh, it does, does it?" inquired Rafe, obviously disbelieving.

"Yes, if you must know. Me grandmother was the cook at Egan House, and she used to let me watch her work, only I must be very quiet so not to bother anyone. I'm told that I was good as gold under the Egan staircase and quite content. So you see, I've many fond memories of staircases in general and that is why I chose this one for me meditations." (Meditations was a word she had learned from her penmanship lessons with Miss Verity and it had finally come in handy.)

Rafe regarded her quizzically for a moment and then his broad shoulders began shaking with tremors of suppressed laughter.

"And what is it you're finding so funny?" Deirdre inquired in a dangerous voice.

"You, to be sure, lass. Putting on such airs, telling me such a Banbury tale, when the truth is I caught you crying your eyes out because you fancy you haven't a friend in the world."

"I was not crying me eyes out."

"No?" he said softly and touched her damp cheek with a gentle finger.

She pushed his hand away. "I'm sure me troubles are nothing to you, so why don't you go away and leave me alone." But even as she said it she couldn't help noticing that Rafe, in his haste, had failed to button his shirt and that he had been blessed with a very pleasing chest.

Rafe folded his arms across his chest and regarded her with that disconcertingly observant blue gaze of his. "You're still out of temper with me, I see," he remarked conversationally.

"And why shouldn't I be? You said dreadful, cruel things, and I can't think why you should have."

The blue eyes continued to watch her intently. "I'll tell you why. I was jealous."

"Jealous?" echoed Deirdre, baffled. "Why?"

"Because all Sir Aubrey needed do to bring you running is to rattle his purse, and there's nothing a common bloke like myself could ever do to match him." The words were spoken quietly, but Deirdre sensed they were fueled by a deep-seated anger. "And then to have you toying with me, and me knowing all the time it was him you really wanted . . . well, it's hard for a man to bear. But now," he went on, grim satisfaction sounding in his voice, "after what's happened, I reckon maybe you don't think Sir Aubrey's so grand anymore."

That was altogether too much humble pie for Deirdre to swallow in one sitting. "You're a fine one to be talking when it was all your fault I went off with him, anyway."

"My fault!" exclaimed Rafe with such vehemence that for a second both of them paused, listening to see if anyone had been roused. "What the devil do you mean, *my fault?*"

"'Twas your meanness that drove me to it. I was trying so hard to please you, and you never gave me so much as a kindly look, for all I was being as proper as a nun."

"Proper as a nun!" hissed Rafe in a furious undervoice. "And when, pray tell, was that? Every time I turned around, it was more of your pretty flirting airs, tripping up and down the stairs all day long driving me to distraction, looking sidewise at me through your lashes, skittering away if I came near you . . ."

Suddenly he broke off with a laugh and a rueful shake of his head. "I think we've been at cross-purposes here. Can it be you're not indifferent to me, after all? Own up to it, why don't you, and put me out of my misery."

A jumble of thoughts whirled in Deirdre's mind, prominent among them the belief that she ought not to let Rafe off so easily in view of all the misery she had endured on his account. But this impulse was immediately replaced by what she dimly recognized to be a more mature course of action. Rafe had been honest with her, so perhaps he was entitled to some honesty in return.

She looked up at him, her lips curving into a flirtatious smile. "Well, I might be interested . . . if you were very, very nice to me."

After a swift look up and down the darkened hall, Rafe pulled her into his arms and kissed her, drowning out her inarticulate protests. Rafe's kisses were a new and dizzying experience altogether. They were vastly superior to Sir Aubrey's wet claret-fumed smacks, or the puppy kisses her Kilkenny admirers had managed to bestow upon her before her grandmother chased them away with her broom. But as much as she liked his kisses, she liked the feel of his strong arms around her even more, the feel of the warm brawn of his chest when he pressed her cheek against his racing heart. It was the first time in a long time she had felt completely safe.

Rafe laughed softly and twirled a scarlet tress round his finger, marveling at it. Even in the dim lamplight it seemed to have a fiery brightness all its own.

"Do you know," he said in a tone of mild wonderment, "I used to dream about touching your hair like this?" He cupped her chin in his strong capable hands and turned her face up to his. "I suppose I'd be a fool to think you ever dreamed of me."

Deirdre's emerald gaze fell before his steady blue one. All her dreams had been about adoring lords, perfectly reasonable dreams for a girl in her position, but now, she felt a little ashamed of those dreams.

Her hesitation was answer enough.

"Well, it's no matter," said Rafe with a smile and shrug that couldn't quite conceal the thread of disappointment in his voice. He sat down on the stairs and pulled her onto his lap. "Now tell me why you're sitting here in the middle of the night, weeping a puddle under the staircase."

All of Deirdre's troubles came back in a rush and she sagged dejectedly against his shoulder. "I'm afraid," she whispered, "afraid of what the ladies are going to do to me."

"They're not going to punish you. You ought to know that."

"Oh, I know they won't make me kneel on dried peas like those poor children in the workhouse—"

"I should think not," interrupted Rafe with a laugh.

"But what if they think the household will be better off without me because I'm such a distraction?"

"You certainly distract me," said Rafe unhelpfully as he traced the curve of her cheek with a fingertip.

"But what if they mean to send me away?"

"They won't," he predicted confidently.

"But how can you know that?"

"Because I asked Miss Verity straight out, for it was worrying me too. You're not the only one who cares what happens to you, you know."

Deirdre clutched at his shirt, her eyes wide and anxious. "Oh, tell me quickly, Rafe, what did she say?"

"She said you had been through enough, and doubtless you'd learned your lesson."

Deirdre was giddy with relief. "Oh, bless you, Rafe! No one's ever done anything half so wonderful for me before." She wound her arms around his neck and rewarded him with a series of ardent kisses, punctuated by deliriously happy expressions of gratitude. The conversation quickly became more chaotic and the embraces more passionate. Rafe's embraces were considerably more intoxicating than Sir Aubrey's furtive fumblings, and Deirdre found herself thrilled from the tips of her toes to the tips of her breasts which pearled through her white nightgown against Rafe's bare chest.

Rafe, his breathing grown ragged, disengaged himself and set his delightful burden on her feet. "Now that's enough of that," he said in a husky voice. "You'd best go off to bed now. It wouldn't do to be found kissing a man in your nightgown at one in the morning."

"No, of course not," agreed Deirdre, flushing a little.

Suddenly she felt overwhelmed with shyness, for she had been sitting on a man's lap with no more than a thin lawn nightgown between him and all of her. But Rafe was such a solid and comforting young man, and she sensed that he would never do anything to hurt her. She gave him a tremulous smile of farewell and then flitted lightfootedly down the long dark hall.

Rafe watched until the floating white nightgown and the bright hair disappeared through the doorway. *I'll make you dream of me yet, girl,* he vowed. *See if I don't.*

Chapter Eight

In Which Verity Undertakes a Good Work Unlike Any Ever Before

Verity had a lot weighing on her mind: an odious cousin who gave her nightmares, a handsome rake who gave her disturbing dreams. Both were forgotten when Chester appeared with a calling card on his silver tray. That someone was paying a formal call caused Verity some surprise, for the Thornrose ladies were far more accustomed to deal in committee meetings than social calls.

"A Mrs. Giles Sedgewick begs to be received," Chester informed her. "I believe the lady is a relation to your late mother—a very distant relation," he added dampingly.

Taking the card, Verity saw at once what was responsible for Chester's disparaging tone. The card was slightly yellowed and engraved in a script that was no longer in fashion. It obviously belonged to someone who had fallen on hard times and could not afford to have new calling cards printed. Verity's curiosity was instantly aroused. She had never been close to her mother's family, and she could not imagine why one of them should be calling on her at this juncture.

The woman Chester conducted into the library could most aptly be described as a beautiful ruin. She was almost gaunt in appearance, yet the fine bone structure of her face still triumphed. Her dress was of the established mode, but looked to have been put to a number of refashionings to appear that way. Verity hastily bade her caller to be seated, for the worn expression on the older woman's face alarmed her.

Mrs. Sedgewick's voice was like her person—genteel, but far from robust. "I must thank you, Miss Thornrose, for receiving me on such short notice."

"Oh, think nothing of it," said Verity warmly. "We mustn't stand on ceremony, for I assume we are related in some way. I fear I must confess to not being well-versed on the Sedgewick family—there being so very many of them to keep track of."

Mrs. Sedgewick smiled wanly. "There are a great lot of them, are there not? Whenever I consider the Sedgewick family tree, I am always reminded of Mr. Malthus' warnings concerning the evils attending unchecked population increases."

Verity eyed her caller with new respect. There were few persons well-read enough to make allusions to Thomas Robert Malthus in the course of casual conversation. And a particularly apt allusion it was, for Verity's maternal grandfather, Baron Sedgewick, had sired nineteen children on three wives. None of these three ladies had the felicity to survive marriage to their very fecund lord, but the baron himself still lived on, gouty and irascible, the terror of his servants and descendants. Verity had not seen him above four times in her life and was always exceedingly glad that he took no notice whatsoever of her existence.

A few additional paragraphs of conversation with Mrs. Sedgewick served to establish exactly where the two of them met on the family tree. To be precise, Verity was the sole offspring of the first daughter of the Viscount's third wife, while Mrs. Sedgewick was the widow of the Viscount's second son by his first wife.

"We met at Oxford," Mrs. Sedgewick recalled in a misty voice. "My father was a professor of mathematics and Giles was one of his students. Giles' father was furious when we married and he cut Giles off without a penny. Even when our daughter was born he did not relent. My husband later entered the army and was killed at Corunna."

"I am so very sorry, ma'am," said Verity softly, her ready sympathy extended to this frail woman who had obviously suffered much in her life.

Mrs. Sedgewick essayed a polite smile which came out rather in the nature of a sigh. "One becomes reconciled—somehow." She straightened her thin shoulders and fixed Verity with an intense hazel-eyed gaze. "I dare say you are wondering why I have called, so I will come right to the point. I am—I am not well, Miss Thornrose. In fact, I am dying of a wasting disease, and so what I am asking you is in the nature of a deathbed request."

"Well, naturally," said Verity, both shocked and saddened by this disclosure, "I should like to do what I can to help."

"My great concern, Miss Thornrose, is for my daughter Drusilla. When I die, my widow's pension will cease and she will be alone in the world with no means of support. Her only hope is to make a suitable marriage. Otherwise she will be forced to become a governess or a companion, and I need not tell you what kind of life that will be." Mrs. Sedgewick took a deep breath as if gathering up the last vestiges of her strength.

"Miss Thornrose, you and your aunts are everywhere known for your good works, and now I entreat you to extend some of your goodness to my daughter. I am asking you to allow Drusilla to stay with you during the Season and accompany you to your various engagements. She is a pretty child, and I believe that if she could be seen in the right circles, she would encounter a gentleman who would care for her and not be concerned with her lack of fortune."

"My dear Mrs. Sedgewick—" began Verity. But in the face of that lady's hopeful, pleading expression, she found herself quite unable to deliver a definitive refusal.

Her guest went on in a hurried voice. "I know there will be expenses and I would beg you to take this to defray them." From her reticule she withdrew a small box which opened to reveal a pearl necklace. "It came to Giles from his mother and I have managed to hold onto it all these years. I know Giles would approve of it being used to present Drusilla."

"Mrs. Sedgewick, please! I beg you to put away your jewelry. It is not the expense. It is simply that my aunts and I rarely go about in Society. May I suggest that you apply to my grandfather. As head of the family, surely the duty to establish your daughter falls rightfully to him."

A flush mounted Mrs. Sedgewick's hollow cheeks. "I did request help from my father-in-law, Miss Thornrose, and he refused it in the most unpleasant terms. I also applied to several of Drusilla's aunts and none of them would offer me any assistance."

"Well, I call that very shabby indeed!" exclaimed Verity, her sense of justice offended. "What is the point of having such a ridiculously large family if no one in it will exert themselves to aid a relative in time of need?"

Mrs. Sedgewick uttered no word, but only continued to regard Verity meaningfully with her great sunken eyes.

Verity smiled ruefully back at her. "I hoist myself with my own petard, do I not?" She fell silent for a moment, considering the matter. That no one among the great herds of Sedgewicks would trouble themselves to aid a dying relation was shameful. Although there were admittedly some unorthodox aspects to this Good Work, it was definitely a Good Work, and therefore she was compelled to do it.

"Very well, Mrs. Sedgewick, I will do my best to introduce your daughter into some of the better circles, but I must tell you that you have probably hit upon the very last person in all London who should be called upon for this particular assistance."

"No," said Mrs. Sedgewick softly, "I think I have hit upon the very person, and I thank you with all my heart."

"I only hope you thank me still at the Season's end," said Verity frankly, "for this will certainly be a case of the blind leading the blind."

Mrs. Sedgewick was in no way discomposed by this observation. "That may be true, Miss Thornrose, but I do not despair. I have often heard it said that the blind develop superior sensibilities in other areas to compensate for their loss of sight. Now when should I bring Drusilla to you?"

"Why, tomorrow, I suppose. You may as well bring your luggage also so that the two of you may settle in."

"Oh, no," demurred Mrs. Sedgewick hastily. "Please understand that I do not intend to impose myself upon you as well. I have very adequate rooms on Thames Street, and I shall remain there."

"You most certainly will not," said Verity decidedly, for she was familiar with Thames Street and did not doubt that the lodgings were not adequate at all. "You will come and stay with us."

"I—I don't know how to thank you, Miss Thornrose."

"I only hope that when all is said and done, you shall have cause to thank me," said Verity with a shake of her head. "I'll send a carriage for you and your daughter tomorrow. Shall I send a wagon as well, or will a carriage be sufficient to convey your belongings?"

A sound suspiciously like a sob caught in Mrs. Sedgewick's throat. "A carriage will be more than sufficient for all our belongings, thank you."

Upon Mrs. Sedgewick's departure, Verity was left to wonder uneasily if perhaps she hadn't let her calling to perform good works overcome her good sense. Although her money and her birth could gain her entree anywhere, she herself had made no formal debut into Society and she hadn't the least notion of how to set about the business of matchmaking. What she needed was a woman of fashion to be her advisor: someone totally frivolous in nature, devoid of serious thought, conversant with the drivel spouted in first circles, and blithely uncaring about what a dreadful mess the world was in.

In short, she needed Belle Toddington.

The Toddington town house was situated at the crossroads between Mount Street and Park Lane. The residence boasted a splendid view of Hyde Park in the front, an elegantly landscaped pocket garden in the back, and one of the loveliest, most vivacious young women in London Society as its mistress. It was also indisputable that Lady Christabel Toddington had no more force of mind than the marigolds that graced her back walk. However, the extreme poverty of her intellect had not prevented her from forming a fast friendship with Verity Thornrose during their school days.

The two young ladies had shared chambers for four years at Mrs. Brompton and Mrs. Purcell's Select Female Seminary for the Daughters of the Aristocracy and the Gentry (known to the irreverent as Mrs. B and Mrs. P's Prize Peagoose Farm). Here, Miss Verity had tried to improve Miss Christabel's mind—and failed. Here, Miss Christabel had tried to initiate Miss Verity into the art of frivolous behavior—and likewise failed.

That their friendship survived and flourished was living proof that opposites attract, for two young ladies more opposite in looks and temperament could hardly be imagined. In contrast to

Verity's slender form and blackberry and cream coloring, Lady Toddington was a Junoesque china doll brought to life, with fluffy golden hair, wide cornflower eyes, and a richly curved figure that had become even more richly curved since the birth of her first child two years ago. While marriage and motherhood had not appreciably deepened the shallow stream of Christabel's intellect, Verity believed that her old friend had developed a more charitable outlook towards the sufferings of others, having herself suffered through thirty-six hours of excruciating labor in the bringing forth of her daughter.

Verity found Lady Toddington in her boudoir, ringed round by dressmakers, incapable of any movement lest she be perforated by a sewing pin. The gown taking shape on her ladyship's well-formed person was a celestial blue crepe topped off by a fraise neck ruff, an accessory which made it appear to Verity's jaundiced eye as if her friend's head was being displayed on a plate of ruffles.

"Verity, darling!" cried her ladyship from her stationary position amidst the billowing swathes of celestial blue. "How wonderful to see you . . . unless," she hastened to disclaim, "you've come to dun me on behalf of another of your everlasting charities, in which case you might as well turn around and go home because my allowance for the quarter is already promised." She cast an eloquent downward glance to the dressmakers crouching at her feet and Verity comprehended in an instant precisely who it was that had levied the previous claim on Christabel's monies. Marriage to the affluent Lord Toddington had not altered this particular aspect of Christabel's nature. Never, it seemed, would she be able to live within her clothing allowance.

"You alarm yourself unnecessarily, Christa. I've not come to dun you for money. I've come to call upon your expertise."

"Expertise! Good gracious, I didn't know I had any."

"Well, you're not chock-full of it, that's for certain," Verity told her dispassionately, for one of the mainstays of their friendship was that each felt herself perfectly free to speak frankly about the other's many failings. "But," Verity went on, "in this you are truly nonpareil, and I hope you'll be willing to help me."

"Nonpareil? Me?" exclaimed Christa, much struck by this vision of herself. "Well, what is it that you want of me?"

Verity's answer to this question left Christa thunderstruck. "*You*, the sober, serious-minded Mistress Reform, you, Verity Thornrose, are presenting a young lady to Society. I can scarcely credit it."

"I can scarcely credit it myself," Verity admitted, "but since the task has fallen to me, I'm determined to do my best."

"But, Verity, you know you are woefully inept in Society."

"Oh, really, Christa. I may not have been an Incomparable—"

"Indeed, you were not!" retorted Christa tartly. "*I* was the Incomparable the first year we were out if you'll recall."

"—but I wouldn't say I bungled all my social engagements."

"Well, I would say it. Every time some poor unsuspecting gentleman approached you, you lectured him on some boring bill in Parliament, which is exactly the kind of talk that men don't like to hear from women. And you're forever telling your hostesses over the dinner table what a shame it was that the poor in the rookeries couldn't eat so well, as if anyone cared to converse about a rookery over a roast. Worse still, your dresses always make you look as if you're in half-mourning and you never laugh. If you weren't going to be so prodigiously rich one day, no one would invite you anywhere."

Verity heard these strictures with equanimity. She had heard them all from Christabel many times before. Her old friend had taken it as a personal affront that Verity would not throw herself wholeheartedly into the shallow silliness of the social world. Christa, of course, had taken to shallow silliness like a duck to water, and the nickname Belle had been hung upon her by those in the *ton* who made it their business to attend to such matters.

"You know very well, Christa, that I did not take in Society because I found it horridly boring and I still do. So you see why I need your help in bringing out Miss Sedgewick."

"Well, I don't know—"

"Oh, you can't mean to fail me in this," implored Verity. "Besides, you know you will love to do it because you may order me to do all sorts of things which I heartily dislike."

A gleam lit in Christa's eyes. "You mean I may dress you as I please, and you will promise to act like a lady of the first consideration and not like a Birmingham Methodist?"

"Oh, if I must," said Verity with a sigh. "But remember, it's Miss Sedgewick we're marrying off, not me."

"Well . . ." Christa paused consideringly. "What does the girl look like?"

"Do you know, I've no notion, now that you mention it. I haven't yet met her."

Christabel was aghast. "Do you mean to say that you have agreed to sponsor this girl in her first Season and you don't know what she looks like? What if she's a hunchback? Or a dwarf? Or crippled? Or freckled?"

"Don't be silly! I'm sure her looks are perfectly well to pass. Her mother must have been quite lovely once."

"What do you mean 'once'?" asked Christa, alarmed.

"It's all rather tragic, I'm afraid. Drusilla's mother is dying of a wasting disease and the poor girl will be left entirely alone in the world unless I—or rather, we—arrange a suitable marriage."

"But this is truly dreadful!" Christa exclaimed.

Verity nodded in agreement. "Oh, if you could have seen the marks of suffering on poor Mrs. Sedgewick's face—"

"I don't mean that," interrupted Christa. "I mean no sooner will you have brought this girl out and found her a husband than her mother bids fair to inconveniently expire, and the girl will have to be in mourning for a year, and have a quiet wedding with no one but the family present and everyone in black gloves. How ghastly!"

Verity regarded her friend with kindly exasperation. "Christa, please try to keep your wandering wits on the matter at hand. Will you help me or won't you?"

Christabel's eyes glazed slightly and she proceeded to gnaw her lovely underlip, sure signs that she was cogitating deep and difficult matters. "All right," she said finally, "I'll do it. But upon terms. First I must see if Miss Sedgewick is presentable. And I warn you, Verity, if she is an antidote, there's no point in either of us wasting our time. If she has no looks *and* no money—and you needn't scruple to say she's purse-pinched, for all the Sedgewicks are—then there's no hope for her."

"Very well," agreed Verity. "Come meet her tomorrow and judge for yourself whether she'll be worth your while."

"And one more thing, Verity."

"Yes?" inquired her friend warily.

"You must put yourself entirely in my hands and do exactly as I say. You may be very needlewitted with your committees and your tracts, but when it comes to matchmaking, you're the merest babe in the woods, so you must promise to let me call the tune."

Verity cast her eyes heavenward. "Oh, all right, Christa. I promise. Word of a Thornrose." Whereupon, Verity took her leave of Lady Christabel Toddington, wondering grimly what manner of absurd tunes her friend would have her dancing to before this Good Deed was done.

The next afternoon brought Christabel to Thornrose House to await the arrival of Mrs. Sedgewick and her daughter. Verity had been teasing herself nearly sick with worry that Miss Drusilla Sedgewick would prove to be knockerfaced and Christabel would decamp, leaving her with a homely eighteen-year-old to provide a husband for—a task she knew was beyond her. As much as she might deplore the male predilection for putting a woman's appearance before every other quality of mind and heart, she knew it was a sad fact about the male sex.

So it was with a heartfelt sigh of relief that she caught her first glimpse of Miss Sedgewick. Surely Miss Drusilla, who had a great look of her mama about her, would pass muster with even so strict a judge of feminine beauty as Christabel, who was even now eyeing the chestnut-haired, hazel-eyed girl as if she were a filly on the auction block.

It was also soon apparent that Miss Sedgewick possessed a decided character along with her pretty looks, for no sooner were they seated than she announced that before matters progressed further she had something to say.

"Drusilla, please!" pleaded her mother.

"Forgive me, mama, but I must be frank with Miss Thornrose. I'm sure she would prefer it that way."

"But of course you must feel free to speak your mind," Verity invited.

Miss Sedgewick fixed her with an unwavering look. "I am aware, Miss Thornrose, that you wish to secure my future by finding me a husband. But before you trouble yourself on my behalf, I wish you to know that I do not shrink from the necessity of earning my own living. I have told my mother many times that I shall go on quite well as a governess."

"Drusilla," implored her mother, "you don't know what you're saying. You've no notion of what such a life is like."

"I couldn't agree with your mother more," struck in Christabel. "I should think you would be willing to do anything to avoid joining the ranks of such unfortunates."

"And I think you should know, my lady," said Drusilla, giving Christabel a very straight look, "that my mother was employed as a governess before she married my father."

Christabel was not one whit abashed. "Then you must understand that your mother knows whereof she speaks when she says that you would not be at all happy in such an existence."

Miss Sedgewick looked as if she were about to say a great deal more, but Verity hastily intervened. "Drusilla, I believe I understand your feelings better than you know. I, too, am able to face a life of spinsterhood with equanimity. Marriage is not for everyone and certainly one can have a tolerable existence without it."

"Oh, Verity, really!" muttered Christabel, appalled by such heresy.

"On the other hand," Verity continued reasonably, "you should not let misplaced pride foreclose you from the opportunity to form an attachment with a suitable young gentleman. It may be that marriage to the right man would suit you very well."

"Hear! Hear!" chirped Christabel brightly.

Indecision was still writ large upon Miss Sedgewick's pretty features. "You are all kindness, Miss Thornrose, but to be blunt, I find it difficult to be an object of charity."

"But I do not look upon this as a charitable endeavor," Verity contradicted her gently. "How should I? I know that were my mother alive, she would gladly undertake this duty for one of her half-brother's children. In her place, I can do no less. And think also of the comfort it will give your mother to see you take your rightful place in Society."

Disarmed at last, Drusilla finally acceded. "But I must insist you let me do what I can to repay your kindness. Surely there are tasks I might perform for you. I am tolerable at embroidery and my handwriting is generally thought to be very elegant."

Verity smiled. "I'm afraid fancy embroidery is not much done in this establishment, but correspondence is plentiful and I would certainly welcome your assistance."

"I only wish I could do more for you, ma'am."

"Well, there is *one* thing you may do for me this very instant," Verity declared with a twinkle in her eyes. "I wish you would call me Verity instead of ma'am. All this ma'aming makes me feel like the ape leader Christabel is forever telling me I am."

"All right, Christa," Verity demanded of her friend after the Sedgewick ladies had departed upstairs, "what's your verdict? Will she do?"

"Well," Christa allowed, "she's rather tall and less handsome of bosom than one likes to see. Still, I think she might take and yes, I will help you launch her."

Verity heaved a sigh of relief. "Surely we won't have any trouble interesting the gentlemen in her," she went on optimistically. "I thought she was quite personable myself."

"Except for those opinions of hers."

Verity blinked. "What's wrong with her opinions?"

"She has altogether too many of them. Men don't like women with opinions. That's why I get on famously with men of all ages. I haven't a single opinion to speak of."

Verity was once again at the point of denouncing her oldest and dearest friend for the rattle-brain she was when Chester appeared on the threshold. "Mr. Octavian is without," he intoned funereally.

Christabel sprang to her feet, arranging her ivory muslin skirts for flight. "Verity, why didn't you warn me that that Friday-faced cousin of yours was coming to call! You know I can't abide that man. I'll never forget all those dreadful nightmares you had about him at school. Ring Chester and have him show me out before the fellow is announced—"

But Verity was looking up at her, violet eyes haunted. "Don't leave me, Christa, I beg you."

As insufficient as Lady Toddington's understanding was,

her friend's distress penetrated into the less airy regions of her brain. "All right, Verity, I'll stay if you wish."

Verity managed a distracted nod, her attention fixed on the heavy tread advancing inexorably down the hall. An instant later, Octavian's massive form filled the doorway. That he was not pleased by Christabel's presence was plain.

"I regret to find you engaged, cousin. There are important matters which we must discuss and I fear that Lady Toddington will be sadly bored by the conversation."

But Christabel was impervious to this broadly expressed hint that she take herself off. "Oh, don't mind me," she carolled to Octavian, "I frequently find important matters boring. Just go on as if I weren't here."

Being outmaneuvered by the simpleminded Lady Toddington did not sit well with Octavian, and he bent her a look of intense dislike. Verity marveled that Christabel couldn't sense it. Then she had no more time to concern herself with Christabel, for now Octavian had turned his attention to her. The weight of his disapproval fell on her like a mountain of cold stone.

"It is regrettable, cousin, that you haven't taken the time to arrange your schedule with more efficiency."

"I . . . do apologize, Octavian," she heard herself stammering in a manner she privately considered pathetic, but was unable to control. "So many things have happened of late that I quite forgot your visit. I can only beg your pardon and assure you it will not happen again."

Christabel watched nonplused as the usually masterful Verity became undone before her odious cousin. In a spurt of ivory ruffles, she shot to her feet and stood before the settee upon which Verity was cowering. "I protest, Mr. Smythe, you are too severe with Verity! This matter of arranging Miss Sedgewick's come-out arose so suddenly—"

"What?" boomed Octavian ominously.

Verity's heart quailed anew. She had been cudgeling her brains for a way to break the news of her latest endeavor to Octavian, whose position as head of the Thornrose Bank gave him control of her fortune until she was twenty-five. She was under no illusion as to how her austere cousin would view her latest Good Work.

"Indeed," said Octavian once Christabel had finished breaking the news in the most bubble-headed manner possible, "I find I cannot sanction this fruitless exercise of frivolity. I must insist, cousin, that you abandon your plans regarding this young woman at once."

"And why should she?" protested Christabel indignantly. "You act as if Verity has done something discreditable. I don't understand you, sir."

Octavian loomed over her, his massive frame dwarfing her ruffled one. His huge hands clenched spasmodically, but Christabel was too undiscerning to sense the latent danger of which Verity was so aware. She merely continued to frown up at Octavian, rather like a poodle facing up to a mastiff.

"Naturally," Octavian informed her in a rumbling sneer, "*you* would not understand the punctiliousness with which I feel compelled to review my cousin's every action. I am somewhat nicer in my expectations of her behavior than I would be of you, Lady Toddington. I would not see her clad in tawdry, drinking spiritous liquors, dancing in the depraved manner that is now the fashion. And, Lady Toddington, I would not have my cousin consorting with women whose highborn titles cannot disguise the fact that they have the besmirched souls of fallen women."

That Octavian Smythe had all but denounced her as the Whore of Babylon did not seem to insinuate its way into Christabel's woolly thinking processes. Regarding him with the greatest bewilderment, she inquired, "But what has all this to do with bringing out Miss Sedgewick?"

Octavian answered with the hissed precision of one who speaks through clenched teeth. "I am attempting to make the point, Lady Toddington, that the world is fraught enough with fleshy temptations without the daughters of our best families displaying themselves in a manner calculated to provoke carnal thoughts in the opposite sex."

Christa emitted a silvery little laugh and plumped herself down in the settee beside the shrinking Verity. "Really, sir! If young ladies did not evoke such longings in young men, then there would be no marriages, no children, and the world would not go forward. If that is your only objection to our sponsoring poor Miss Sedgewick, then it is a very silly one."

"Christa . . . Octavian," Verity managed weakly. "I beg of you not to quarrel over my affairs."

"I should not dream of quarreling with Lady Toddington," said Octavian. The words were urbane enough, but Verity was certain that her cousin was enduring near-murderous frustration at Christabel's obtuseness. "I perceive," he went on, "that you are much engaged this afternoon, Verity, and will have no time to consider my remonstrations properly. I will call again when you are not so plagued by distractions."

With a last brimstone glance at Christabel, he bowed and took his leave.

"What an odious man!" huffed Christa once the floor had ceased to vibrate from his passing. "No wonder he is never invited anywhere. I wonder that you receive him."

"I've no choice really," said Verity shakily. "My father named him trustee of my estate, and my aunts' as well. He means well, but I do wish he would not watch over me with such diligence."

"Well, I am excessively glad he does not watch over me," declared Christa. "He makes my flesh creep."

The horrid thought of being watched over by Mr. Smythe did not leave Lady Toddington's mind for a whole quarter hour. As her carriage clattered back to Toddington House, she found herself falling prey to a strange, frightening fancy, an odd mental start for one usually so devoid of troubling imagination. Whenever her carriage came to a pause in the Mayfair traffic, she half-expected to see Octavian Smythe standing on the street corner beside a large pile of stones, waiting for her to appear within range.

Octavian Smythe retired to his cavernous, pillared office in the Thornrose Bank on Threadneedle Street. Here, he brooded upon the designing female who had insinuated herself into Thornrose House. He brooded upon the shocking sums of money Christabel Toddington would suborn Verity into spending on sinful female finery. And most of all he brooded upon the worldly influences, the worldly *men,* that Verity would now encounter.

At length, Octavian summoned his carriage. The rows of

clerks who labored over quill pen and inkwell counting his fortune bobbed respectfully to their feet as he passed.

Octavian directed his carriage to the home of a wellborn matron of good family, a lady prominent in many charitable societies. The lady's husband, a respected clergyman, was prominent in a far more secret and select political society. He, along with Octavian Smythe and a number of other gentlemen, believed that England had not been well-governed since the time of the Roundheads. They yearned for the day when the idle, glittering monarchy and its fool of a Regent would fall, and England was once again ruled by the stern and worshipful black-clad men of iron. They worked in numerous clandestine ways for this cause, and if it one day led again to revolution, so be it.

The wellborn matron and her clergyman husband were kindred spirits to Octavian in this endeavor, and he trusted them implicitly. Where trust failed, however, there was another safeguard. The husband owed a considerable sum to the Thornrose Bank on Threadneedle Street.

So it was that the matron was anxious to comply with Octavian's bidding. She would be his eyes and ears. She would report to him all that his cousin said and did in the course of her social engagements. She would be the voice of Octavian Smythe's conscience whispering into Verity Thornrose's ear. Whether at the banquet table, on the ballroom floor, or in the ladies retiring room, she was never to let Verity Thornrose forget how Octavian Smythe expected his future wife to behave.

Lapses in Miss Thornrose's behavior were to be duly noted and reported to him. When Verity became his wife, he would, as was his husbandly right, mete out her punishment accordingly.

Chapter Nine

In Which the Earl of Brathmere Masquerades as a Man with Honourable Intentions

*A*laric stood atop the arched staircase of his Aunt Mont's townhouse, monumentally bored. Wending their way up the staircase toward him in a plumed, bejeweled, perfumed herd were the fashionables of the *ton*, rigged out in full evening regalia. Fans waved, jewels flashed, snuff boxes snapped, expensive perfumes warred against one another. There was hardly room to breathe, much less move.

My dear aunt must be in ecstasies, thought Alaric dourly, for no hostess could count her affair a success unless she put her guests in danger of being either trampled or suffocated. Scaling the Mont staircase this particular evening offered both these dangers.

Lady Mont, in cerise crepe, presided over the fashionable crush from the top of the stairs, greeting her guests before waving them on to salon, card room, or ballroom. Her ladyship still possessed much of the acclaimed beauty of her youth, although giving birth to five children had somewhat impaired her acclaimed figure. Beside her on the stairhead was her third daughter, Georgiana, who unfortunately was the image of her gingery-haired father and not her lovely mother. Also in indentured servitude on the receiving line was the Monts' only son, Laurence, who wore an expression of long-suffering, an emotion that Alaric was in perfect sympathy with—

It was then that he saw her.

She was standing halfway up the packed staircase, looking upward. It was her. It was, by God. The same oval face, the same deep-of-the-night hair. It had to be her, he exulted as he elbowed his way to the railing . . . unless his wits were abandoning him or his eyes were playing tricks on him.

When her upraised gaze crossed his, all doubt was erased. A spark of mutual sensual awareness jumped between them. Her eyes widened, the color drained from her face, and she gripped the curving stair rail so as not to topple over.

I'll be damned! thought Alaric. *I look for her high and low, and now I stumble upon her right in the middle of the most insipid affair of the Season.*

Even as the thought formed in his mind, she contrived to conceal herself behind another woman he vaguely recognized as Belle Toddington. *She's going to bolt!* he thought, and he was seized by the strongest impulse to charge down the stairs, and carry her—willing or no—off to Brathmere House, where they would come to a singularly sweet understanding in his waiting bed. But uncharacteristic caution cooled his ardor. He didn't know what kind of a game she was playing here in his aunt's house. Better to reconnoiter first.

"Laurie," he hissed, pulling his startled cousin to one side. "She's here."

"Who? You mean—"

"Yes, it's her, I tell you. The one in purple, standing next to Belle Toddington."

"That's mulberry, not purple," stated Laurie, the brother of four fashion-mad sisters.

But Alaric brushed past him without answering and stepped into the receiving line next to Lady Mont. "May I be of assistance in greeting the guests, Aunt Louisa?" he asked her with his most charmingly insincere smile.

Lady Mont, both gratified and mystified by this sudden stroke of civility from her scapegrace nephew, gave him a vague nod before returning her attention to a beribboned ambassador. Laurie elbowed his way between Alaric and an annoyed Georgiana, determined not to miss the forthcoming meeting between Alaric and his mysterious lady.

She's knows I'm lying in wait for her, thought Alaric, for now she seemed to be looking for an avenue of escape but could find none in the back-to-back, toe-to-toe crowd on the staircase. *Don't run away,* Alaric willed her silently, *for I swear I'll come after you here and now, though all of London watches.*

"Verity!" Christabel was exclaiming in an annoyed voice. "You're standing on my flounce."

Verity was incapable of replying. He was here. Dear Lord, he was here! She risked another look upward to find his eyes glittering darkly down at her. Guilty panic threatened to overwhelm her. Would he denounce her in front of everyone? Would he bow and say, "Ah, Miss Thornrose, how nice to renew our acquaintance. I've not seen you since the night you accosted me in the front of the Pantheon like a common streetwalker and I laid lustful hands upon your unchaperoned person in my private box."

Merciful God in heaven! Octavian would boil her in oil!

"Verity!" repeated Christa sharply. "What is the matter? You're pale as a ghost. You're not going to faint, are you?"

Verity could only shake her head dumbly and allow herself to be nudged another step upwards. She felt as if she were mounting the gallows. Step by upward step, she came closer to where the handsome hangman waited.

And now the moment was upon her.

Lady Mont was discoursing upon their mutual charity, the Royal Infirmary for Disorders of the Eyes, but the only reality for Verity was the dark gaze that rested on her face like a hot branding iron.

Said Lady Mont, blissfully unaware of the undercurrents swirling about her, "Miss Thornrose, I don't believe you have the acquaintance of my nephew, Alaric Tierney, Earl of Brathmere."

Verity hesitated. Lies, whether circumstantial or direct, were repugnant to her, for after all, her very name meant truth. On the other hand, the truth was tantamount to suicide, and she had a lot of widows, orphans, and unvaccinated persons depending on her.

"Lord Brathmere and I have . . ." she swallowed hard and then prevaricated shamelessly, "never been formally introduced."

She extended a hand to his lordship, and he carried it to his lips. She waited, heart pounding, for him to denounce her and watch her dance on air before all of London Society. But the hangman wasn't hanging tonight, for he did no more than to repeat her name. Yet the look he gave her promised a further encounter, as did the way he murmured her name, silken and intimate, as if he knew that she had dreamed dreams of him in her virgin's bed.

Verity felt herself trembling. In all her well-ordered life, she had never had a guilty secret, never done a deed that need be hidden from the light of day. But now all that was changed. She walked away from that dark, watching gaze knowing that a little piece of her soul had been chipped away.

The minute that Laurie was freed from his servitude in the receiving line, Alaric clapped hands on his young cousin and propelled him unceremoniously to an out-of-the-way alcove. "Laurie, you dolt, you knew her all the time!" he accused.

"Dash it all, Alaric, how could I have known?" retorted Laurie, stung. "I barely even noticed her when she came to call on my mother."

"Good God, Laurie! A man would have to be dead or gelded not to notice her. Now tell me what you know of her."

Laurie shrugged over his champagne glass. "All I know about Miss Verity Thornrose," he informed his impatient cousin, "is that she's rich, a high-stickler, and mad to reform the world, just like all the Thornroses before her. My mother says the whole family acts like a parcel of leftover Roundheads. They all have names like Thrift and Moderation and are depressingly upright. The only reason your precious Miss Verity has condescended to enter into frivolous society is because she's trying to snare a husband for her cousin, Drusilla Sedgewick, who's as poor as a church mouse. Too bad about Miss Sedgewick, don't you think?" he went on reflectively. "She's dashed pretty. Georgie thought so too, of course she gave her the cold shoulder when they were introduced."

Alaric had no interest in this minor drama. There was a glitter in his dark eyes: the hot-blooded Tierney male pursuing a conquest. "I have to tell you, Laurie, that this Miss Thornrose paragon intrigues me. I mean to turn her pretty Puritan head, and no mistake."

"Ha! I wish you luck in that little endeavor, cousin," exclaimed Laurie, tossing off another gulp of champagne.

"You'd better be warned that your pretty Puritan lives with two—or maybe it's three—spinster aunts who will flay you alive if you so much as look in her direction. Besides," he went on thoughtfully, "Miss Thornrose doesn't strike me as the sort of woman who would succumb to your blandishments."

"Care to make a bet on that, cuz?" inquired Alaric silkily.

"She's devilish high-principled, Alaric."

"But not, I don't think, cold-blooded." He relieved Laurie of his champagne glass and took him by the arm. "Now come along, my worthy host. I need you to help me set a snare for our Miss Verity. She's certain to lope off the moment she sees me coming, and it's confoundedly hard to mount an assault on a lady's virtue if she won't stand still."

Alaric's rake's blood was up for the hunt. The conquests of his past would be as nothing compared to the seduction of Miss Verity Thornrose.

Having sent Miss Drusilla Sedgewick off for punch in the company of a promising young fellow known to be in line for five hundred a year and an estate in Chislehurst, Christabel pounced upon Verity. She bundled her friend into a secluded niche behind some potted palms and demanded without preamble, "All right, my girl! Out with it. What's between you and Brathmere?" Shallow-witted she might be, but Christabel was a veritable bloodhound when it came to scenting romantic intrigue.

Verity was near tears. "Oh, Christa, I fear you will think me the most awful fool outside Bedlam when I tell you what I've done."

Her fears were entirely justified. "Verity, you've put your reputation in the hands of the most heartless, ruthless rakehell in London."

"But surely," faltered Verity, remembering her Good Samaritan of the Pantheon, "surely, heartless and ruthless is too severe . . ."

But then Christa recited several doggerel couplets that were currently being circulated by Society under the title, "The Return of the Lock," and Verity had to agree that heartless and ruthless summed up the earl very aptly.

Worse anecdotes followed. The Earl of Brathmere had won

and lost several fortunes at play. He had killed a man in a duel. He had been expelled from Cambridge for sheer hell-raising. At nineteen he had become the lover of the beautiful and notorious Lady Jane Harley, Countess of Oxford, preceding Lord Byron in the countess's practiced and promiscuous affections.

Verity paled at hearing the last. "Merciful heavens! Don't tell me he's thought to be the father of one of the Miscellany." Even Verity had heard the gossip that Lady Oxford's five children were all reputed to have different fathers and that they had been collectively dubbed the "Harleian Miscellany" by the cruel *ton*.

This question caused Christa to ruminate briefly upon the ages of the Harley progeny. Finally she declared, "I don't think we can convict Brathmere of fathering a bastard on her ladyship. Although," she added tartly, "I'm sure it's not for lack of trying."

Verity shook her head, feeling very much at sea. "If only I knew the right thing to do."

This untimely moralizing caused Christabel to throw up her hands in frustration. "The only thing you can do, Verity, is to lie low and hope he'll forget about you. We'll have my carriage brought around back, and you can slip out that way. I'll make your excuses and chaperone Drusilla."

But the more Verity considered this course of action, the less she liked it. Thornroses did not "lie low." Nor did they skulk out of back entrances. They faced their tribulations unflinchingly, though it took them to the headsman's block—a fate that actually did befall one unregenerate Roundhead Thornrose who, according to a contemporary chronicler, "blenched not a whit" as the ax fell.

Can I do no less? Verity asked herself sternly. Now that she had recovered from the shock of being confronted by her Samaritan in the all-too-real male flesh, she was heartily ashamed of herself for having blenched so cravenly before him.

She drew a determined breath. "I'll not run, Christa. I shall approach Lord Brathmere forthrightly and ask him to swear on his honor to never speak of what occurred between us. And if he will not, then at least I will know his intentions and be prepared."

Christa, who had been peering out from among the palm fronds at the gentleman in question, turned to her with a worried frown. "Well, if you're going to speak to him, you had better do it now. He's over there with that Mont boy fairly smothering Drusilla with gallantries, and I'm sure you'll agree no good can come of that."

He's lying in wait for me, Verity apprehended. *He knows that sooner or later, I must return to Drusilla's side. Very well then, my lord libertine, I will meet you face to face and bring all into the open between us, for I have no liking for these intrigues and dark secrets.*

And so with her chin lifted and her expression set, Verity left the shelter of the potted palms, and marched across the ballroom to engage the rakehell earl.

In her estimation of why the Earl of Brathmere and young Mr. Mont had attached themselves to Drusilla, Verity had done Laurie an injustice. The desire uppermost in that young man's mind was to become better acquainted with the various perfections of the pretty Miss Sedgewick. But Verity was on the mark as to Alaric's motivation. He knew that sooner or later Miss Thornrose would have to return to her protégé.

And soon enough she did, sweeping across the floor toward them, slender as a wand in her mulberry gown, her violet eyes fixed on him very particularly as she joined their company. After the exchange of socially correct nothings were undergone for the requisite period of time, Miss Thornrose, the veteran of many an organizing committee meeting, proceeded to take charge of the Fateful Encounter with a briskness that left the gentlemen speechless.

"Mr. Mont," she said crisply, "I desire a breath of air and would have his lordship escort me to the garden. Will you be kind enough to return Miss Sedgewick to Lady Toddington?"

"Yes . . . of course," said Laurie, slightly stunned by this swift and masterly dismissal. But having gotten his marching orders, he obediently possessed himself of Drusilla's arm and led her away. Shooting Alaric a sidewise glance, he detected a triumphant gleam in his cousin's dark eyes. Alaric had to be extremely pleased at this unlooked-for opportunity for a private talk with Verity Thornrose. It seemed the virtuous Mistress Reform wasn't going to require much seducing after all. In fact, she appeared unmaidenly anxious to hurry Alaric off to a rendezvous without delay.

Alaric bowed to her, eyes glinting. "I am entirely at your disposal, ma'am—for a walk in the garden, or anything else you desire."

"You gratify me excessively, sir," said Verity in a cool voice. "Let us hope you remain so pleasantly biddable."

Alaric smiled, offered his arm, and strolled off with her into the garden. He wasn't at all sure why she was taking him in hand like this, but he was willing to allow her to call the tune—for now. In the end, he would have her dancing abandonedly to his tune, of that he was certain.

In the farthest reaches of the garden, Verity found a spot that was to her liking and came to a stop.

"Should you like to sit?" her escort inquired politely, gesturing to a stone bench set amidst a clump of shrubbery.

"I think not," said Verity in an austere voice. "There are some things better said while standing."

"You terrify me, Miss Thornrose."

Verity doubted that. It was she who felt uneasy in the presence of this disturbing man who was reputed to have committed every one of the seven deadly sins—except possibly gluttony. Casting a quick glance up and down the earl's well-formed person, she decided that gluttony was certainly one thing he could never be accused of.

She clasped her gloved hands together as she always did when preparing to make a speech. "My lord, I would like to explain to you how I came to be at the Pantheon that particular evening." She gave him a brief account of Deirdre's history and how she was enticed to the masquerade by the unprincipled Sir Aubrey. "And of course," she concluded, "I wish you to know that my gratitude for your aid to us remains undiminished."

"Ah, yes," he observed somewhat sardonically, "as I recall, you pronounced yourself to be forever in my debt, and then promptly decamped without giving me the courtesy of your name."

"But surely—in retrospect—you see why."

He smiled faintly. "Oh, I quite understand that the excellent Miss Thornrose of the reforming Thornroses would not want her sterling reputation compromised in any way."

"And it is this precise matter which still concerns me, my

lord. I have recently been apprised of your reputation, and to be frank, what I have heard is not to your credit."

"And just what have you heard, Miss Thornrose?"

"That you are a gambler, a duelist, and a libertine." Warming to her subject, she went on, "I have also heard that you drink to excess, that you are idle in the extreme, that you are a haunter of the lowest dens, and that your name has been scandalously linked with several married ladies."

"You neglect to mention," he said softly, "that I have also been known to consort with women who importune me in front of the Pantheon."

Verity felt her color rise, but she was too practiced a debater to be rocked from her balance. "You put your finger on the crux of the matter, my lord. I realize now that I was foolish to go to the Pantheon as I did. Were the details of our encounter to become known I would be held up to public notoriety. You have it within your power to do me great harm. I would like to know if you intend to do so."

There was a pregnant pause, and then the Earl of Brathmere said in a voice of black velvet, "Surely, you don't think, Miss Thornrose, that I would ever bring myself to do you harm."

Verity's usually quick debater's wits promptly abandoned her. None of her debating opponents had ever said anything remotely like that to her. None of her debating opponents had ever looked remotely like the way this man did in the moonlit garden . . . like the answer to a maiden's prayer for a happy end to her maidenhood.

She was still trying to formulate a coherent reply when she heard the sound of her name being hallooed shrilly through the nighttime air. A woman hurried toward them, a plumpish matron, possessed of a doughy face and a pair of protuberant blue eyes that seemed to be perpetually staring about in appalled disapproval at the world around her. Verity knew herself to be acquainted with the lady, but such was the disarray of her thinking processes that it was only at the last possible minute when she was positively forced to make the introduction that the name came to her.

"My lord, may I present Mrs. . . . Mortlock."

Mrs. Mortlock acknowledged the introduction stiffly and drew her silk shawl more closely across her ample bosom as if to shield her matronly charms from the gentleman's view. It was apparent that Mrs. Mortlock knew all about Lord Brathmere's reputation and didn't approve. And it was equally apparent from the earl's negligent stance that he didn't care what Mrs. Mortlock thought of him.

Feeling that the responsibility for facilitating this awkward encounter fell rightfully to her, Verity observed brightly, "Mrs. Mortlock and I are old acquaintances. We are both members of the Society for the Suppression of Vice."

"Ah," said Alaric, "then perhaps I should take my leave lest you ladies feel obliged to suppress me." Ignoring Mrs. Mortlock's offended gasp, he turned to Verity, "I must thank you for your enlightening discourse on the issues of reform. I can't say that any of them stir me to any great passion, but your efforts are certainly admirable, and it is my earnest wish that nothing will occur to diminish the esteem in which you are universally held."

"You are too kind, my lord," replied Verity in an emotional voice, for she understood quite well the message couched within his flowery phrases, and she was forced to acknowledge the cleverness of the manner in which he had conveyed it. Not only had he reassured her that her reputation was safe, but he had managed to give Mrs. Mortlock the impression that they had retired to this secluded corner of the garden solely for the purpose of discussing reform.

Rake and libertine he might be, but Lord Brathmere was no fool. Nor was he totally without a sense of chivalry, Verity reflected as she watched his tall figure stride away into the dark. Surely she need have no more worries that her honor would suffer at his hands.

Chapter Ten

In Which Verity Goes to a Garden Party and Encounters Tigers, Sheep, and a Wolf

The Season was proceeding apace and a gratifying number of invitations had found their way to Verity's desk. Christabel came regularly to Thornrose House to pass judgment upon the engraven pasteboard squares, ranking each on the basis of the number of eligible bachelors likely to be served up by the hostess. The latest invitation to pass muster was to the Marchioness of Lansdowne's garden party.

"For," Christabel opined, "I believe Dru will show better amongst the greenery than under the drawing room gilt. You'll wear marigold yellow, Dru, with a bonnet to match. Verity, you'll wear delphinium blue and carry a pink parasol. And remember, no talking about reform. In fact, Verity, dear, no talking, whatsoever. You may open your mouth only to eat."

In the matter of garden parties, Lady Lansdowne could be certain of outshining every other hostess in town, for the Lansdowne House garden park was so spacious one might almost imagine oneself on a country estate instead of in the southwest corner of Berkeley Square. Drusilla and Verity had determined to walk the length of the square down to Lansdowne House, but an invitation to join them was roundly declined by Christabel, who never stirred outside under her own power if she could avoid it. She would take her carriage like a sensible person, she informed them with a sniff, and then convey them home at the end of the day when they would doubtless be exhausted from all this debilitating exercise.

Verity and Drusilla set off, Rafe walking the proper three paces behind to see them safely to their destination. Along the way, they observed a fine collection of phaetons, curricles, and various other sporting vehicles drawn over until their owners should send for them. The current fashion in coaching circles was to have such vehicles attended by tigers—young servant boys who wore diminutive coachman's costumes complete with cockaded hat, driving coat, and boots. The sight of the tigers, most of whom could not have been above twelve, was one which afforded Verity no pleasure.

"What an appalling custom!" she exclaimed to Drusilla. "It fairly wrings my heart to come out of a late-night meeting and see the poor little fellows yawning hugely, drooping with weariness, or shivering with the cold. It is shocking that these children should be obliged by their masters to hang about to all hours of the night outside public houses, greeking establishments, gaming hells, or worse, when by rights they should be in their beds. I certainly could not respect any man who employed a child in such a manner," she declared, and then suddenly found herself wondering if Lord Brathmere had a tiger.

"Perhaps," Drusilla ventured, "Parliament will pass a law protecting the tigers, just as they did for the factory children."

Verity's eyes flashed. "You mean that pathetic excuse for a reform measure that says children may work only ten hours a day instead of twelve? Oh, I did support the measure, but only because I knew we'd get nothing stronger passed—" She broke off abruptly, perceiving that she was preaching from an inappropriate pulpit. "Forgive me, Dru! I have the sensibilities of tartar. No young girl off to a party wishes to hear a lecture about the woes of the world." She twined her delphinium clad arm through Dru's marigold one. "Come, onto the garden party where we can enjoy the beauties of nature, which, happily, we are not dependent on Parliament to provide for us."

Lady Lansdowne had reached new heights in the planning of her alfresco entertainments. Musicians dressed as shepherds played country melodies. Singing milkmaids danced round a maypole. Shepherdesses led about flower-wreathed sheep, while several black rams, ribbons trailing from their curling horns, frisked among the phlox. Had the shade of Marie Antoinette happened upon the scene, she might have thought herself back at her toy farmstead at Versailles.

They found Christabel standing under a striped marquis being harangued by Mrs. Mortlock. Christa promptly hailed them in the manner of one who beholds a savior. Mrs. Mortlock greeted them with equal effusiveness, glad of an expanded audience: "I was just expressing my amazement that Lady Lansdowne should have opened her billiard room to both sexes. I am of the strong opinion that the sexes should never mix while playing billiards. It encourages indelicacy among the women and gives the men too much opportunity to ogle the ladies' posterior portions. Alas, if only more young ladies were being raised according to Hannah More's *Hints Toward Forming the Character of a Young Princess*, then we might have a more seemly tone in society. You must procure a copy of it, Lady Toddington, and consult it in the raising of your own daughter."

"I don't see why," retorted Christabel. "To judge from Princess Charlotte's recent behavior, Holy Hannah's improving tome hasn't done her an ounce of good."

Mrs. Mortlock frowned and seemed about to unleash another preachment when her voice suddenly escalated into a screech. "Merciful heavens! That creature there! What is it doing?"

Verity and Christa, no experts in animal husbandry, were not altogether sure what the beribboned ram was doing with the flower-wreathed ewe. Country-bred Drusilla knew, however.

"I fear, Mrs. Mortlock, that the ram is doing that which a ram was born to do, and that which he does best."

Mrs. Mortlock proclaimed herself faint with disgust and was taken away by a maid. The errant ram was set upon by a footman and banished to the carriage house, shortly to be joined by a lamb who had answered the call of nature while being cooed over by a lady guest. Once the excitement had subsided, Christabel took Drusilla off to sniff out eligible young men. Verity was not allowed to join the hunt lest she inadvertently spout a reformist slogan.

Barred from the company of her friends, Verity settled upon a secluded wrought-iron bench set among some tall rhododendron bushes. Several strolling gentlemen, certainly unaware of her presence, paused nearby to converse. They unwittingly informed her that the play at Crocker's gambling house was deep and constant . . . that a certain Mrs. Massingberd who ran a bawdyhouse in Piccadilly was also in the moneylending line . . . that the new barbering establishment on the Strand was staffed by exotic females clad in harem draperies . . .

Sitting enrapt on her bench, Verity realized that she had just caught a glimpse of the raffish twilight world which gentlemen were permitted to frequent, but ladies were never supposed to hear of, a world of which she could never approve, the world which Lord Brathmere inhabited. She found herself wondering about Brathmere, his duels, his gambling, his women. Did they make him happy, these women . . .

"Miss Thornrose! Well met!" A male voice sounded close at hand—Lord Brathmere's voice.

Verity lept from her bench as if from hot coals.

"My lord," she stammered, looking up into his rakishly handsome face, wondering if her guilty thoughts could possibly be showing on her own. "You've roused me from a brown study," she went on, recovering a degree of her customary composure. "It seems that Lady Lansdowne's gardens are most conducive to silent meditations."

"So it would seem." The dark eyes held hers speculatively. "I've been watching you at your reflections, Miss Thornrose."

"Watching me? Whatever for?"

"For the sheer pleasure of it, Miss Thornrose."

Verity's expression became troubled. Could it be that she had misjudged him after all? Was it possible that he saw her as just another female to be courted and cozened?

A little hesitantly, she inquired, "My lord, are you by chance trying to strike up a flirtation with me?"

"As it happens, I am," he replied equably.

"Well, I'm afraid you're wasting your time. I never flirt with gentlemen."

"Oh, and what do you do with gentlemen, Miss Thornrose?"

"I serve on committees with them, I compose tracts with them, I circulate petitions with them."

"Good. Then I needn't be jealous of them."

"Jealousy cannot possibly enter it," retorted Verity positively, "because where there is no heartfelt feeling, there can be no jealousy."

The black brows lifted. "You think I have no heartfelt feelings for you, Miss Thornrose?"

"How could you? By common report you have no heart at all."

"And you believe that?"

"In substance, yes."

He regarded her with a slight, mocking smile. "Shall I tell you what common report says of you, Miss Thornrose? Common report has it that you are a bloodless icon of reform, cold as charity, and distant as the moon."

Before Verity could protest this unflattering assessment, he went on, "Perhaps the two of us should form a pact to prove common report wrong. You will prove that I have a heart, Miss Thornrose, and I will prove that there's hot blood in your lovely veins after all."

He had drawn very close to her, in their own secluded world within the maze of garden shrubbery. She wondered how he had accomplished it. He's probably very good at closing upon mesmerized females, cried a warning voice in her brain. But the voice was lost amid a host of other impressions: his hands closing gently over hers, his fingertips caressing the vulnerable place on her wrists where her pulse jumped betrayingly with a strange, unprecedented excitement she had never felt before.

As if pulling herself out of deep water, she managed to say, "My lord, this really will not do."

"Oh, but it will do, Miss Thornrose, it will do very well, indeed."

He breathed the words softly across her cheek and the long-fingered hands slid up her forearms, pulling her closer. The glittering dark eyes looked into hers and shut out the world and all the duties that she had to perform in it. There was only herself and the man who held her. He was going to kiss her, her first kiss, a rake's kiss from a handsome mouth that seemed expressly made to draw her lips to his. Only divine intervention could save her now.

A spattering of raindrops fell across their nearly touching

faces. Verity recoiled, and after favoring Alaric with a single horrified look, fled toward the house.

"Blast," muttered Alaric, glowering up at the darkening sky, which glowered back and thundered for good measure. Racing against the coming storm, he followed Verity Thornrose's fleeing figure toward Lansdowne house.

Chaos reigned on the ground floor of Lansdowne House.

Fully two hundred people had been strolling in the gardens when the skies opened, and in a body they rushed for the shelter of the townhouse. As her garden party sank beneath the storm, Lady Lansdowne was gallant in the face of disaster. She had fires lit in every fireplace, caused hot beverages to be circulated, and threw open her medicine chest to dispense remedies for the warding off of colds.

Servants ministered to the doused fashionables, but most people were choosing to take themselves and their sodden finery home. Drusilla, too, had fallen victim to the storm. She had had the misfortune to be admiring a tulip tree in the furthest reaches of the Lansdowne property and was all but drowned, her marigold muslin dress clinging to her figure in a way she could not like.

Christabel was much vexed, for she had been hot on the trail of a likely young man who had just inherited a baronetcy in Derwentwater. Now she must call off the chase to take Drusilla home, as well as providing transport for the tiresome Mrs. Mortlock, who was still swooning from her exposure to the licentious sheep.

And Verity was nowhere to be found . . .

Having escaped the voluptuous terrors of the garden with only a few water spots on her delphinium dress, Verity was hiding in that female rabbit hole known as the ladies lounge. She was quite certain that if she—poor palpitating spinster that she was—were to come out of hiding, she would be set upon by a certain handsome and hungry wolf.

Eventually, she did venture to the side portico of the house, only to see the Toddington town carriage clatter away without her. Thrown to the wolves by my dearest friend, she thought bitterly, and turned around to find herself face-to-face with the Earl of Brathmere.

"Are you in need of transport, Miss Thornrose?" he inquired, knowing perfectly well that she was.

"No!" she told him with frigid finality. "I have my parasol and I am determined to walk."

His lordship eyed the flimsy pink silk confection with the scorn it deserved. "I must insist on conveying you home, Miss Thornrose." He said this in the manner of one who does not intend to be thwarted of the object of his desire, which in this case happened to be her. Verity could tell this by the way the dark eyes lingered on her mouth as if he had not yet given up the preposterous idea of kissing her.

After a moment of frantic thought, she said stiffly, "I do not wish to discommode you, sir."

"You do not discommode me, Miss Thornrose."

"Then perhaps you will be good enough to summon your vehicle so that we may proceed without delay."

"Be assured, Miss Thornrose," he told her with a quite wolfish smile, "that I am no less anxious than you to retire to the privacy of my carriage."

Gullible man! thought Verity as his lordship went off in search of a footman. *As if I would ever set foot in his rolling den of iniquity.*

As soon as he was out of sight, she took her parasol firmly in hand and hastened out into the rain. Once, she would have scorned to play such a petty, deceitful trick as this on another person. But she consoled herself with the thought that if there was any man who deserved to be the victim of such a trick, it was the rakehell Earl of Brathmere.

For an overpriced trifle, her pink parasol did not serve her too badly. It was the hem of her skirt that suffered the most on the puddle-filled walkway. She had crossed Berkeley Street and was proceeding prosperously enough when she happened to catch sight of a young boy slumped limply across the driving box of a high-perch phaeton. From his uniform the child was obviously a tiger, and so he should rightfully be occupying the phaeton box. Still, it seemed a very odd posture for someone to adopt in the middle of a rainstorm.

"Boy," she called softly, "are you all right? Are you sleeping?"

The tiger did not stir. She shook him gently, and when he did not move, she reached up and put a hand to his forehead. It was blazing hot, burning with a child's fierce fever, so hot that it was a wonder that the raindrops that beaded his face did not sizzle to steam. The tiger that belonged to this fashionable phaeton, the child that was probably not nearly as well-fed or well-treated as the horses he waited upon, was ill, seriously ill.

But what to do? She paused, biting her lip with indecision. She supposed she must return to Lansdowne House and try to discover who owned the phaeton—

An iron hand fastened on her shoulder and spun her around. Lord Brathmere, looking wet and unpleasant, gripped her arm and shook her for good measure.

"I'd like to know," he inquired in tones of suppressed violence, "why you felt obliged to run off and leave me to stand about like a fool—"

"Oh, do hush up, for pity's sake!" Verity flared back at him with a fierceness that left him temporarily silenced. Her color was high, her eyes blazing violet fire. She was no longer the virginal spinster flustered by a rake's wiles. She was a Thornrose in the full flame of reformist passion.

"This poor child is dreadfully ill, and I must think of what can be done for him. I cannot think while you are manhandling me, so will you kindly release me."

Alaric let her jerk her arm free. His eyes flicked over her shoulder to take in the sight of the child sprawled on the phaeton box.

"Well, what the devil ails him?" he growled. "He seemed fit enough this afternoon."

Verity stared at him with dawning comprehension. So it was his vehicle. His poor little tiger.

Her words tumbled out in righteous indignation. "Didn't you even notice the poor child was ill? But of course you didn't. Concern for a mere servant would be beneath you, wouldn't it, you inhumane, exploitive—"

"Madam!" Alaric advised her in a roar, "this is not my turnout, nor is this unfortunate child in my employ."

"Oh," said Verity.

"The rig belongs to Collier Thane. He's been showing it—and his tiger's costume—off to everyone today. The boy's name is Jerry or Jeremy or something like it."

Verity stood on tiptoe and reached up to pat the tiger's cheeks. "Jerry . . . Jeremy, can you hear me?"

The boy stirred and muttered something unintelligible in a hoarse voice, but his eyes did not open and he did not seem capable of sitting up.

Alaric frowned. "Well, you're right about one thing. This boy's not fit for anything but the sickbed."

"Then we must find this Mr. Thane and tell him to take the child home at once."

Alaric gave a brief, derisive laugh. "Mr. Thane is engaged at the card table and I doubt he'll withdraw until he is either drunk or bankrupt. But I might be persuaded to do something for the boy in the meantime." Seeing that he had her attention, he went on, "Yes, I think I might be persuaded to help him . . . but on terms, Miss Thornrose, on terms. Agree to go driving with me tomorrow and I'll rescue the lad."

Miss Thornrose gave him a look that would turn sand to glass, but did not hesitate to meet his terms. "Oh, very well," she snapped, "I promise I shall let you drive me tomorrow— but only because it happens to suit my plans."

He grinned down at her. "So you have plans for me, do you? I'm gratified to hear it."

Verity regarded him grimly. She had plans for him, though she doubted they would gratify him in the least. But that was for tomorrow. First she must deal with the crisis at hand.

"My lord, please! Tell me what you propose to do about the boy."

"The first thing I propose to do is to get us all out of this rain and into my carriage."

He signaled to a rig waiting across the street. As it approached, Verity noted that the coachman and the groom were both grown men.

Alaric guessed her thoughts. "I pay too much for my horses to put a youngster like this in charge of them. He'd never be able to control them."

In short order, the tiger was laid on the seat inside the carriage, with Brathmere's groom installed in his place on Mr. Thane's phaeton. Inside the shelter of the carriage, Verity insisted on taking off the lad's sodden coachman's jacket and tucking a traveling rug about his feverish form. She had been half afraid that he might come to his senses and panic at being borne away by strangers, but the boy was so ill he was entirely unaware of his surroundings.

Alaric lounged in his seat, watching her at her ministrations. "Very touching," he said softly. "Pray don't forget that there is another who is equally desirous of experiencing your sweet attentions."

Verity ignored this preposterous sally and settled herself at the far end of the coach seat. "You've still not told me how you will help him," she reminded him.

"I intend," he replied with a shrug, "to place him in your care until he recovers. In fact, if you like him you may as well keep him."

"But this boy is not yours to dispose of as if he were chattel," protested Verity, appalled at this cavalier attitude. "And surely Mr. Thane will be outraged if we take away his servant without his permission."

Alaric smiled thinly. "Oh, you needn't worry about dear old Colley. You won't hear a peep of protest out of him, I assure you." He produced a calling card case from his coat, extracted a card, and handed it to her.

It was Mr. Thane's card, Verity realized, and on the back was a badly penned notation with the figure £200 standing out prominently.

She looked up in astonishment. "Do you mean to say that Mr. Thane owes you money?"

"Colley owes everyone money. He's the most abysmal card player to ever come out of Dorset. I'll simply tell him I took his tiger as payment. You keep the lad and fuss over him as long as you please. Colley won't squawk about it."

Verity wasn't at all sure that she should approve of this. Still, she could not help but admire the ruthless panache with which his lordship had disposed of Mr. Collier Thane, whom she already heartily disliked without even having met him.

"But what of Mr. Thane's horses?"

"I'll leave my groom to watch them until Colley returns. They're fine animals and shouldn't suffer just because their master is an idiot at the card table."

"'Tis a great pity," Verity could not refrain from observing, "that the gentlemen of your set aren't half as concerned about the people in their employ as they are about their horses."

His lordship merely shrugged, his dark eyes on her face. The carriage was in motion now, and Verity could not help thinking with relief that very soon she would be able to escape this close confinement with his lordship's very disturbing presence.

"Miss Thornrose," he was saying in a voice that she found equally disturbing, "should you like to dine at my house some evening?"

Verity frowned. "Our bargain was for an afternoon drive, my lord, no more than that."

"Ah, but perhaps you will see fit to change your mind."

"Why should I?"

"Because I can give you several things that you need very badly."

Much against her better judgement Verity inquired as to what these might be.

"My vote in the House of Lords, for one." He leaned close to her, saying in a silken and beguiling voice that surely would have melted the bones of a reformer of lesser character, "Just think of it, Miss Thornrose. My vote would be completely at your disposal. And perhaps I could influence others as well. But, as I take no interest in politics, I would need instruction as to how I should cast my vote—a great deal of instruction. Surely, you won't pass up this opportunity to reform me."

Verity was briefly tempted. Another two or three votes might turn the tide in the Lords on several close-fought issues. Still, the man was too dangerous, and the price he obviously had in mind to charge for his vote was far too high.

"My aunts would not like me dining at a gentleman's residence."

"And do you always do what your aunts wish?"

"Of course. I would never unduly distress them."

"But why should it distress them for you to dine with me? You are of age, after all, and your own mistress."

Verity looked him squarely in the eye. "Yes. I am my own mistress, and no other's, nor ever shall be, my lord."

My lord leaned back in his seat, not at all dismayed by this bold declaration. Luring Miss Verity Thornrose from the path of virtue was becoming a fascinating undertaking.

Just you wait, my sweet Verity. Just you wait . . .

Chapter Eleven

In Which the Earl of Brathmere Is Amazed to Find Himself Doing Several Good Deeds

*T*he next afternoon, Alaric made a timely appearance at Thornrose House. He had expected to find the terrifying aunts lined up to inspect him, but the aunts, as it turned out, all had errands of mercy to run and had previously bespoken both the Thornrose carriages. Alaric was now possessed of the dark suspicion that he had been granted the pleasure of Miss Verity's company today only because she needed transport.

Now that he considered it, the hour that she had named for their ride in the park was an unusually early one. Five was the conventional hour for driving along Rotten Row, during which time many agreeable stoppages were made to show off one's clothes, carriage, and horse millinery. But Verity wished to depart at the unfashionably early hour of one. Alaric had raised no objection. Being private with the object of his desire without out a mob of tattlers about suited his taste exactly.

Verity came rustling down the stairs in another of her dove-grey dresses. She vouchsafed him the most coldly formal of greetings and met his eyes with a straight unwavering look that held a definite hint of defiance. Miss Thornrose, Alaric apprehended, was going to require a deal of thawing.

He watched her covertly as she made her preparations to depart, wondering if she realized how well the subdued color of her grey gowns suited her. She had probably never thought about it, he decided, for vanity about her appearance was not in keeping with her character. She obviously had no notion of what to do with that lovely body of hers. He was perfectly willing to instruct her in the matter, however, and surely she deserved to experience passion before she dwindled into a permanent fixture on one of her numerous reform committees.

A cool voice intruded into his reflections. "You've not asked after Mr. Thane's tiger," Miss Thornrose reproved him.

Recalled to reality, Alaric responded dutifully, "Ah, yes. And how is poor little what's-his-name?"

"His name is Jeremy." There was a decided edge to Miss Thornrose's voice. "He is twelve years old, an orphan, and he has been shockingly underpaid by your Mr. Thane, to whom, by the way, I have returned that ridiculous costume. As for Jeremy, I have decided that I will keep him here at Thornrose House."

"A lucky boy, Jeremy," murmured Alaric, watching as Miss Verity took in hand a market basket containing a stoppered stoneware jug. He cocked an eyebrow at the jug. "Dare I ask what that's for?"

"I shouldn't if I were you," she advised him austerely. "I fear you'll find it highly discomposing to your vanity."

You think so? murmured Alaric's unregenerate inner voice as he followed her to the carriage sweep. *We'll see whose vanity is discomposed before the day is done, madam.*

The sight of his horses stirred Miss Thornrose to a little more warmth. She paused before the phaeton, admiring the matched bays. "Your horses look wonderfully well cared for. I can see we'll not have to report you to Mr. Martin's Society for the Prevention of Cruelty to Animals."

A society to prevent cruelty to animals! marveled Alaric inwardly. *What would these reformers be up to next?*

"Don't you ever run out of reforming societies to refer to?" he inquired, watching enviously as she fussed over his horses' velvet noses.

"Hardly, my lord. There are currently in the city some 704 benefit societies for charitable and humane purposes, eight societies for the purpose of promoting good morals—"

"I particularly beg you not to report me to them."

Miss Thornrose wisely ignored this witticism and continued as if he had not spoken. "—twelve societies for promoting the learned and polite arts, 122 asylums and alms houses, ninety hospitals and dispensaries for the sick, the lame, and the delivery of poor women."

"And do you support them all?"

"Oh, no! My aunts and I consider very carefully which among the many we can sanction. There are some whose principles we do not agree with and others that are shoddily run." Her expression darkened. "And many of the workhouses are no more than places where sweated labor is extorted from the unfortunates who are consigned there. If only," she concluded with a sigh, "we could induce Parliament to take an interest in these matters."

"I think you could induce me to take an interest in anything you wished," said Alaric in a velvety voice.

Verity brightened. "Could I interest you in making a speech in the House of Lords?"

"Alas, anything but that. The truth is I never go to the Lords unless I need a nap."

Her eyes clouded. "You disappoint me, my lord. And unfortunately you are not the only one to ignore the responsibilities of your title. The Lords is shockingly behind-hand on many important issues." Sudden passion ignited her voice. "If I were a man and a peer, I should wake up those slumbering Lords soon enough."

Alaric gazed down at her. Her eyes were alight, her color high, and she'd certainly, he thought to himself, woken everything there was to wake up in him.

"You'll forgive me if I disagree with you in one matter," he said softly. "I find myself most grateful that the Creator in His infinite wisdom did not see fit to make you a man."

She gave him a swift, aware look and then turned quickly away. "I think we'd best be on our way. Tempus fugit, you know," she added in a too-bright voice.

Alaric smiled to himself. Miss Verity Thornrose was the only young lady he knew who resorted to Latin quotations when cast into confusion by a compliment. She was adorable and a darling, and the only female he had ever been prepared to seduce discreetly.

Verity secretly enjoyed the ride to Hyde Park. She had never been in a high-perch phaeton, and she concluded that the expe-

rience of riding high up in the fresh air must certainly be beneficial to the circulation. And she admired the competent way
that his lordship feathered his spirited team through the Mayfair traffic.

Once they were in the park, she directed him to pass by the
various drives and proceed directly to the Keeper's Garden
where several freshwater springs bubbled up from rocky en-
closures.

"Good God," muttered Alaric as Verity, defying every con-
vention, leaped lightly from the phaeton and put her jug to the
mouth of one of the gushing springs. "What the devil do you
want with that?" he called down to her.

"The water from this spring reputedly has medicinal quali-
ties," she explained as she corked the jar and handed it up to
him. "It's believed to be particularly good for bathing weak
eyes. Personally," she confided as she settled herself in the
seat beside him, "I think it's all a hum. But if it comforts people to believe it, then I see no harm in it." She turned her clear
gaze full upon him and said crisply, "And now, my lord, if you
would be so kind as to drive me to Soho."

"Soho! Why the devil do you want to go there?"

She gave him a look of the greatest innocence. "Because,
my lord, now that we have gone to the trouble of procuring the
medicinal spring water, it only makes sense to deliver it to its
intended patient. Don't you agree?"

Notwithstanding the fact that he had not the least desire to
go to Soho to deliver spring water to a weak-eyed person un-
known to him, Alaric soon found himself driving thither. He
now understood that he had been gammoned by the virtuous
Miss Verity into helping her perform a charitable act on behalf
of the Friendly Female Society. This worthy group, entirely
under the management of the ladies, took it upon themselves
to extend the hand of kindness to indigent females of genteel
character.

Verity's errand of mercy took them to a part of Soho occupied by the lower orders of tradespeople—carters, coal agents,
lacemakers, coopersmiths. The habitats of these persons were
second-rate public houses, stores selling used clothing, plain-
bread bakeries, and when times got bad, pawnshops. To be
sure, it was well above the horrors of a slum rookery like

Seven Dials, but this corner of Soho was filled with its own quiet desperation. It was a place of yesterday's fashions, reduced circumstances, and constant shifts to retain one's dignity and make ends meet. In short, it was shabby-genteel and it made Alaric feel uncomfortable to be there.

Not only, he thought resentfully as he maneuvered his smart rig among the wagons and peddlers' carts, had he been gammoned into this ridiculous adventure, but he was now informed that he must proceed incognito.

"For you see," Verity explained as they pulled into a bystreet of narrow houses without a flower or a foot of greenery between them, "it would put poor Mrs. Rimmel into a quake to know that she was entertaining an earl. So I shall simply introduce you as plain Mr. Tierney, a gentleman who is interested in our charitable endeavors." She shot him a glance that was almost roguish. "Since her eyesight is very bad, we should have no trouble fobbing you off as a philanthropist, as long as you don't talk too much."

Alaric promised faithfully not to talk too much, all the while marveling at the indignities he was prepared to endure in order to beguile Mistress Reform into becoming his mistress.

Their destination was a boarding establishment of dingy brick, its narrow windows curtained with net instead of lace. Alaric shot a quick glance up and down the teeming street, wishing he had brought a groom to watch over his rig.

Verity guessed his concern. "Don't worry. The landlord's son will mind your team."

As if on cue, a boy in worn nankeens streaked toward them, shouting, "'Alloo, Miss Verity!" in appalling cockney accents. He careened to a stop before them and bobbed an unpracticed bow.

Verity laughingly ruffled the lad's straw-colored curls. "Good afternoon to you, Master Tom. I'm glad to find you at home for I've brought you something special."

The boy's eyes lit up as Verity produced a handful of peppermints from her basket and deposited the candies into a grubby, outstretched hand. "Now be a good lad and watch the gentleman's carriage."

Tom eyed the phaeton with approval. "Lor', she's a fine one, miss. It'll be a pleasure to keep a peeper on it."

Leaving Tom at his post, happily gorging himself on peppermints, they entered the rooming establishment and walked along an unlit passageway. Crude sconces were nailed to the walls, but apparently none of the inhabitants could afford to keep candles in them. Alaric looked around curiously. Although he had been to his share (more than his share actually) of seedy gin mills, notorious gambling hells and low bawdy houses, he had never before ventured into the lodgings of the working classes, this particular specimen being filled with the sounds of crying babies and the palpable smell of boiled cabbage. Verity led the way up the stairs, which were steep, dark, and worn to splintery unevenness. Alaric plunged manfully after her.

On the third floor, their knock was answered by Mrs. Rimmel, a rabbity-faced little woman who exclaimed titteringly, "Miss Thornrose and a gentleman!" Bowing over her proffered hand, Alaric noticed that her fingertips seemed to have been nibbled upon by mice.

Mrs. Rimmel hastened to utter many apologies about the cluttered state of her apartments, a rather grandiose term, Alaric thought, to apply to her bare one-room domicile. In his opinion, Mrs. Rimmel didn't own enough possessions to make a respectable clutter.

There were just enough chairs for the three of them. In the far corner of the room was a narrow bed behind discreetly hung chintz curtains. A caged thrush twittered softly, a threadbare rug lay before the meager hearth fire. Warming over the fire was a kettle of what Alaric's nose led him to believe was parsnip soup. There was such a conscious air of genteel poverty and diminished circumstances about the little room that Alaric felt even more uncomfortable than before. But Verity, he noticed with reluctant admiration, was as easy in these mean surroundings as if she were in her own drawing room.

"I do hope," she was saying to Mrs. Rimmel, "that the spring water shall bring you some relief."

Mrs. Rimmel took the jug eagerly. "How good of you, Miss Thornrose. I'm sorely in need of it, I can tell you that. I've a dozen shirts due by Saturday and I find myself much-tried in completing them. The pay is but ten pence per and the work is quite beneath me really—but one must do something to get by in these difficult times."

"Mrs. Rimmel has sewed for some of the very best ladies in Society," Verity explained for Alaric's benefit.

It was easy to see why Mrs. Rimmel was no longer sewing, however. The red-rimmed, watering eyes told the story too well. Yet, she sewed on still, puncturing her fingers in her efforts to complete the shirts and thereby earn her ten pence per.

"I can't begin to name all the famous beauties that Mrs. Rimmel sewed for," Verity went on.

Mrs. Rimmel, however, was perfectly well able to name each and every one of them. She pulled out a sheaf of yellowing sketches, each of which was inscribed with the name of the Great Lady who had commissioned the gown: the Duchess of Devonshire in blue taffeta, the Princess Louise in a morning gown for her trousseau, Lady Hamilton in clinging Indian gauze.

Alaric was acutely bored with this discussion of historical frills and furbelows, but behaved himself for Verity's sake. He sensed that providing Mrs. Rimmel with an audience was the greatest kindness that could be done for her. Salving the pride of a shabby-genteel female was not a thing that Alaric in his wildest dreams could ever imagine himself doing, yet, here he was, thanks to Miss Verity and the Friendly Female Society. What next? he wondered ruefully.

Playing with dolls, apparently. It seemed that Mrs. Rimmel had also sewn for the best dollmakers in London, and she was now taking down each of the elaborately dressed dolls displayed upon her hearth mantle and expounding upon them at length.

He glanced at Verity—his eyes seemed bent on wandering to her face at every opportunity—just in time to see the color drain from her face and her gloved hands press to her lips as if to stifle a cry. She stood and said in the strangest whisper, "Please don't drop the dolly in the kettle."

Alaric stood too, his whole frame instinctively tensed to fight, though he couldn't have put into words what danger it was they faced. In the next instant Verity had dropped back into her chair in the manner of one whose knees were trembling while Mrs. Rimmel, quite oblivious, stood before the bubbling parsnips on her hearth nattering about her handiwork.

At length, Verity, who had been making a visible effort to collect herself, brought the visit to a merciful end, and they were able to make their escape from Mrs. Rimmel's dreary room.

Outside in the unlit hall, Alaric, fearing for Verity's balance on the dark flights of stairs, put an arm around her and was rewarded beyond his wildest dreams. The bonneted head drooped upon his shoulder, and she clung to him for a sweet breathless instant, but then the moment was gone.

"I beg your pardon," she whispered, "the stairs are so steep. I felt a little dizzy."

Alaric didn't believe it for a minute. "What happened in there?" he demanded bluntly.

She closed her eyes and he felt her fingers tighten convulsively on his arm. "Something that happened when I was a child, something I'd rather forget. Please, let's go." And she went with him down the stairs, clinging to his arm as if she were an invalid.

To Alaric's immense relief his rig was where he had left it, and he tossed Tom a guinea in payment. This was apparently so vast and unanticipated a sum, that the lad felt obliged to bite the coin to establish its authenticity.

"Where to now?" asked Alaric quietly, once they were under way.

That Verity was still not her old self was apparent. She turned to him, her eyes alight with a strange longing. "I want to be away, away. I should like to go for a long ride in the country. Somewhere green and private where no one can watch you. A place where you can drive as fast as you please with no one to tell you any different."

Alaric hoped his jaw wasn't dropping. Nothing could have suited his purpose better. Before his fair passenger could recover her senses, he turned his carriage northward, and drove toward Marylebone, a sprawling royal preserve of tall woodlands and bright wildflowers that bordered the edge of the city. The secluded pastoral beauties of Marylebone made it a favorite haunt of duelists, landscape artists, and lovers. The Regent's favorite architect, John Nash, reportedly had great plans for Marylebone. So did Alaric.

Once they were inside the meadowland, Alaric gave the

bays their heads. The matched thoroughbreds surged forward, grateful for the chance to go swiftly after all the neat, disciplined show required on the crowded city streets. Verity was in a like mood, leaning forward into the rush of country-scented air.

Alaric turned off the track and pulled his team to a halt in a quiet dell carpeted by dancing bluebells. Hedgerows sheltered them from sight of the track, and nearby was a green pond with water flowers luxuriating on its still surface. The air was full of May, and Alaric knew he would never come upon a more perfect setting for seduction.

He pulled the bays to a stop and turned his attention to Verity. Her bonnet had blown back and her hair had fallen in a trailing tangle about her neck. In the bright sunlight, her black hair was shot through with glistening ruby gleams. *My, what high-flown poetics your lust drives you to, Alaric, old boy,* he told himself with a twisted, self-mocking smile.

Verity had dropped from the phaeton and was reveling in the pastoral scene as if she were newly let out from close confinement. Eyes half-closed with pleasure, she breathed sighingly of the fresh country air, and Alaric felt a sudden stab of hot desire at the sight of her high breasts outlined beneath the taunted bodice.

Verity looked up at him inquiringly. "Aren't you coming down to join me?"

Of course I am, you foolish girl, thought Alaric, hastening to secure the reins.

"What a beautiful place," she sighed when he had sauntered to her side. "Thank you for bringing me. I needed to be . . ." Her eyes clouded, and suddenly her clear features were drawn with apprehension and her voice caught in her throat. "Sometimes I'm so afraid. In my own house, I'm afraid and I don't know why."

She looked up at him through unshed tears, her eyes like drowned violets in a storm. Alaric found himself lost.

With hands that trembled with eagerness, he gathered her against him, his lips tasting her tears as his long fingers tangled themselves in the shining mass of her hair. He covered her mouth with his, and it was her first kiss—he sensed that instantly—yet she responded to him at once, her mouth warm and alive under his. When he drew away from her, she looked up at him in radiant wonderment.

He kissed her again and she let him part her lips with the tip of his tongue. He pressed her closer, his hands searching out the soft curves and slender planes of her.

"Oh, Alaric," she whispered. She'd never spoken his Christian name before, and the sound of it on her lips was piercingly sweet. He dipped deep into her sweet mouth again.

Her head fell back beneath his kisses, her hair spilling across his arm like a fall of black water. His mouth sought the hollow of her throat and then slid to where he could feel the wild leaping of her heart beneath the grey bodice. She sighed voluptuously against him, and offered her breasts to his kisses. He brought his mouth back to hers and she let him fill her mouth with his tongue, a delicious harbinger of the possession to come. His hands slid down her back over the swell of her slender hips to lift her up against his hardness, a rake's surest test of whether the lady would or whether she would not . . . and Verity would, for she clung to him still, her body ready for his. A few more passionate caresses and she would be his to lay down on the secluded, grass-softened bank.

He had triumphed. He held that virtuous icon of reform, Verity Thornrose, in the palm of his rakehell hand. The chaste citadel was crumbling, and all he need do was to lay her down among the May flowers and administer the joyful coup de grace that she in her innocent ardor was craving.

And yet, and yet . . .

He could not forget how she had clung to him as if he were her safe harbor. He could not forget that he had seen her with tears in her eyes, and he knew that after he had had his rake's way with her, tears were all she would have, tears and bitter regrets. In the end, he could not do it. Though he stood trembling on the brink, hot with longing, hard with desire, the wild Tierney blood driving in his veins, he could not do it, not when he was aware of every breath of her mouth and every beat of her heart as he had never been aware of anything before. He was undone by better instincts he did not know he possessed.

Dear God! Can it be that I care for her? The thought frightened him.

Regretfully, painfully, he stepped away from her and began the litany of male apologies. "Verity, forgive me. You are distraught and I have taken advantage of you."

She looked up at him dazedly as if she had just awakened from a dream and found reality far less pleasant. Then the scalding color rose in her cheeks, and her hands clenched at her sides as she struggled for self-control.

"I am not myself," she said in a low, unsteady voice. "You are certainly correct on that score. I wish you would take me home without delay."

"As you wish," said Alaric wearily.

Conversation did not flourish on the return trip. Verity was a frozen statue. Alaric drove his fine horses with a hard, ruthless hand. As the afternoon sun sank beyond the city's west end, he deposited the inviolate Miss Thornrose at her abode.

It was the beginning of the end of the rakehell earl.

Chapter Twelve

An Invitation to Swords

*T*he Earl of Brathmere lounged against one of the white-washed walls of Angelo's Fencing Academy, watching his cousin Laurie flourish a button-tipped rapier. Young Laurence, he thought sourly, had obviously been reading too many of Mr. Scott's epics, else he wouldn't be wasting his time swishing a weapon that the pistol had rendered obsolete.

Alaric's mind was fixed on neither swords nor pistols. His thoughts ran—as they often had of late—on Verity Thornrose, and brooding thoughts they were. A thousand times over, he regretted his decision to allow her to retire unscathed from the field at Marylebone. What a fool he had been, allowing her to slip through his fingers on account of a misguided notion of chivalry. He should have seized the moment and set his seal upon her. They say a woman never really forgets her first lover. He would have seen to it that she never forgot him. He would have gained a hold over her that would not be easily broken. He was disconcerted to discover just how desperately he wanted a hold over Verity Thornrose.

A shadow fell across the whitewashed wall, and he turned frowning. The shadow belonged to a great hulking fellow with arms longer than even his great stature warranted, shoulders like a bull and no neck to speak of.

Alaric regarded the man narrowly. He himself was taller than most. He had never met another man who could intimidate him physically, but he had to admit there was something nastily impressive about the massive fellow who stood before him, suppling his sword meaningfully with fingers as big as street corner sausages. It was an impressive sword, too, Alaric noticed—as far above the average in length as its owner was above the average man in height and breadth.

"Octavian Smythe, at your service," the outsized fellow informed him in a rumbling voice that held more than a trace of a sneer. "Would your lordship care to exert yourself to the extent of offering me a match?"

"I don't fence," said Alaric shortly.

"Surely your lordship jests."

"I don't do that, either."

"Perhaps your lordship is afraid." The tone was an unmistakable insult.

Alaric stiffened. It was obvious that this man was trying to provoke him. He was succeeding, too. "I don't think," he said in the gentle voice that always preceded an explosion, "that I caught that last remark of yours."

"Then I'll repeat it." And he did, in rolling tones that would have done credit to a divine on the pulpit. "I said the Earl of Brathmere is afraid to take up swords against me. Perhaps he knows that I fight without a mask and he fears to do the same lest he mar the pretty features that give him so much success with foolish ladies."

Good lord! thought Alaric in grim amazement. *Can it be there's a woman behind this quarrel? Have I bedded Mrs. Smythe at some point in my career? If so, she must have been a singularly forgettable female.*

He eyed Octavian Smythe measuringly, noting the winter cold eyes, the unyielding mouth set in a permanent expression of contempt for the weak, unrighteous world around him. They faced each other in acute silence, the reckless, hard-living nobleman and the ascetic zealot, two men as opposed by nature and beliefs as the Roundhead and the Cavalier.

The other fencers had become aware that something was in the wind. Foils were lowered, matches broken off, and an ominous silence rolled across the long, polished floor of the fencing academy.

Alaric could feel his temper rising to its notoriously low

flash point. He had no idea why Smythe was trying to engineer an altercation, but he was perfectly willing to oblige.

"Very well. Since you're so devilish hot to tread a measure or two at sword's point, I'll accommodate you."

Smiling coldly, Octavian Smythe called to Harry Angelo to bring sword and fencing costume (but no mask) for my lord.

But the famous fencing master was reluctant to comply. "Gentlemen, this is most ill-advised. Mr. Smythe, I beg you to consider that his lordship does not often frequent these rooms and is not in practice."

This was, alas, true. The sword was not Alaric's weapon, although like most young men of his class, he had been taught fencing. Swordplay was not his preferred method of inflicting mayhem on his fellows. He had no taste for slicing up other men with cold steel. He'd much rather blast a hole in them with a pistol, his weapon of choice.

He had the cool nerves and steady wrist necessary to become a dead shot, and pistols appealed to the gambler in him . . . win or lose, all or nothing, life or death hazarded on the single moment of concentration needed to loose one leaden ball. One never quite knew what would happen with a pistol; it was a great leveler of men. A dwarf could dispatch a giant with a pistol, which was why Octavian Smythe had no truck with them, but preferred the sword, where his great strength, long arms, and specially forged Birmingham blade gave him the advantage.

None of these rational considerations mattered to Alaric at the moment. Eyes dangerously aglitter, he buckled himself into the canvas vest that Angelo provided. That he had been up half the night, drinking and disporting himself with a brunette opera dancer who bore a passing resemblance to Verity Thornrose was not a consideration. He was confident that he could give Octavian Smythe a decent match. And he was in the mood for venting his spleen on someone.

Laurie, his face drawn with concern, pulled him aside. "What's between you and Smythe, Alaric?"

Alaric gave a mirthless laugh. "Nothing that I know of. The fellow seems to have taken me in instant dislike."

Laurie cast a worried glance across the fencing floor to where Octavian Smythe waited impassively, his blacksmith's arms folded across his huge chest. "He's more than good with a sword, Alaric. I've seen him in here often. You're no match for him. Can't you contrive to cry off?"

"The devil I will," snapped Alaric, jerking his arm from his cousin's grasp. "This has gone too far. Besides, I just may surprise you."

I hope so, thought Laurie.

Angelo, looking unhappy, declared he would act as referee. It would be his task to strike apart the combatants' blades if a hit was made or a violation of the rules occurred. Since the rules also required that the swords be of a length, Octavian Smythe was forced to lay down his Brobdingnagian blade and take up one of Angelo's blunted rapiers.

The other students had gathered round, eager to see what promised to be a dramatic clash. Brathmere was at it again, they told themselves. Not content with risking his neck in fast chariots and taproom brawls, he now proposed to fence with Octavian Smythe, the roaringest blade around. Bets on how many bouts he would last were made in murmured undertones.

Angelo raised his sword and announced the beginning of the match. "Gentlemen, salute! Present! Onset!"

Octavian Smythe wasted not an instant, but attacked Alaric like a Knight Templar hacking down infidel dogs. His expression, unguarded in combat, showed a fanatic's cold-eyed hate for the object of his ire. Octavian Smythe's gaze had become particularly baleful this morning upon encountering the Earl of Brathmere, so cool, so aristocratic, so disdainfully handsome, taking his lazy ease in Angelo's fencing rooms.

The blunted rapiers crossed and clashed, scissoring together and then flashing apart. It was immediately apparent to the watchers that Octavian Smythe was the stronger man and the better fencer. Brathmere, however, was the quicker, and whipcord tough, for it took a strong constitution to live the life of a Tierney man.

Alaric's fencing was almost totally defensive. Yet, he took chances that a more technically correct fencer would not have, which served to put Octavian Smythe slightly off his rhythm. Still, the first hit went to Smythe. The blunted sword drove past Alaric's guard, hitting him in the chest with painful force. Brathmere would have a fine bruise to go home with, thought the watching students.

"Do you wish to continue?" asked Angelo, looking very much as if he hoped they did not.

Alaric showed his teeth. "But of course we must continue. Our Captain Hack'em here is far from satisfied, I'm sure."

A muted murmur of laughter arose from the watching fencers. Octavian's broad face went brick red to hear himself compared to a character in a theatrical farce, and he vowed inwardly to cut out Brathmere's mocking tongue.

The two men engaged again, Alaric fencing a little more neatly as his old lessons came back to him. This bout was longer and more complicated than the first. The two blades banged and beat against each other in a subtly altered pace. Alaric was performing better, but he was far from congratulating himself. Smythe had passed up several opportunities to thrust home and thus end the second match. Alaric realized that his opponent was not trying for a conventional fencer's hit. So what was the overgrown oaf up to? Alaric wondered.

The answer soon came—a slashing downward slice aimed at Alaric's face. This was a gross impropriety of fencing etiquette, and a chorus of disapproval arose from the assembled students. Only Alaric's extreme agility saved him from falling under the blade that Octavian wielded like a steel whip. Even though the swords were blunted, a blow like that, with all of Octavian's gargantuan strength behind it, would have laid his face open to the bone.

Mr. Smythe harbors no great liking for my pretty face, that's for certain, thought Alaric, as the two men once again engaged.

Octavian Smythe's strategy was now obvious. He fenced conventionally only to protect himself from Alaric's thrusts. His own lunges were high, seemingly aimed at depriving the Earl of Brathmere of his eyesight or his nose. So irregular was this behavior in a match between unmasked combatants within the confines of a fencing school, that Alaric would have been perfectly within his rights to demand that Angelo end the bout. But Alaric would not break. He fought furiously on, managing to defend himself against the glistening blade that repeatedly parted the air in the immediate vicinity of his unprotected skull.

Harry Angelo, seeing that the earl, stubborn young fool that he was, would not call it quits, determined that the bout would cease. His rapier flew up and dashed apart the combatants' swords.

"Mr. Smythe, you forget yourself!" he cried out sharply. "I'll have no bully swordsmen in my establishment."

"Stand aside, fencing master," growled Octavian Smythe. "The bout's not over yet."

"And I say it is, sir!"

Angelo's sword flashed, and Octavian's weapon suddenly became airborne, flashing out of the giant hand, and clattering to the floor across the room.

Alaric threw down his sword and advanced toward Octavian, eyes blazing, face furiously pale, the ghosts of his wild Tierney ancestors thundering for vengeance. The watching students drew in their collective breaths waiting for the fateful challenge . . . all but Laurie, who grabbed his cousin's arms and pinioned them behind his back.

"Alaric, don't!" he hissed in a desperate undervoice. "If you challenge him, he'll have the choice of weapons."

This hardheaded sense penetrated the red haze of anger that fogged Alaric's brain, and he forced himself to take a deep calming breath. Laurie was right. The man challenged had the choice of weapons, and there was little doubt which weapon Octavian Smythe would choose, and this time there would be no blunted sword, no Angelo to make sure the rules of fairness were observed. In the end, Smythe would probably kill him.

I can't walk through the gates of hell just yet. Not until I've seen Verity one more time . . .

The thought of her was calming. Mastering himself as he never had before in all his wild, undisciplined existence, he faced Octavian Smythe. "All right, Smythe, you've had your day. I promise you though that one day we shall meet again, and then, by God, I shall have mine."

He turned and walked away.

Chapter Thirteen

In Which Octavian and Christabel Unite to Save Verity from the Earl of Brathmere

On this particular afternoon, the Thornrose library served as the setting for a particularly charming tableau. Disposed about the room in various graceful attitudes were four young ladies whose attributes of form and coloring spanned the palette of feminine beauty. The playful gambolings of the two lapdogs, Prudence and Comfort, added a note of humorous whimsy to the scene.

At the writing desk sat Deirdre, her fiery head bent low over her copybook as she struggled to penetrate the further mysteries of literacy under the tutelage of her young mistress and Dr. Bell. Occasionally during the lesson, a worlds-away look came into her green eyes.

Verity did not chide her, for she guessed that Deirdre's wavering attention had something to do with her recent betrothal to Rafe Bowen. She understood Deirdre's preoccupation, for had not she herself recently learned a sharp and salutary lesson on how very potent romantical yearnings could be. The torturing memory of Brathmere's caresses still made the color roar into her cheeks.

She looked quickly around to see if any of her companions had noticed, but Christabel and Drusilla were entirely taken up with the day's post. Christabel was winnowing through the invitations, exclaiming gleefully at some, tossing others aside disdainfully, while Drusilla perused the replies to the latest circulating letter that she had penned for the Thornrose aunts.

Then Chester appeared and uttered a single sentence that put a quick end to the charming tableau. "Mr. Octavian is without."

The effect was instantaneous.

Deirdre bobbed to her feet in a crackle of starched apron. "I'm sure Mrs. Allen must be wanting me for something."

Drusilla, fully aware of Mr. Smythe's objections to her presence at Thornrose House, decided it would be a good time to go look in on her mother. Christabel rolled her blue eyes heavenward in annoyance. The lapdogs hid.

Verity took a white-knuckled grip on the arm of her chair, for it seemed that Octavian's footsteps were cannonading down the hall with particular emphasis. He came into the room, frowning balefully. His eyes lit first on Christabel and a low disgusted growl issued from his throat. Eschewing any semblance of polite greeting to either lady, he grated out to Verity, "Cousin, I must and will have a word with you. In private."

But Verity was determined not to be deprived of Christabel's comforting presence. "You may speak freely in front of Lady Toddington. I can conceive of no secret that I would keep from her." *Save one,* amended her conscience's inner voice.

To her horror, Octavian seemed once again able to read her guilty thoughts.

"Then let Lady Toddington stay," he acquiesced grimly. "She'll hear the gossip about you and Brathmere soon enough."

Christabel suddenly assumed an attitude of attention. "What does he mean, Verity? Have you seen Brathmere since the garden party?"

Verity's stricken expression confirmed it.

"So she has deceived you as well," said Octavian with venomous satisfaction. "Permit me to inform your ladyship that Verity was seen driving with that blackguard into the Marylebone preserve."

"Verity! Is this true?"

"Yes," said Verity in a dull voice.

"You have made a degrading spectacle of yourself," intoned

Octavian, "that will live in infamy in the annals of the Thorn-roses."

Christabel took Verity's icy hand in her warm plump one. "Verity, what's come over you? Can't you see it won't do at all? He will take advantage of you."

"He will debouch, besmirch, and befoul you," Octavian intoned further. "He will drag you and the good name of Thorn-rose through the public mire."

"He has only been trifling with you, dearest," said Christabel. "Brathmere is not an honest suitor."

"What he is," thundered Octavian, "is a Sybarite, a sensualist, a swine of Epicurus."

"If you are foolish enough to accept his advances, Verity, he will ruin you."

"He is an uncontrite sinner, a worker of iniquity, a demon incubus who delights in enticing women into perdition with his fleshly—"

"Stop!" shrieked Verity, leaping to her feet. "I beg you to stop, both of you."

Her tormentors fell silent, watching as she paced the room in terrible agitation.

"You are right, of course," she said finally in a low trembling voice. "Both of you are completely right. I will take immediate steps to remedy the situation."

Octavian's pale eyes glowed. "I would be with you, little cousin, when you deliver this declaration of righteousness. Allow me to stand beside you and buttress your frail female will against the blandishments of this seducing scoundrel."

"I'll do better than that," put in Christabel pugnaciously. "I'll tell him for you. Give me five minutes with him and I'll send him packing."

"No." Verity faced them, wan-looking, but firmer of tone than before. "I thank you both, but I must do this myself. It is I who must put an end to this unseemly familiarity that has sprung up between us. It is I who must stand up against his . . . blandishments and tell him that our association must end. No one else can do this for me."

Alaric came to Thornrose House in all haste. He had been cudgeling his brains to think how he might manage to be private with Verity again when, like a bolt from heaven, the note came, penned in her own neat hand, asking him to be so good as to call at his earliest convenience. Such an abject surrender was more than he could have hoped for. He had won the day after all. He had kissed all the nonsense out of his dear, prim Verity, and now she was waiting for him. His mouth curved into a slow half smile at the thought.

Verity came downstairs all in black, even to the lace at her throat, her ebony hair caught round her head in a sleek style that allowed not a curl to escape. She swept into the room with the grace of a black swan, but her face was troubled, and Alaric wondered if perhaps someone in her family had died unexpectedly.

He said her name softly and held out his hand.

She took a quick step back, a deliberate movement that put her beyond his reach.

His eyes narrowed. "Is something amiss?"

She did not answer immediately. Her hands twisted together and he noticed a sodden handkerchief clenched between them. He looked closely at her face and realized she had been crying. He had had occasion to witness a few women in tears and he recognized the signs.

She took a deep breath and raised her eyes to meet his searching gaze. "There is a certain matter which must be settled between us. I know of no easy way to say this, so I will be brutally frank with you."

Alaric smiled faintly. "I find it hard to believe that you could be brutal to anyone—even to me."

In a spate of evenly spoken, precise words, Verity proceeded to disabuse Alaric of this hopeful notion. "My lord, I do not wish to see you ever again. If we should meet in public, you will please refrain from addressing me. If you do speak to me, I will not acknowledge your presence. From this moment on, I do not wish to be acquainted with you."

The smile disappeared from Alaric's face. He listened to her declaration in silence, his mouth set in a thin line.

"May I ask what I have done that you should wish to sever our association so completely?" he asked when she was finished. His voice was cool, but there was an angry glitter in his hooded eyes.

"My lord," sighed Verity, "the blame is mine, not yours. You have done nothing but act according to your character."

"And is that so terrible?"

"It is when all you are known for are your follies and your philanderings and the blood of a dead man on your hands."

Alaric stiffened. He was getting deucedly tired of having that duel forever thrown up in his face. He was actually beginning to wish he'd missed his shot.

"If you are referring to the late unpleasantness with Westcott," he said evenly, "you may rest assured that the duel was conducted in all honour and propriety."

She looked at him sadly. "You have killed a man honourably and properly over trifling words at the card table. Is that anything to be proud of?"

Alaric stifled his rising Tierney temper and forced himself to the unusual effort of offering an explanation. "Westcott knew what he risked when he crossed me. He made certain accusations that he knew I couldn't swallow without a fight. No man of honour blames me for calling him out."

"Oh, will you not see?" cried Verity with sudden passion. "I blame you. I must. I must. I write tracts against duelling. I have spoken against it at reform meetings. I have lectured members of Parliament on the necessity of strengthening the laws against it. And now I make a public spectacle of myself in the company of an infamous duelist who has killed one man and wounded heaven knows how many others—"

"Three others, to be precise," said Alaric through his teeth. It was beginning to sink in that his dear, prim Verity had summoned him here not to fall into his arms but to give him his congé.

Verity turned to him imploringly. "Surely you must see that our lives are set unalterably upon opposing paths. You are a notorious gambler who has ruined other men at play. I am the granddaughter of one of the men who introduced the anti-gambling statute of '65. To consort with you in any way would make me guilty of the rankest hypocrisy. Even honourable marriage to you would be injurious to my chosen mission in life and the good name of Thornrose."

"I think you exaggerate the danger I pose to your good name," Alaric retorted in a cold, careless voice. "I assure you that I never had the slightest intention of asking you to exchange the fair name of Thornrose for my sullied one."

"No," said Verity quietly, "I never thought you did. It's just as well. I could never marry a man who ranked pleasure above all else."

"You seemed willing enough to be pleasured when last we met," Alaric pointed out, his tone soft and deadly.

Verity looked whipped and defeated. "I don't deny it," she whispered. "I acted the wanton, just as my cousin said I would. There can be nothing honourable between us, my lord. I beg you to let me go from this trap I've fallen into. I beg you."

She stood before him, her violet eyes aswim in her distressed countenance, her abused handkerchief fluttering from her fingers like a flag of surrender.

Only I'm the defeated one, thought Alaric bitterly.

His pride demanded some small victory and he achieved his most nonchalant shrug. "You needn't resort to beggary, my dear. I'll depart the scene quietly, as you request. And," he went on, his voice light but stinging as the lash of a whip, "as unprincipled as I am, it is the famous Mistress Reform who makes love like the lustiest wench to ever lay down in a May field. And now I'll bid you good day, madam." As he turned to leave, he had the empty satisfaction of seeing her flinch visibly under the lash of his tongue.

Be damned to you, Verity Thornrose!

Lady Fanny Sherbourne was preparing to ornament a dinner party at Holland House when Lord Brathmere's note was brought up to her. She seated her sumptuous form on a chaise lounge to consider the message at leisure.

The note was abrupt, and there was no apology for his odious conduct concerning her lock of hair, only a brief request that he be permitted to call upon her later that night to renew their friendship. She knew well enough what that meant. He expected to tuck his boots under her bed again. How like Alaric that was, arrogant to the point of cruelty. She ought to have no more to do with him.

At the thought of his coming, however, a tiny flame of excitement began to uncurl deep within her. He did have certain

talents, and she would so enjoy flaunting him on her arm
again. How gratifying, the envious female glances that would
follow them, for every woman secretly yearns to be the one to
throw the harness over a rogue like Alaric. And surely the best
way to recover from the embarrassment he had caused her
would be to have him dancing attendance upon her once more.
The gossips would then be talking out of the other side of their
mouths.

Alaric came to her not entirely sober, his dark eyes holding
the dangerous glitter she always found arousing.

She received him in gauzy splendor, reclining in the shadows cast by the canopy above her bed. It was a gothic splendor
of a bed, hung round with red velvet bedcurtains and adorned
with golden tassels and cavorting cherubs. Gilded candelabra
cast a softening glow about the chamber and upon Lady
Fanny's fulsome person. Heavy curtains shut out the night sky.

A bland-faced serving maid attempted to assist my lord off
with his coat, but Alaric only snarled, "Get your hands off me,
and get out." The maid curtsied and slipped away.

Alaric came and stood over the bed, untying, unbuttoning,
unbuckling as he stared down with a hot, fixed gaze at the
woman posed upon the satin counterpane.

Lady Fanny stared up at him with limpid eyes. "You've
been a naughty boy, Alaric," she told him reproachfully. "I've
a good mind to have no more to do with you."

"Ha!" His laugh echoed jeeringly through the velvet-hung
bedchamber. "Don't play your strumpet's games with me,
Fanny. You mean to have quite a lot to do with me, or you'd
never have received me at your bedside dressed in all your
tart's trumpery."

Lady Fanny pouted and lowered belladonnaed lashes, but
not quite quickly enough to conceal the sensual gleam that
kindled in her eyes at the sight of Alaric stripped to his masculine glory.

Without further converse, he dropped down on her, pressing
her deep into the satin-covered bed, crushing her mouth with
hard scornful lust, then moving farther afield to leave his mark
on her white neck.

A few token protests emerged from the lady's panting lips.

"My lord, you are too precipitate . . . you'll bruise me sure . . ."

But Alaric paid no heed to her words, only to the eager hands that clutched at him, the lush flesh that shifted abandonedly beneath him. Dear Fanny was healing balm to his wounded masculine soul. No moral ambiguities would plague him in her bed. He knew well enough how to treat this lady.

He hooked his long fingers into the bodice of her negligee and tore the translucent material away from her bosom. Fanny gasped rapturously. In the course of their torrid affair, Alaric had destroyed a small fortune in expensive lingerie. There was something about rending fabric that stirred her to amazing heights of passionate demonstration.

And Verity Thornrose was very far away, an unreal paragon enthroned in an ivory tower, high, high above him.

There were certain persons who made it their business to observe whether or not the Earl of Brathmere's high-perch phaeton and well-known set of bays departed from the stables of Lady Sherbourne's townhouse at any point in the warm spring night. When they did not, a note was dispatched to the marble-vaulted business chambers from which Mr. Octavian Smythe superintended the Thornrose wealth on Threadneedle Street. Octavian perused the contents avidly, then crumpled up the paper, and fed it slowly into the candle flame.

So, he thought with grim satisfaction, the blue-blooded hound has gone back to sniffing round Fanny Sherbourne. Well and good. Let Brathmere amuse himself with whatever strumpet pleases him as long as he leaves to me what is rightfully mine.

Chapter Fourteen

~~~

Deirdre Runs Away — Again

*D*eirdre tiptoed down the darkened back hall of Thornrose House, a tear-stained, ink-smudged letter in one hand, a small sack containing her belongings in the other. She angrily dashed away the tears that persisted in gathering in her eyes, for she had come so close, so close to having her dreams come true.

In her mind's eye she had pictured herself returning to Kilkenny in triumph, a handsome husband in tow. Perhaps she would even have an adorable baby on her knee (but naturally the travails of childbirth would not have diminished her beauty). She would have a fashionable traveling outfit of which the good wives of Kilkenny would be green with envy, and she would refer with casual sophistication to such fabled London places as Vauxhall and the Exeter 'Change.

But it was not to be. All her hopeful dreams had been obliterated by a chance-heard conversation between Rafe and Mrs. Allen. She had stood rooted to the floor outside the kitchen door, face burning, heart breaking.

"She'll be the ruin of you, Rafe! And just when you've been promoted to under-butler and are on your way up. In time, you could move on to a position in any of the great houses."

"Now why should I do that?" Rafe asked in his reasonable way. "When Chester is pensioned off, I'll become butler at Thornrose House, and no one here objects to Deirdre."

"You'd best not count your chickens before they hatch," retorted Mrs. Allen amidst a violent clanking of pots. "Things may come about as you say, and then again they may not. The aunts won't live forever. Miss Verity may marry and move to her husband's establishment. Then where will you be, shackled to that Irish snippet? What future have you outside this house?"

The rattling of cookware rose to a crescendo, and Deirdre nursed a dark suspicion that it was her head that Mrs. Allen would prefer to be knocking about rather than the pots.

"A butler's missus," Mrs. Allen went on, "should be able to act as a cook or housekeeper and keep the female servants in line. Deirdre couldn't keep a sheep cot in good order, much less a grand establishment. And what about her past? To have a wife who was known to have been turned off for dallying with the master and to have been found walking the streets for—"

"You're wrong about Deirdre," said Rafe steadily, but with considerably less energy than Deirdre would have liked to hear. "She's not a strumpet."

"Oh, no?" countered Mrs. Allen shrewdly. "And how is it that she got this sudden proposal out of you, Master Rafe? Not, I'll warrant, by saying her prayers and going to bed early like a good girl ought."

There was a long pause, during which Deirdre held her breath, waiting for Rafe to passionately declare his undying love for her. But Rafe only said, "It doesn't matter why I asked her to marry me. I have done, and I'll keep my word no matter what. It's time I married, and Deirdre suits me."

"Oh, for pity's sake, lad, think what you're doing." A pleading note sounded in Mrs. Allen's voice, for it was she who had taken the battered five-year-old Rafe under her maternal wing when he had first come to Thornrose House. "That girl will ruin you. She'll be nothing but a millstone about your neck . . ."

Deirdre fled, able to bear no more, and took refuge in the coziest maid's quarters in London. She looked about the comfortable, familiar room and stifled a sob. Rag rugs woven by the inmates at the Refuge for the Destitute brightened the floor, hangings sewn by the girl orphans at the Welsh Charity School adorned the walls. But Deirdre Lanahan, distressed Irish serving girl, did not belong in this room nor in this house.

This was just one of several things that had been forcibly borne in upon her. The other was that Rafe did not love her as she loved him. It was also apparent that by marrying her he would ruin his prospects. She couldn't bear to be the ruin of Rafe, and she was wise enough to know that a man with ruined prospects would not be very pleasant to live with. And what's more, she thought, her pride rallying, Deirdre Kathleen Lanahan would be a millstone to no man.

She sat down at the table that also served as a writing desk. After many false starts, blottings out, and crossing overs, a letter gradually emerged from her faltering pen.

> *My dearest Rafe,*
>   *When you read this I will be Gone. I depart in order to spare you my Burdensome Presence which will Blight your Bright Prospects. Please remember me fondly.*
>
> > *Yr. very obed serv't,*
> > *Deirdre Kathleen Lanahan*

It was long past midnight when she groped her way below stairs, leaving her letter where it would be discovered. After a last look around the shadowed kitchen, she undid the bolt, and slipped into the cobblestone alley. Having learned from her previous attempt at clandestine departure that it would be wise to avoid the notice of Hackett the stableman, she steered clear of the stable area. She allowed herself only one quick look back to bid a final farewell to that extraordinary place known as Thornrose House, where she had found—and lost—her first true love.

"Come in, child. Come in," urged Mrs. O'Grady, her brogue a poignant echo of home. "What's amiss, girl? You look peaked as a polled cow."

Deirdre gave a tearful rendition of the circumstances surrounding her discovery that she would constitute a blight on her beloved's future. "And I couldn't stay after that," she concluded brokenly. "To see him everyday and know he didn't care for me . . . and everyone thinking I wasn't good enough for him, and how long before he'd be thinking the same?"

"Well," allowed Mrs. O'Grady, "there's no denying that some of these London folk won't have an Irish servant in their house. And while I think Rafe's a fine man, when it comes to marrying, sometimes it's better to stick with your own kind. A nice Irish lad and a wedding in the Holy Mother Church is what's best for you, I'm thinking."

Deirdre gave her a hopeful look. "Does that mean you'll help me, Mrs. O'Grady? That you'll take me in?"

"Aye, child, and so I will. But I'll write Miss Verity tomorrow and tell her you're safe and well, and looking for a new start. I'll not have her worrying, for she's looking sadly pulled with that cousin of hers always hanging about like a mourner at a funeral."

Deirdre nodded gratefully. "And in the meantime I'll look for another position, for I'm not meaning to be a charge on you. But I can't go to any of the domestic registries on account of being turned off by Lady Stanhope."

Mrs. O'Grady frowned. "That will be a problem, unless . . ." She paused and regarded Deirdre consideringly. "I might know of a position for you, though it's not the kind of work you're used to, and I daresay that Miss Verity wouldn't think it fitting, either. But as it happens, I've got an old friend from me army days, Lucius Donegal, by name. He owns a chophouse and he's always looking for pretty table girls to fetch food and drink to the customers. He pays decent and the place is popular with the fancy gents, so the tips are good. But there's a certain peculiarity about Lucius' place . . ." her voice trailed off in hesitation while Deirdre waited, curious and expectant.

"Well, the thing of it is," Mrs. O'Grady resumed, "Lucius runs a gambling hell on the floor above the chophouse. Not that I'd let him put you to work upstairs, but even so, you'll probably see more of the sporting set than a young girl should. But beggars can't be choosers and you must have honest work and soon, for me army pension won't keep us both for long, I'll tell you that. And Lucius will keep you safe. Now what do you say to paying him a call and asking him to take you on?"

Deirdre hoped her eyes weren't gleaming too eagerly. The terms "fancy gents" and "sporting set" had not escaped her notice. Hobnobbing with gentlemen gamesters might be the very thing to put Mr. Rafe Bowen out of her mind.

Lucius Donegal of Donegal's Prime Chophouse was a bantam of a man with merry blue eyes and a slight limp caused by an American musket ball that had caught him while he was serving as a drummer boy in the battle of Yorktown. He also seemed to have kissed a goodly hole in the blarney stone, for he greeted Mrs. O'Grady with such a torrent of effusive and fantastic compliments that the beefy matron actually blushed. On the subject of Deirdre, he pronounced himself delighted to employ a colleen whose face put the angels to shame. But the contract was not made without some severe words from Mrs. O'Grady on the subject of Deirdre's care. In the face of these strictures Lucius Donegal was moved to swear on his mother's grave that any man who dared to ogle Deirdre would soon be looking out from an empty eye socket, and any man who dared to lay a hand upon her would draw back a bloody stump. These assurances satisfied Mrs. O'Grady and Deirdre could now consider herself employed.

First she must have working clothes. Mr. Donegal directed her to a used clothing shop on Cloak Lane and Deirdre came away from the place tricked out in a low-cut clinging magenta muslin, her red curls sprouting a trio of matching magenta plumes. The costume made her look very different from the matronly Mrs. Rafe Bowen of her recent imaginings.

There was powder and paint, too. More than she'd ever worn before. Red, red rouge for lips and face, and kohl for her lashes, and although she felt that the lavish cosmetics heightened her looks to new dramatic heights, when she looked in the mirror it was as if a stranger stared back at her.

Donegal's Prime Chophouse was a place of late hours, loud laughter and fortunes won and lost. In the public rooms downstairs, it was like any other eating place, filled with the savory smoke of grilling beefsteak, chops, and kidneys. Lucius Donegal was everywhere at once, greeting the guests effusively, grilling the chops personally for the gents at one table, ordering a round of stout on the house for another, showering outrageous flattery upon anything in skirts.

On her first evening, Deirdre was taught how to turn the roasting spit and how to manipulate the iron fork used for grilling the meat, all of which was cooked over a huge grill in a smoke-blackened alcove just off the dining room. Both these tasks were vastly more difficult than they appeared—and not for nothing was the smokey grease-spattered alcove known as the Pit. Fortunately, the table girls were never required to work the Pit steadily, for the grease was injurious to their dresses and the heat made their plumes wilt. Their real job was to look pretty, and smile for the gentlemen.

And smile Deirdre did. She smiled as she never had before. She smiled as she carried ale mugs four-in-hand amongst the packed tables, smiled as she labored throughout the crowded rooms bearing a steaming game pie above her head, smiled as she offered goblets of sherry to men who waved her away as if she were a faceless beast of burden. She even smiled when brassy females of uncertain character shrilled "You, girl!" at her and sent her scurrying.

It didn't take her long to realize that despite all the smoke and bustle, the chophouse was only a facade for the real business, the gambling that went on upstairs. And despite Lucius Donegal's promise that she would never see the inside of his hell, when the place got busy and help was short, this stricture was ignored.

Lucius would sidle up to her with a broad wink and the promise of an extra guinea if she would help out in the gaming room. "But not a word to the sainted Mrs. O'Grady," he would say with a conspiratorial grin, "for she would take her baton to us both if she ever found out." So Deirdre would hoist up her tray, filled this time with free champagne for the gamblers, and enter the sanctum sanctorum of Donegal's place.

Left behind were the rustic wooden benches, the pewter lamps and dinnerware, the easy bonhomie of the chophouse. Here were to be found soft carpeting, glittering chandeliers, and gilded bowlegged chairs with seats of velvet. Pale-faced, quick-fingered croupiers stood at their posts behind the green baize tables, presiding over exotic games of chance that she'd never heard of before: roly-poly roulette with its dancing ball and spinning wheel, rouge et noire with its diamond-shaped board, and card games like whist and piquet and silver loo, and of course, the eternal rattle of the ivory dice. Dark curtains held back the dawn so the gamblers would never know the sun had risen on a new day. It was the first time Deirdre had seen the gambling fever close at hand, men risking all on the turn of a card, caring for nothing in the world except the markers they made out to each other and to Lucius Donegal.

The clientele at Donegal's were an interesting mix. There were plenty of fancy bucks as Mrs. O'Grady had promised, and they did tip well—at least when they were winning. But there were also plenty of men who were not gentlemen born. It showed in their dress, their waistcoats always too showy, and in their manners, which lacked the polished ease of the beau monde. As the nights passed, Deirdre learned a little about these "flash gents" as these men were called, a higher class of criminal than White Willie's street coves. Among the flash gents that congregated at Donegal's were the proprietors of crooked skittles games, professional gamblers, turfites of uncertain business addresses, and pawnbrokers who didn't always inquire rigorously into the legal ownership of the property they received.

"Why do you let them in here, Mr. Donegal?" she asked him one evening. "Aren't you afraid it might keep the gentlemen away?"

Lucius Donegal gave a great hoot of laughter at her naivete. "Lord love you, child. It's mixing with the raff and scaff that brings the gentlemen in, don't you know. When they get bored with the drawing room jiggery-pokery they come here looking to mix with the flash gents and the dragsmen and the bruisers and the highfliers. They want a taste of the low life and I give it to them—within reason, of course—and they give me a bit of their blunt in return." He gestured expansively to the crowded gaming room. "It makes a fine show, don't it, Deirdre girl? The flash gents from the streets doing their best to mimic the Quality and the Quality coming to rub shoulders with the lower orders. And all of them paying me for the pleasure of each other's company."

"What about the girls, Mr. Donegal?" Being female, she was naturally curious about the other females to be seen in the place. The customers always had pretty girls on their arms—actresses or opera dancers, or so they claimed.

"What about the girls?" shrugged Lucius Donegal. "They come and they go, and there's always more of them to be had, a new crop every year, like pretty weeds."

Deirdre shivered a little as the shadow of her own fate fell coldly upon her. She had come here wanting to be like these girls, drinking champagne every night, queening it with the sporting set, being the petite aimee of some high-living gent, having him set her up and pay her way.

But she was beginning to see that the gay life didn't last very long. She never saw a girl in the gaming rooms who looked a day above two-and-twenty. The ultimate fate of the faded belles of Donegal's gambling house didn't bear thinking of.

It promised to be a dreadful night at Donegal's Prime Chophouse. The cook was in a froth because the dressed rabbits hadn't been delivered. One of the table girls was sick, another had discovered herself pregnant and was worse than useless. As a result, Deirdre was assigned to the Pit—but not before a clumsy customer had managed to spill ale on the bodice of her magenta gown.

Eyes smarting, face flushed, she struggled to wield fork and spit over the grill, occasionally muttering a prayer to the blessed St. Adamnan, who according to legend had enjoined Irish men from forcing their women to labor in the cookpits with the spits upon their shoulders. The cookpits of ancient Ireland couldn't have been worse than this, she thought morosely. An ominous spurt of flame caught her eye, and she hastily scooped up a row of sizzling sausages, biting back a cry as a spatter of hot grease singed her wrist.

Nursing her burnt wrist, she became aware that she was not alone in the pit. A strangely silent figure was standing behind her. She spun about, sausage plate still in hand.

"Rafe," she whispered.

His face tight with anger, his blue eyes steely, he gave her such a look of searing contempt that a hot blush spread from her painted cheeks to her throat to where her breasts showed above the low bodice of her dress. She knew she must look the veriest draggletailed drab, with her stained gown, her curls plastered to her perspiring forehead, and her plumes drooping exhaustedly.

"H . . . how did you find me?" she stammered.

The steely look didn't waver. "Not easily, since you made it clear you didn't want to be found. I've been spending my days off looking every place I thought you'd run to. It was only a matter of time before I got round to Mrs. O'Grady."

"She told you I was here?"

"No, she sent me packing with some nonsense about you marrying a nice Irish lad as soon as one happened along. But the landlady at her rooms was very helpful," he went on in a cold, uncompromising voice. "She knew you right off. She told me that every night a red-haired girl in purple tawdry leaves Mrs. O'Grady's rooms to work in Donegal's gambling den."

Deirdre lifted her chin. "Don't you be looking down your nose at me, Rafe Bowen. 'Tis honest work I do and it suits me just fine to be here, thank you very much."

With a muffled expletive, Rafe jerked the sausage tray from her hands and tossed it clattering onto the grill.

"Get your cloak," he said between his teeth. "You're coming back to Thornrose House where you belong."

"And why should I? You've got no claim on me, Rafe."

"Haven't I? We were to be married. Or did that little detail escape your mind?"

Deirdre's eyes flashed and all the hurt and anger came spilling out in a torrent. "Oh, I was fair crazy with happiness at the thought of marrying you, Rafe. Oh, yes. Until I found out how you really felt about me. I heard you telling Mrs. Allen that as you had to marry sometime, it might as well be me as anyone. Well, I'll tell you right now, I'll not be marrying a man who thinks so little of me. Now get out and let me earn me keep."

Rafe had the grace to look a little ashamed. "So that's what set you off? I wondered. Look here, I wasn't about to speak my true feelings about you to Mrs. Allen."

"Oh, but I think you did speak them," said Deirdre shrewdly.

"All right, maybe I was having a bit of bridegroom's nerves. Maybe I was feeling a little trapped—"

"Oh, now it's trapped, is it?"

"But that was before you went away. I've missed you like the very devil, Deirdre. I haven't had a night's peace for worrying you might be hurt or hungry or in trouble. I want you to come back with me."

"No," whispered Deirdre. "People will always be holding your Irish wife against you. Sooner or later you'd regret marrying me and want to be rid of me. I won't go back with you, even though I have to stand over this grill for the rest of me natural life."

Rafe's jaw set. "You'll come with me, like it or not. I'll not go off and leave you in this—"

A menacing purr of a voice cut across his. "This bloke wouldn't be giving you any trouble, would he now, Deirdre, darlin'?"

It was Lucius Donegal, and he was not alone. Two of the hulking ex-boxers he paid to keep order in his place stood like battered colossi at his back. He came to Deirdre's side and put a proprietary arm round her shoulders.

Rafe stiffened, his eyes narrowing.

"You wouldn't be pestering our pretty Deirdre now, would you," Donegal purred, "because, if you were, the lads here"— he gestured to the looming boxers—"well, they wouldn't take kindly to that at all."

Rafe ignored him. "Deirdre, for the love of heaven, come away from here. You don't belong in a place like this."

"Rafe, just let me be," implored Deirdre, fearful of what would befall him at the hands of the boxers. "Just go away and forget you ever knew me."

Rafe gave her a long measuring look and then turned on his heel and left.

"Go after him, lads," Lucius Donegal commanded his boxers, "and see that he doesn't go astray on his way out."

"They'll not hurt him?" asked Deirdre anxiously.

"Not unless he makes trouble. You're wise to be rid of him, Deirdre, girl. He doesn't understand the way things are here."

No, thought Deirdre bitterly as she gathered up the blackened sausages, he doesn't understand that I'm just another pretty weed, and that there'll be a new crop to take my place when I wither away.

At night's end, just before the grey dawnlight broke through the mist rising off the Thames, Deirdre walked slowly home. She was weary to the bone, not only from her toil at Donegal's Prime Chophouse, but from the burdens of life itself. Her progress through the sleeping streets was followed by several interested observers, among them Cut-Throat Jem, who was White Willie's chief kidnapper and assassin.

Chapter Fifteen

Too Full of Adventure to Be Briefly Described

A hand came out of the dawn mist and fell on Deirdre's shoulder. Terrified, she tried to twist away. Her struggles brought her face to face with her assailant.

"Rafe!"

Amazement made her cease struggling for an instant, and Rafe neatly pinned her against his chest. "You didn't think I'd give up so easily, did you?" he inquired, looking pleased with himself.

Deirdre regarded him speechlessly, and then emitted a few interrogative sputterings.

"I'd have carted you out of that place," he informed her as he took a tighter grip on her straining person, "but I didn't think I could handle you and those two bullies of Donegal's. But now the odds are more to my liking."

"I'll have you know—" began Deirdre.

"And I'll have you know," he said huskily, "that I'll never let you run away again."

His kiss caught her on the corner of the mouth, and her resistance seeped with such rapidity that in the next instant she let him kiss her foursquare. They stood locked together for a timeless moment, until dimly, through the haze of bliss, Deirdre saw a shadowy figure creeping up behind Rafe . . . an evil face swimming toward them out of the fog.

Cut-Throat Jem.

She stiffened and screamed a warning. Rafe whirled around, fists cocked to fight.

There were two—no three—men around them now, materializing out of the fog like ragged phantoms. They approached warily at first, for Rafe was much the bigger man. Though he had the advantage in strength and size, his years in the Thornroses' peaceable kingdom had not made a street fighter out of him.

One of the men managed to get behind him and send him sprawling forward with a vicious blow to the back of the neck. As he went down, Cut-Throat Jem's knife flashed out and cut the tendon that ran along the back of Rafe's calf. Deirdre, shrieking like a Celtic war queen, flung herself on the nearest cove's bony back, holding one throttling arm across his throat, the other hand crooked to claw at his eyes just as she'd seen the village brawlers do in Kilkenny.

But where Deirdre had been to school, White Willie's man had graduated with honors. He launched himself backwards, smashing his strangling, clawing burden against an alley wall. Deirdre's head snapped back against the bricks with a sickening crack, and the air was wrenched from her lungs. She slid off the man's back and collapsed into a stunned heap on the cobbles. She was spared the sight of Rafe staggering to his feet, only to fall forward again, a dagger buried to the hilt in his back.

"But where could both of them have got to?" Verity asked worriedly. "I cannot rid myself of the notion that something is terribly wrong."

Mrs. O'Grady nodded somberly. " 'Tis agreeing with you, I am, Miss Verity. Deirdre wouldn't have gone off without leaving me word."

Deirdre's failure to return to their shared rooms had alarmed Mrs. O'Grady, who promptly took herself off to Donegal's Chophouse to make Inquiries. Learning that a bothersome young fellow had paid Deirdre a visit the night before, it did not take much intuitive deduction to conclude that Rafe had discovered the whereabouts of his elusive sweetheart. It also occurred to Mrs. O'Grady that perhaps Deirdre had undergone a change of heart and run back to Rafe as precipitously as she had run away from him. Despite the earliness of the hour, she bent her steps toward Thornrose House, and was making Fur-

ther Inquiries of Verity when the door to the library flew open
and Chester entered much more hurriedly than usual.

"Rafe's been found, miss!" he announced, "but he's badly
hurt. We've laid him down in his room."

Rafe was being tearfully tended by Mrs. Allen, and by the
Thornrose family doctor who by fortuitous circumstance happened to be in the house looking in on Mrs. Sedgewick.
Though the knife had gone through Rafe's right shoulder
blade, it had mercifully missed his lung and struck no vital
spot. He was dangerously weak from shock and loss of blood,
and it would be touch and go for the next twenty-four hours.
While the doctor cleaned and stitched, Verity and Chester went
into the kitchen to speak to the helpful pie man who had
brought Rafe home in the back of his cart.

"You'll be kind enough," Chester directed the pie peddler
loftily, "to tell my mistress what has transpired."

"'Tarn't much to tell, guv. I were 'awking my pies and I see
this bloke lying in the alley. I gives him a shake and 'e moans
and groans and tells me to take 'im to 32 Bruton Street. So I
put 'im in the cart and brings 'im 'ere."

"You saw no one else," asked Verity anxiously, "no sign of
a young girl with him?"

"No, mar'm. Not a sniff of anyone else around."

"Well," said Verity, swallowing her disappointment, "we're
most grateful to you for your trouble."

"Aye, mar'm. And trouble it were, too, if I may say so,"
added the pie man in insinuating tones. "I missed my morning
trade altogether, for no one will buy from a pie man wot's got
a bleeding 'uman carcass in 'is cart, if you take my meaning."

"We are not interested—" began Chester repressively, but
Verity interrupted.

"Yes, we quite understand. Chester here will give you ten
pounds for your trouble."

"Ten!" exclaimed Chester, looking pained.

"Ten," said Verity firmly. "With our grateful thanks."

Muttering under his breath, Chester went to fetch his
strongbox, the pie man following in lockstep, determined not
to let the source of his windfall out of his sight.

It was not until the afternoon of the next day that Rafe was
conscious long enough to relate how he and Deirdre were set

upon in the alley. Verity was off to Bow Street in an instant, for this could only be White Willie's work, though why the Arch Cove should trouble himself over Deirdre so particularly she could not imagine.

The Bow Street magistrate, Sir Nathanial Conant, was, as usual, happy to do anything in his power to oblige Miss Verity Thornrose. He dispatched his Runners to roust White Willie in his flash house lair. Though the Runners searched the place high and low, they found nothing except an attic full of women who swore that they were naught but innocent table girls. The whole lot of these unfortunate females were piled into prison carts and duly trooped for inspection before Verity and Mrs. O'Grady, but Deirdre was not among them. The day was not entirely wasted, however, for Verity took the opportunity to deliver a homily to the girls about the various societies that stood ready to help them should they choose to abandon their present unhappy and unhealthy situation.

Mrs. O'Grady was more to the point, declaring, "Go on with your scummy way of living, me girls, and you'll be rotted with the pox before you're twenty."

Of White Willie himself, there was not a trace.

"That white-headed rascal is lying lower than Holland," opined Sir Nathanial. "But never fear, we'll run him down in due time."

But time is what they didn't have, Verity thought grimly. Deirdre had been in the hands of her captors for nearly two days. Who knew what dreadful things might already have been done to her?

Deirdre awoke painfully, her aching head full of visions of Rafe and Cut-Throat Jem's knife. She was possessed of a terrible fear that Jem had finished Rafe off permanently, for it was Jem's way to lame his victims first, and then dispatch them while they were down. She was desperate to help Rafe, but first she had to get out of wherever she was: a cold, dimly lit place that reeked of mold—a dungeon, obviously. What's more, she was in a cage inside the dungeon. She knew that because her cheek lay upon a mat of dirty straw, and a few inches from her nose a row of iron bars rose upwards. Groaning she lifted her head, and what she saw made a new thrill of fear shoot through her. Sprawled all about her were still, white-clad bodies.

Dear Holy Mother in Heaven, 'tis the shrouded dead I've been thrown in with!

Terror prodded her to her feet. Through the bars, she saw an even more eerie sight. She was in a forest of hangman's nooses. Loops and coils of rope dangled from nearly every inch of dungeon ceiling. Enough rope to hang every miscreant in London. She wanted to scream, but her tongue was frozen in her mouth. She took a swaying step forward, and her bare foot made contact with an encrusted bucket, which to judge from its aroma was being used as a chamber pot.

But what use would the shrouded dead have for a chamber pot?

Screwing up her courage, she bent unsteadily over the nearest of the white-draped bodies. It was a flaxen-haired girl dressed only in a lawn nightgown and, Deirdre discovered to her unutterable relief, the girl was alive and breathing, though deep in sleep. The other bodies were all the same, all young girls sleeping in their nightgowns or underdresses. Deirdre looked down at her own self in sudden comprehension and saw that she, too, wore only her thin white slip.

The distant sound of metal scraping against metal froze her in place. Footsteps sounded, coming closer. Acting out of a deep instinct for survival, she collapsed face down in the damp straw, feigning the strange deep sleep that possessed her fellow prisoners. A slot in the bottom of the cage was opened and a tray slid through it. As the footsteps began to recede, Deirdre risked a quick glimpse and saw that her gaoler was a woman. Deirdre also saw what had happened to her clothes, for the female gaoler was wearing the magenta muslin outfit, feathers and all.

Maybe she knows I'll have no more need of it, thought Deirdre sickly.

When the figure disappeared, she made herself crawl over to investigate the tray. Surprisingly, the food was not nearly as appalling as the surroundings. There was a whole cheese and several loaves of fresh bread, along with a pitcher of what looked to be small beer and several bowls for drinking. She didn't feel particularly hungry, but knew it was important to eat. Who knew when she would be fed again?

The bread and cheese were as good as they looked and it was only after she had eaten her fill that she began to wonder uneasily if she and the other prisoners weren't being fattened up for a sinister purpose. She poured herself a bowl of the small beer, but found it had an odd taste. Still, it was all she had to drink, and she had learned from her time on the street that thirst could be as debilitating as hunger. By the time she finished the small beer, she felt unaccountably drowsy, and though she struggled to keep her eyes open, she was dragged unwillingly into a leaden sleep.

She dreamed of Rafe.

She awoke to find herself on her feet. She was swaying in someone's bruising grasp and her cheeks were being smartly slapped. An unfamiliar voice buzzed in her ear like an irritated gnat.

"Too much, you fool! Too much! Do you want to lose another one? Especially a fine one like this. Look at this hair. 'Tis like the morning sun on the white cliffs." A hand was upon her now, touching shoulders, arms, breast, fondling her as if she were a melon in a stall. She wanted to protest but she felt too sleepy.

"Cut the dose in half, I say," the irritated voice continued. "We want them pretty and lively with roses in their cheeks. I'll come again in two days and I want to see them looking sound as roaches."

The bruising hand let go and she slumped gratefully into the blessed darkness. Gradually after that, her mind became less murky, her limbs less leaden. Her fellow prisoners stirred to consciousness as well, and eyed her in puzzlement.

"Where's Betty?" they wanted to know.

Deirdre didn't have an answer for them, although she vaguely remembered some ominous references to "losing another one." She began to suspect that she had been brought in as a replacement for the permanently lost Betty. A terrible heart-freezing dread began to grow inside her, and she curled up in the corner of the cage, shivering convulsively.

At the next feeding time, the female gaoler appeared again, still clad in the magenta dress. The imprisoned girls, rousing

now from their stupor, begged their wardress to say what
would be done with them. She remained unmoved and merely
shoved the food into their cage with callous indifference.

The answer to their questions came soon enough, however,
when two men entered their prison. One of the men was White
Willie. The Arch Cove was immediately identifiable from his
skewed walk, his stolen, mismatched finery, and the eerie halo
of white hair that glowed like phosphorous in the lantern light.
His companion was a man of entirely different character. Well-
dressed, plump and cheery-looking, he seemed bizarrely out of
place in this dark prison. He twirled a fine cane in a gloved
hand and generally looked more fitted to presiding over a
prosperous guildhall than this awful place.

He came to the cage and pressed a pink-jowled face between the bars. "Now, my good Master Willie, let's see what
we've got here."

He walked around the cage, in his snuff-colored suit, looking like a plump partridge. Occasionally he poked his cane
through the bars and prodded a girl who wasn't showing herself lively enough.

"Very good, very good," he approved, beaming rosily.
"They'll bring a breath of England to our poor lonely lads at
the India Station."

The barred cage whirled sickeningly about Deirdre. Now
she understood what White Willie meant to do with her, what
he had probably meant to do all along. She was to be sold into
prostitution and shipped to India. No wonder White Willie had
been annoyed when she disappeared. He couldn't sell his flash
house girls who had lovers and family among the flash coves,
and he was too cunning to strain the loyalty of his mobsmen
by exporting their women against their will. But Deirdre Lanahan—homeless, friendless, a stranger, Irish, with a head of
hair that would shine like a flaming star among the dark-
haired Indian people—she could be sold away to living death
in a Delhi bordello and no one would care.

The sight of his cargo seemed to put the chubby-faced merchant into an even better humor, and he began to expound expansively on the whys and wherefores of the India flesh trade.

"I'll tell you, Master Willie, there are few enough English
females there as it is. And genuine English whores—especially

ones who look as good as this lot—why they're scarce as hens' teeth. Just look at them. Don't they make you think of mornings on the moor, hedgerows in the spring, sunset on the lochs."

Deirdre could stand no more. "You can't do this," she protested, her voice wavering on the edge of hysteria. "For the love of God—"

The cane wrapped smartly against her fingers where they clutched the bars. Deirdre shrank back, nursing her bruised knuckles.

The flesh merchant's eyes sparkled with piggy glee. "My dear pretty child, these alarums are most unseemly. You should count yourself fortunate to be able to console John Company as he labors for British commerce in a foreign land."

Deirdre stared at him, stunned into silence by the cheery inhumanity of this reply.

White Willie was less jovial. "It's no more than wot you deserve, puttin' me to so much trouble to find you. But you're one slut those meddling busybodies won't snatch out from under my nose." He turned to the other flesh merchant, who was still inspecting the recent acquisitions. "You want 'em fed tonight?"

"No, just give them the beer," said the merchant with a significant look. "Tomorrow my men will load the cage into a covered dray and take it to the ship."

Tomorrow, thought Deirdre, horrified, *tomorrow was the day.* After tomorrow, what hope had she?

Alaric Tierney, Earl of Brathmere, restlessly paced the length of his mistress's boudoir, waiting for her to arrange herself. They were to dine and go to the opera, after which they would retire to the delights of the lady's opulent bed. A full and pleasant evening, to be sure; however, it would bring Alaric no joy.

He paused before one of the gilt mirrors (Lady Fanny was fond of mirrors) and studied his somber reflection. All good things in life were his for the taking, yet his existence seemed empty and burdened. What had happened to the care-for-nothing Earl Brat, reckless reprobate and despoiler of dames of high and low degree? What had happened to him?

You know what happened to the poor devil, he told his re-flection bitterly. *She happened.* He poured himself a good measure of wine from a decanter displayed on the table be-neath the mirror and raised his goblet in a silent toast to Verity Thornrose, the woman who had sent him into everlasting dis-array.

He had seen her today, standing in front of Parliament with her black-clad aunts. She wore her usual light grey, and in the midday sun she looked like a silver rose set amid iron thorns. She had turned toward him and his poor abused rake's heart leaped with hope, but no, the thorny aunts bore her away, leav-ing him yearning more than ever. Oh, he could make a count-ess of her if she would have him, but she considered her duties as a Thornrose to be far more important than the string of earls that preceded his name in the stud book. And yet . . . and yet . . . he believed that he had touched her unspoiled young heart.

He wondered, as he often did, what she was doing at the moment. Writing a tract perhaps, or reading an improving tome, or perhaps she was asleep by now, lying slim and grace-ful between cool sheets.

The image of his loss brought an ache of pain like a knotted fist driven into his middle. God help him, but she was the one he wanted. No other woman would do. He put down his wine and left his mistress's boudoir without a backward glance.

Deirdre had been gone for four long days. Rafe tossed on his sickbed, weak and feverish and calling for her.

Verity took every measure she could think of to aid the search for her abducted maidservant. She put up a reward of a hundred guineas for Deirdre's safe return. She took out a miss-ing person's notice in the Hue and Cry, the police gazette pub-lished by the Bow Street Runners. She commissioned the printing and posting of handbills bearing Deirdre's likeness. Yet it all seemed futile, for she knew too well that the twisted streets of London swallowed up a dozen girls like Deirdre every day.

A tiny frown was permanently etched between Verity's brows, for she felt her responsibility keenly. Other matters weighed heavily upon her as well. In her capacity as a patron of the Society for Bettering the Condition of Chimney Sweeps, she was aiding the reform-minded politician Henry Bennett in his efforts to gain passage of a law forbidding the use of small boys in the hazardous work of cleaning chimneys. This meant reviewing pages of testimony about the dangers and abuses to which these unfortunate children, some as young as four, were subjected. It was like looking into a hell where the innocent suffered instead of the guilty, and it did nothing to lighten her already bleak mood. She felt tired and defeated, and very much in need of a strong shoulder to lean on, and it was not her cousin Octavian's monstrous shoulder of which she was thinking.

What was he doing tonight, at this moment? When she remembered the alluring Lady Sherbourne, she had little doubt what the bold Earl Brathmere was up to at the moment. Yet, it didn't stop her from thinking about him in a way that caused a slow burning flush to mount in her cheeks. Who was this handsome dark wizard who could make her forget her moral principles? She should be glad that she had had the good sense to send him away. But she wasn't glad. Her mind wondered relentlessly: *Why doesn't he come to me? Doesn't he know I need him?*

While Verity worried over Deirdre and wrestled with her conscience, Peggy O'Grady moved into action. She took her baton in hand, summoned her faithful fellow-volunteer, Riley the coachman, and once more traversed the night streets of Covent Garden, searching for Distressed Irish Serving Girls in general and Deirdre in particular. On the second night, her endeavors bore fruit. This happy development was heralded by the clatter of Riley's coach into the mews behind Bruton Street, and by the issue from the coach of the most virulent string of billingsgate to ever disrupt the dignified precincts of Thornrose House.

Believing that Mrs. O'Grady had rescued yet another fallen female, Verity and her aunts hurried to the kitchen to inspect the newly saved lamb. The newly saved one was anything but lamblike, however. She clawed and flailed, looking like a maddened hen in her bedraggled magenta plumage.

"Good heavens, Peggy!" shouted Verity, straining to make herself heard above the invective. "I believe you've made a mistake. This girl is no more Irish than I am." And indeed the girl's cockney accent proclaimed her to have been born within the sound of Bow bells.

"Aye, I know it," panted Mrs. O'Grady as she endeavored to wrestle the writhing girl into a chair. "That's not why I snatched her. Hold still!" she roared at the resisting captive, "or I'll snap you cross me garters like a twig."

Temporarily cowed, the girl retreated into a corner, her eyes darting about like a trapped animal's.

"We'll have to get some rope and tie her up," said Mrs. O'Grady.

"Surely you can't mean that," protested Verity.

"Aye, but I do. We need to get the truth from this one, I tell you. She's wearing Deirdre's dress."

The import of this was not lost on Verity. "Are you sure?"

"As sure as anything. I helped Deirdre sew on that flounce meself. Do you think I wouldn't know me own dressmaking? I tell you, Deirdre was wearing this when she left Donegal's place. And now I find this doxy parading in it, walking the streets bold as brass. For a second, I thought she was Deirdre."

Verity turned to the cornered captive. "No one is going to hurt you. Please be calm and tell us your name."

"Wot's it to you?"

"I should like to know what to call you."

"Name's Iris," was the sullen reply.

"What is your last name, Iris?"

"Don't got one."

"Where do you live?"

"Nowhere."

"What do you do for a living?"

"Nuthin'."

"How did you come by this dress?"

"Found it."

"I'm afraid I don't believe you."

"Don't care."

"Iris, if you don't tell me the truth tonight, I must hand you over to Bow Street tomorrow morning."

"Ha! And too late you'll be for all yer trouble."

"What do you mean?"

"Nuthin'."

"You must tell me what you know. What happened to the girl who wore this dress? Why will tomorrow be too late?"

"I don't know nothin', I tell you."

"Listen, Iris, I will pay you a hundred guineas if you help me find the girl we're looking for."

"'Undred guineas won't do a corpse no good," opined Iris darkly.

And that was her final word. Despite all of Verity's pleas and all of Peggy O'Grady's threats, no more was to be gotten from her.

"Verity, darling, may we have a word with you?" It was the aunts, who had observed all from the doorway.

"Dearest, we've been thinking," whispered Aunt Faith, "that it might be wise to question the girl a little more forcefully."

"Perhaps we could tickle the soles of her feet with feathers?" suggested Aunt Hope.

"Or drip water on her head the way the mandarins do," put in Aunt Charity. "I have a lotion dispenser that will do nicely."

Verity stared at them. "Are you suggesting that we torture her?"

"Only the tiniest little bit, Verity, dear."

The discussion got no further, for a tall figure clad in a nightshirt and dressing gown hobbled into the kitchen. It was Rafe and he had overheard.

Moving with remarkable speed for a nearly dead man, he seized the girl with his one good arm and shook her. "Where did you get that dress? Tell me or you'll be sorry."

Iris shrieked and broke free, only to find her way blocked by Mrs. O'Grady, who was hefting her baton suggestively. Menace came from the other direction in the form of a pair of small but savage-looking dogs who nipped viciously at her ankles. Like a vixen run to earth, the cockney girl dived into the pantry and crouched in the corner as Mrs. O'Grady locked the door behind her. Rafe took a staggering step toward the pantry door and then hunched over with a cry of pain, his torn leg giving way beneath him. Samuel the groundsman and Hackett the stableman were summoned to carry him back to bed while he protested vociferously. Mrs. Allen commanded him equally vociferously to stop being a fool unless he wanted to be lamed

permanently. The aunts admonished him similarly in trio while
the lapdogs yipped piercingly.

At this moment Chester descended the kitchen stairs to an-
nounce above the general din, "Miss Verity, the Earl of Brathmere demands to see you at once. He swears he'll not take no
for an answer."

A shining look came to Verity's face. He has come after all.
The turmoil in the kitchen was forgotten. She ran up the stairs
without a backward glance.

Chapter Sixteen

In Which the Earl of Brathmere Makes a Timely Entrance

Alaric stood in the front salon of Thornrose House, mentally congratulating himself. So far, his darling had not seen fit to have him thrown out into the street. Nor did she keep him waiting, but hastened to him almost at once. He wanted to look his fill at her, for it had been a month since he had seen her.

"Forgive me," he said simply. "I couldn't stay away."

"Oh, but I am glad you've come," she said with astonishing warmth and held out her hands. "I knew my Good Samaritan would not fail me in the end."

The warmth of her greeting astounded him. He took her hands in his and was rewarded when she suffered them to remain there. "Is something amiss, Verity?"

"Oh, everything, everything. Deirdre has disappeared—"

"Don't tell me that fool girl has loped off again!"

"No . . . well, actually, yes. First she loped, then she was abducted. Rafe tried to save her and was stabbed and now he won't go to bed. My aunts want to genteelly torture the girl that Mrs. O'Grady found wearing Deirdre's dress, but I don't think it will answer." Seeing his look of confoundment, she collected herself. "Forgive me. I'm babbling." Gently she disengaged her hands from his grasp and provided him with a more cogent rendition of events.

Alaric listened intently. "So," he concluded, "I gather you must make this Iris creature talk tonight."

"Yes, I think we must. I'm convinced that she spoke the truth when she said that tomorrow would be too late. I've threatened her with Bow Street, but I believe she's more afraid of White Willie than the magistrate."

Alaric frowned. "And what could the magistrate do in any case but throw her into the Fleet? A few days in prison might loosen her tongue, but by then it would be too late . . ." He paused for a moment and then went on in a silken voice that boded no good for Iris. "I think I'll have a word with your little guttersnipe if you don't mind."

Verity smiled brilliantly at him, thinking, *Strange how I never doubted for a moment that he would come to my aid.*

"Where is the girl now?"

"I blush to admit it, but I've allowed Mrs. O'Grady to lock her in the pantry."

"A wise precaution, I would think. I need a word with my coachman first and then we'll see to Iris."

Having procured what he needed from his coachman, Alaric had no trouble finding his way to the pantry, being led thither by a string of shrilled vulgarities. "One hears so much about the malnourished constitutions of the lower orders," he observed to Verity as she unlocked the door, "but I must say this one's constitution seems to be in remarkably fine twig— though I can't say much for her vocabulary." When Verity would have gone in with him, he stayed her with a hand that lingered warmly on her shoulder. "I think I'll do better without you. You hardly have the face of an inquisitor."

"All right," said Verity, a little breathlessly, for his touch dazzled her, "if you think it best."

"I do," he assured her. Because, he added silently, Miss Verity Thornrose, champion of the oppressed, would never countenance what I'm about to do.

The captured Iris had wreaked havoc in her prison, destroying a small fortune of jelly jars and tea canisters. Her eyes held a mixture of fear and cunning, and Alaric knew she was old beyond her years. She'd not have survived the violent city slums otherwise.

But I've matched wits with the best gamesters in England, Alaric told himself, *and I'll be damned if I don't make this little gutter jade show her hand.*

His entrance caused her to leave off destroying the contents of the pantry. She pressed herself into the farthest corner, suspecting that she was now in the hands of a gaoler of a vastly different kidney.

Alaric turned round a chair, straddled it, and took from his pocket a small, silver-chased, and lethal pocket pistol made by the premier gunsmith Joseph Manton. In her young, brutal life the girl must certainly have seen what a pistol ball could do to human bone and sinew.

Still saying nothing, Alaric began to inspect his gun, cocking it experimentally, wiping a speck of dust from the silverwork, sighting it at various angles off the back of the chair. He let the charade stretch out for a number of nerve-wracking moments.

"Well, my girl," he said at last, and had the satisfaction of seeing her jump at the sound of his voice, "I should like to know how you came by that dress."

The girl opened her mouth, but Alaric held up a weary hand. "Spare me your tedious denials, Iris." He continued with sinister softness, "Do you see this pretty pistol here? If you don't tell me what I want to know, I'm going to put a bullet into one of your feet. I haven't decided precisely which foot, but I daresay I will have made up my mind when the moment comes. And then if you don't tell me what I want to know, I shall shoot you in the other foot. And there's an end to your streetwalking days. There'll be nothing for you to do but crawl into the gutter and beg."

He sighted the pistol at her and was pleased to see her cringe into the corner and screw her eyes shut.

"Of course," he went on with dreadful affability, "there's always a chance that you possess an extremely high resistance to pain and loss of blood. If you still haven't told me what I want to know, I will shoot you next in the hand, which will greatly hamper you in your begging career, as you will have only one hand with which to hold your cup. Then if you still refuse, I will put a bullet into your other hand, and you'll have to hang your cup around your neck. Doubtless you will make a most arresting beggar at this point, but whether you'll profit by it is another matter. You'll have to spend most of your pennies to hire a street arab to brush the flies off you. You'll not be a pretty sight, I fear, scuttling about with children throwing garbage at you and women turning away from the sight of you."

A muted whimper escaped her as Alaric swung himself off the chair. He made a final inspection of the pistol, pointed it at her, but then shook his head and re-aimed, then shook his head again, changed his stance, took a step toward her, and sighted the pistol downward at her quivering ankles.

There was a long silence and then Alaric lowered his pistol. The girl seemed to resume breathing until Alaric spoke again. "Would you be so kind as to lift your skirts slightly? They're preventing me from taking proper aim."

The girl gave him a glassy-eyed look, and then fell to her knees and babbled frantically about a cage of drugged women held in the basement of a boarded-up ropemaker's shop on Ratcliffe Highway.

"Oh, Alaric, to threaten the poor girl with a pistol," chided Verity.

"I had no intention of actually shooting her, dear heart, and let me tell you, yon poor girl is in thick as thieves with White Willie and the Jolly Merchant Man, whoever he may be. And they're about to ship a consignment of young girls—your Deirdre among them—off to India for no good purpose."

The thought of white slavery made the Thornrose lightning flash in Verity's eyes. "We must stop this," she said fiercely. "I'll send a message to Sir Nathanial at once, but who knows how long it will take him to rally his men."

"I don't mean to wait on the Runners in any case," said Alaric. His voice was cool, but there was an air of excitement about him. He was fairly straining to be away, an idle thoroughbred who had finally found a race worthy of being run. "I'll take my coachman and go to Ratcliffe Highway immediately. The girl swears there's but one guard. It should be easy enough to take him unawares."

Verity shook her head. "I cannot ask you and your servant to take such a risk on my behalf. It is for me to—"

"Verity, if you think I would let you set out upon such a dangerous endeavor, you are greatly mistaken. Ratcliffe Highway is full of drunken sailors and all the trouble that comes with them. And suppose the girl is lying. Suppose there are a dozen men on guard. What would happen to you?"

"But what would happen to you?"

"You would care?"

Her gaze fell beneath his.

"You would care?" he repeated softly.

"Yes," she whispered, "I would care."

"Then, have no fear. I will return. How could I not?"

She smiled up at him, a quiet twinkle in her violet eyes. "Oh, you'll come back. We'll see to that."

"And just who is 'we'?" Alaric inquired, his expression narrowing.

"Mrs. O'Grady, Riley, and myself."

"Don't be ridiculous. The three of you may do well enough snatching serving maids, but you're no match for underworld criminals."

"You have obviously never seen Mrs. O'Grady wield her baton. And Riley has a blunderbuss. As for myself," she went on in her crispest reformer's manner, "I'm well aware that the only weapon I'm proficient with is my hatpin, and that will do us no good tonight. However, I'm quite capable of minding a team and keeping watch, which is what I intend to do so that both Riley and Mrs. O'Grady can go with you and your coachman and guard your back. You surely cannot think," her voice was softer now, "that I would remain behind while you were in danger on my account."

Alaric's eyes gleamed at this further evidence of Verity's concern for his rakehelly backside, but he only said, "No, I see now that you would never countenance such a thing."

Ratcliffe Highway ran through the river district and had an evil reputation. For hundreds of years it had been the place of execution for pirates, who were hung in chains at the low water mark, and left hanging until the three tides had flowed over them. The highway was lined with docks and warehouses along with the taverns and cheap lodgings favored by sailors. The names of the cross streets bore evidence of the area's hard and violent history—Gun Alley, Dung Wharf, Hangman's Gains. Occasionally, Ratcliffe Highway offered its traversers a glimpse of the Thames, its dark waters

crowded with barges and merchant ships riding at anchor
under a fitful moon.

Several blocks from the ropemaker's shop, Riley stopped,
turning the reins over to Verity so that he and his long-
barrelled blunderbuss could join the others. Mrs. O'Grady had
out her baton, gleefully anticipating its encounter with the
noggins of White Willie's minions.

Alaric's weapons were a pair of silvered Manton pocket pistols, the one that had so forcibly impressed Iris, and its exact
twin. Eyes glittering purposefully, he took them out and gave
them a final check, running his long fingers over them caress-
ively. For all his duels and tavern brawls, he knew that until
tonight he had had no fight worthy of his manhood.

Verity, watching him, thought that at this moment, she
understood him as she never had before. She saw in him that
breed of English gentlemen born with a lust for adventure
where their bump of respectability ought to be—men who
turned easily to outlawry or privateering or knight errantry,
men like the courtiers of King Charles, who became the fighting cavaliers, or Earl Huntingdon who robbed the rich as
Robin Hood, or Sir Francis Drake, who turned privateer in the
service of Good Queen Bess. But in these settled days of
Prince George's Regency there was no place for such men except in Wellington's army, and the very idea of Alaric Tierney
being amenable to military discipline was ludicrous. And so
Alaric had fallen victim to his own restless devils.

May the angels protect them, she thought prayerfully, as she
watched Alaric lead his motley little troop toward the abandoned shop that served as the last way station on the road to
the living hell of a Delhi brothel.

A cautious advance brought the rescuers to the sloping bulk-
head door that covered the stairway into the cellar. Alaric
eased it open and led the way down the slimy treads of a stone
staircase. Ahead of them stretched a cobwebbed passageway.
At the end of it shone a thin sliver of light in the outline of a
door and they stole silently toward it. Voices floated out under
the door—more than one voice. Alaric swore inwardly. Either
there had been a change of routine, or Iris had been lying
through her cockney teeth.

He pressed his eye to the crack and caught a glimpse of a

barred cage filled with motionless white forms—the kid-napped women! He was forced to admire the ingenuity of White Willie and company. How easy it would be to simply lift up the cage of unconscious prisoners and conceal it within a covered wagon. No one would look at it twice as it rolled through the busy dockside streets and was loaded onto an East Indiaman. The unfortunate women would probably remain in this unholy pen for the duration of the voyage.

His elation at having actually found the abducted women was tempered by the fact that there were four rough-looking men guarding them instead of only one. They were sitting round a fat barrel drinking and playing cards. Above their heads a lantern swung from one of the hundreds of coils of rope that hung from the ceiling. How and if they were armed he couldn't determine, but it was likely that they would be. On the other hand, the number of empty bottles scattered on the floor gave him reason to hope that at this juncture their wits would not be sharp.

Still, the odds against the rescue party were worse than he had anticipated, and he had no intention of taking the guards on, en masse. Eight people, shooting, bashing, and stabbing at each other in the confined space of the cellar would be danger-ous. Riley's blunderbuss with its scatter shot pellets was as likely to hit one of the captive women as it was one of their gaolers. Another plan was called for. Happily, he had one.

Once everyone was in place, Alaric applied a hefty kick to the door and sent it flying open. A look of enormous surprise spread over the faces of the card players. Before they could move, Alaric shattered the lantern with a single, well-placed shot, and the cellar was plunged into darkness. Simultane-ously, he shouted, "Surrender in the name of the King."

Of course the men did no such thing, knowing it meant the gallows. Caught flatfooted, they sought frantically to escape by any means they could find. Nor did Alaric mean to stop them. He and the other rescuers stood pressed quietly against the wall as the men fought to get out of the cellar door, but the last man out blundered too temptingly close to Mrs. O'Grady, who felled him with a crunching blow to the head.

A prisoner, by God! thought Alaric happily.

Finally there was silence in the ropemaker's cellar.

"Strike the light," Alaric commanded his coachman, who had foresightfully brought along tinder, flint, and candle.

The flickering light showed the cellar to have been won.

"Now," said Alaric, "let's see what we've rescued."

Quite a nice collection of comely damsels, as it turned out. Alaric recognized Verity's servant girl instantly from her unmistakable hair. A surge of elation shot through him, as if he had just won a fortune on a single cast of the dice. Success! And he had thought reform work dull. There was obviously more to it than he had supposed.

"Listen!" hissed Mrs. O'Grady suddenly.

There was a commotion on the street, the noise of running feet thudding on the floor of the shop above them. It sounded like an army gathering overhead. Alaric slipped his unfired pistol from his pocket while Riley raised up his blunderbuss.

A voice boomed out. "You in the shop! You're under arrest, by order of the Bow Street Magistrate."

A universal sigh of relief wafted through the cellar.

Alaric pulled out a handkerchief and gave it to his coachman. "Go upstairs and surrender us to Bow Street, Phillips, and try not to get your head blown off in the process. And one thing more," his voice crackled urgently around the cellar, "no one is to reveal my name to the authorities. It won't do for me to be associated with Miss Thornrose in this venture. However," he added with a grin, "if you're pressed for particulars about my identity, you may describe me as a private gentleman interested in preserving the virtue of English womanhood."

Chapter Seventeen

Pistols at Dawn

*D*eirdre tiptoed carefully into Rafe's sickroom. It was against the doctor's orders, of course, but that didn't matter. A whole day had passed since she had slept through her rescue from the ropemaker's shop, and she had had no word with Rafe. She couldn't bear not seeing him any longer.

She found him lying pale and hollow-faced on his pillows. Penitent tears sprang into her eyes at the sight of him, but he smiled at the sight of her.

"Don't come to me with tears in those green eyes," he whispered.

The tears spilled anyway. "I can't help it . . . to see you like this . . . knowing your leg will never be the same . . ."

Rafe's mouth tightened determinedly. "My leg will bear me up to the end of my days, Deirdre, girl, and that's all a man needs from a leg."

She shook her head. "Oh, but downstairs they're saying that no one will want a butler who can't stand as straight-legged as a sergeant on parade—" She could have bitten her tongue then that she'd let the awful worry that had been plaguing her spill out.

But Rafe merely cocked an eyebrow at her. "Who's to say I'll want to be a butler to the end of my days? It's a good enough life for a single fellow, but a married man wants more—land and a house of his own."

Deirdre stared at him, certain that it was the fever talking. "And where is all this land coming from, Rafe?"

"It's waiting for us, Deirdre. In New South Wales."

"New South Wales!" He might as well have said the Land of Faery. "You can't be wanting us to go there." Half the population of Kilkenny spent their entire lives trying to avoid transportation to New South Wales, and now here was Rafe, wanting them to go there of their own free will.

"There's land there for the taking, Deirdre." Despite his weakened condition, excitement sounded in Rafe's voice. "I'm not saying I mean to go right away, for we must have some money put by first. But I promise that if you go with me, one day I'll build you a house fit for the prettiest girl to come out of Kilkenny Village. What do you say to that?"

"A house of our own," breathed Deirdre.

Rafe smiled drowsily. "Aye, with white pillars and a staircase for you to meditate under if you've a mind to."

But Deirdre did not hear that, being lost in dreamy contemplation of this new and vastly interesting vision of her future. "Why, land of your own would make you as good as a squire, Rafe. And the place must have a name, just as if it were a squire's estate. Do you fancy the sound of Bowen Farm? No, that's not grand enough. What about Bowen Grange? Or Bowen Court? That sounds quite grand, don't you think?"

There was no reply. Rafe had—very sensibly from his point of view—gone back to sleep.

Deirdre smiled down at him tenderly and smoothed back the thick brown hair. She wondered if he was dreaming, but it didn't matter. She had dreams enough for them both.

Verity was the heroine of the hour, praised at reform meetings, commended in the press, and lauded from the pulpit. The invitations to society affairs trebled overnight.

As for the rescued females, they were admitted to the Magdalene Hospital to recover from their ordeal. Most were found to be friendless country girls who had been snatched from the streets, although a few had actually been sold to White Willie by avaricious relatives. The Magdalene Hospital Committee (of which Miss Hope Thornrose was a patron) quickly set about arranging situations for the girls so that all would be provided for when discharged.

The success of the night's work on Ratcliffe Highway was not total however. The cove who had fallen victim to Mrs. O'Grady's baton proved to be only a common street bully who knew nothing of those who had hired him. The cockney girl Iris, who obviously knew more than she was telling, managed to escape Thornrose House that same evening by tripping Mrs. Allen to the floor when the unsuspecting cook brought her a tray of food.

As for White Willie, he had gone to earth in the blind courts and tenement slums of Seven Dials and was not to be found. Also not to be found was the Jolly Merchant Man, believed to be the financial backer of the scheme.

Of the anonymous gentleman interested in preserving the virtue of English womanhood, only passing mention was made. Of that gentleman it may be said that he once again ended his relationship with Lady Frances Sherbourne, albeit this time in a more civilized manner, despite the expensive knickknacks crashing about his head as he made his exit.

Miss Verity Thornrose was now often seen in the company of the Earl of Brathmere. They sat together at a concert given by the newly formed Philharmonic Society; they attended a lecture given at the Royal Horticultural Society. The earl was not seen at any reform meetings, but Miss Thornrose was seen with his lordship at a cricket match at Lord's. Yes, said the Interested to themselves and to anyone else who would listen, it was certainly a case with these two. Very astute, the Interested of London Society.

Alaric's restless devils were stilled in Verity's company. In all his wild, rudderless existence, he had never known anyone with her sense of purpose. He watched fascinated, admiring the way she lived her life, trying not to be jealous of the time she gave to her committees. He tried also not to let her feel the desire that ran hot beneath his gentlemanly manners. Verity felt that heat and basked in it, though this was a secret she kept in her own heart. She was no longer content in her dutiful, disciplined existence. She craved the unsettling excitement that the sight of a lean, restless face had brought into her life. She craved the clash and thrill of passionate love. She craved it—yet she was afraid.

* * *

"Must we dine out again tonight?" lamented Miss Drusilla Sedgewick. "I believe I shall go distracted if I must endure one more evening of insipid conversation to gain my supper."

"I'm afraid you must," decreed Verity. "Christabel wrangled this invitation for us most particularly. Be of good cheer, though. Lord Brathmere informs me that Mr. Mont accompanies him tonight. I'm certain he will do his best to rescue you from boring table talk."

And so to dine they went, Drusilla in Pomona green and Verity in rosette white.

There were twenty guests at table, and Alaric, Lord Brathmere, was seated beside Miss Thornrose, for London hostesses had begun to account the two of them an "item." Verity felt a rush of warmth whenever she felt Alaric's dark eyes upon her, and a rush of unease when she noticed how often other women's eyes were upon him. *Women flutter about him like moths, and they always will. How will I bear it when he leaves me for another, for surely he will.*

Verity's victory over the Nabobs of the Flesh Trade was still fresh in everyone's minds and she was made much of this evening. One who did not praise her was the Right Honourable Baron Lord Pollard, a Tory Lord and a vociferous opponent of reform. A blustering red-faced man whose stomach marched well in advance of his chest, Lord Pollard was content with a social order that gave him a hundred tenant farmers to work his land, and a plentiful supply of tenant farmers' daughters who dare not complain of his attentions. Lord Pollard found the world just as it ought to be and not in need of reforming. Between him and Verity Thornrose dispute was inevitable.

"Well, Miss Thornrose," he boomed at her over a laden plate and an oft-filled wine glass, "it seems that once again I shall have the honour of killing your chimney sweep bill when it is presented to the Lords."

A particularly vivid Thornrose look sprang into Verity's eye as she considered Lord Pollard. "It may be, my lord, that you shall succeed in killing the bill. But whether the deed will enhance your reputation is another matter altogether. I rather think that when the judgment of history is writ, it will be recorded that Lord Pollard was on the wrong side of a great issue."

"Now, now, Miss Thornrose," his lordship admonished her in jocularly patronizing tones, "there is not a great issue at stake here. This is a matter for cooks and householders, not the government. A young lady of your station has, of course, no notion of what occurs in her kitchen, but I assure you our cooks could not do without climbing boys."

Verity gave Lord Pollard's waistcoat straining belly a speaking look. "I don't doubt, my lord, that you are considerably more knowledgeable about kitchens and cooks than I." A ripple of laughter went around and Verity was gratified to see the target of her barb flush to a port wine color. "Nevertheless," she went on before he could recover, "I assure you that there are ways of cleaning chimneys that do not involve inhumane cruelty to young children."

"Faugh, young woman!" Pollard brought a meaty fist down on the table. "No doubt you mean drawing a fluttering goose up the chimney the way they do in Ireland. But surely," he went on with ponderous sarcasm, "that would be unkind to our feathered friends? And we can't have that can we, Miss Thornrose, for surely you belong to some infernal society that aims to prevent unkindness to geese."

The laughter was aimed at Verity now, and she knew she must counter quickly, for great issues could be won and lost at the dinner tables of the influential as much as in the Halls of Parliament.

She favored Lord Pollard with a dazzling smile. "My lord, your concern for our feathered friends surely makes liars out of those who say that Lord Pollard is a champion of every thing that is cruel. You show the world, my lord, that though you care nothing for our nation's children, you do have the most tenderest regard for our nation's geese."

Oh, well done, my darling, thought Alaric, hiding his grin in his wine glass. Other diners were not so circumspect. There was a scattering of "bravos" to see the boorish Pollard so neatly pinked.

Lord Pollard fixed on Verity like an enraged bulldog. "Poppycock, young woman! Sheer poppycock! You reformers bleat the same nonsense year after year. Replace the climbing boys with mechanical brushes, you whine to Parliament. Force the sweeps to acquire these expensive devices and pass the cost on to every householder. Never mind that there are idle slum children to be picked off the streets and worked for a fraction of the cost. Ridiculous radical nonsense! This bill to ban the use of climbing boys will die a quick death, Miss Thornrose. I intend to see to it personally."

Every head turned to see how Mistress Reform would react to Lord Pollard's declaration that the sufferings of tens of thousands of children were less to him than the cost of a comparable number of elongated horsehair brushes. Miss Thornrose seemed to grow very tall in her chair, her face luminously expressive of her outrage, her violet eyes blazing at the fat, self-complacent man before her, and more than one of the watching guests was put in mind of King Solomon's verse about the woman "who looketh forth, fair as the moon, clear as the sun, and terrible as an army with banners."

"My Lord Pollard"—Verity's voice was low but carrying—"I will pray tonight that the Almighty gives you the wisdom to deal fairly with this bill. But if that prayer is not answered, I will offer up another on your behalf. I will pray that when you stand before that last great judgment seat, you will understand what it must be like to be a terrified child forced up a blackened, burning chimney, suffocated in the soot, pins stuck in your bare feet to make you climb faster, open sores on your hands and knees, your growth stunted, your body riddled with wasting diseases that will bring you to an early, agonizing death. I will pray that you gain enlightenment in the next world, my lord, so that you may atone for your appalling deficit of understanding and compassion in this one."

There was a deep silence around the table as the guests watched the playing out of the age-old conflict between the young visionary and the entrenched defenders of the status quo.

Lord Pollard threw down his napkin and hefted himself to his feet, his face empurpled with fury. "How dare you preach at me in this manner, you impertinent chit? How dare you try to foist yourself off as a succoring angel when all the world has watched you make a scandalous byword of yourself with that notorious libertine that sits beside you?"

Verity went white, for she had been struck in her soul's

most vulnerable part. A sickly silence fell over the long table. Alaric rose slowly to his feet, his eyes glittering murderously in his set face. The guests looked on, helplessly fascinated.

"You'll meet me for that insult, my lord," said Alaric in a low, deadly voice.

"Gladly," snarled Lord Pollard, still in a fury.

A protesting murmur arose from the diners. Lady Pollard plucked imploringly at her husband's sleeve, but he shook her off.

"Name your weapons," said Alaric inexorably.

"Pistols, damn you!"

A slow, satisfied smile spread across Alaric's face, and there was not a person there who did not remember that pistols were his chosen weapon and he had killed with them before. With remorseless efficiency, Alaric proceeded to the next step required in the Code Duello. "Mr. Mont, will you serve as my Second?"

Laurie nodded mutely, knowing there was no hope of amicable resolution.

"In the meantime"—Alaric's hand was on Verity's arm, literally lifting her out of her chair—"I will remove Miss Thornrose from his lordship's boorish presence."

Verity went with him in a nightmare fog, followed by Drusilla and Laurence Mont. Outside, the cool night air had the effect of lessening the shock.

"Alaric, you must not do this."

"It is a matter of honor, Verity."

"Alaric, I beg you."

He looked down at her, his face hard. "Verity, you were not the only one insulted. My own honor demands satisfaction."

"Alaric, in the name of God, is there no way this can be prevented?"

He studied her agonized face for an instant and a little of the hardness left his eyes. "Very well," he said with reluctance. "I'll send Pollard a note saying that if he offers you an apology, I will withdraw the challenge. But nothing else will avert our meeting."

And with that she had to be content.

Verity passed a tortured night and arose the next morning convinced that among other torments to be faced this day

would be a visit from Octavian. Yet, as the day stretched end-
lessly on, she had no word from either Alaric or her cousin.

At dinnertime, Christabel arrived at Thornrose House, looking uncharacteristically somber and bearing news. "It is for
tomorrow, Verity. At dawn, on Hounslow Heath."

A lightning stroke of fear pierced Verity's heart. "Are you
sure?" she whispered. "I've heard nothing of it."

Christabel nodded. "My husband heard talk of it at White's.
It seems Brathmere sent a note to Lord Pollard, telling him he
would settle for an apology, but the overstuffed blockhead refused."

Verity was on her feet, pacing distractedly. "I must put a
stop to this. I must."

"But can you?" asked Christabel worriedly. "You know men
have no sense in these affairs. I swear that bullheaded Pollard
will never back down, and we all know what a fire-eater
Brathmere is. What can you do?"

After a long pause, Verity said in a low voice, "I shall offer
Lord Brathmere what he has wanted for some time."

Christabel gave her an alarmed look and hastily gathered up
her skirts. "I have no notion of what you intend doing, Verity,
and I'm sure I don't wish to know, either. Send for me if I can
comfort you, but otherwise I wish to know nothing, absolutely
nothing."

Verity sat in silence for a long time and then went to arrange
herself and her affairs for the evening. Once this was done, she
summoned Kirby the coachman and ordered him to drive to
the back entrance of Lord Brathmere's Albemarle Street residence.

The ringing of his booted feet on the marble stairs alerted
her to Alaric's presence. He came down in loose white shirt
and breeches, looking black-browed and thunderous. The Earl
of Brathmere was in fact in a perfect fury of discretion that
would have astounded the previous ladies who had called at
his bachelor establishment.

"Verity, have you lost your mind?" he demanded. "To have
your coachman leave you here at this hour of the night?"

She hastened to reassure him. "Kirby is completely loyal.

You see, my aunts rescued him when he was apprenticed to this dreadful hackney driver—"

Alaric, in no mood for a recitation from *The Book of Good Works*, cut her off with a swift angry gesture. "But what if you were seen by someone else? Wouldn't a note have served just as well?"

"No," she whispered, clutching her cloak about her, "a note would not have served as well. Tell me, is it true that you meet Lord Pollard tomorrow?"

"I'd hoped," he said after a moment, "that you'd not hear of it."

"Alaric, you must not. What if he were to kill you?"

"What?" The straight black brows rose incredulously. "Do you actually think that old blowhard could do me harm?"

"But might he not get off a lucky shot?"

He shrugged. "It's remotely possible, I suppose, but if it's any comfort to you, my wagering cronies inform me the odds are four to one I'll kill him with the first shot."

"Dear God in heaven," said Verity, covering her face with her hands.

"I'm sorry," said Alaric less flippantly. "I shouldn't have told you that. I meant only to reassure you."

"Reassure me of what, Alaric? That you will have another death on your head because of me?"

He looked at her quizzically. "So you worry for my immortal soul, do you, Verity? But of course you do," he answered his own question softly. "All right, I promise that if at all possible, I shall miss my shot at Pollard. I daresay it won't be easy, for he makes a substantial target."

But this was not enough for Verity. "This duel must not happen, Alaric. It must not. Withdraw your challenge." She stepped closer to him, her eyes huge in her cameo face. "Don't fight for me tomorrow, Alaric," she whispered, "and you may have all that you wish from me tonight."

Alaric was suddenly very still. "Verity, what are you saying?"

"I'm saying I cannot let you go out to kill or be killed in my name. Let me stay with you tonight, and I do not think that you will wish to leave me in the cold dawn to fight this senseless duel."

"Verity . . ." His tone was disbelieving.

"I know you desire me. I have seen it in your eyes."

She let her cloak fall away. Under it she wore a frothy chemisette dress that she ordinarily reserved for reading in her room on hot summer days. She thought herself very daring to wear it outside her house, never knowing that the effect she hoped to achieve failed because she had neither damped her skirts nor rouged her nipples. Nevertheless, the object of her attentions was gratifyingly affected. His eyes were dark in his set face and she sensed that he was holding himself in check at very great effort.

Tentatively she reached out and slid her hand inside the loose shirt to feel his heart drumming through the ridged muscle and the black ram's fleece on his chest. She had, she realized suddenly, been wanting to do that for ages, to caress him and feel his rake's heart leap for her. She looked up and saw the fire surfacing in his eyes, but in the next moment, he drew a ragged breath and caught her hand and returned it to her side.

"Verity, if only you knew how often I've dreamed you would come to me like this. But it's no good. I can't let you use your body as a bribe, though God knows"—his eyes lingered hungrily on her face—"I've never been tempted more than at this moment. But when it was done, you would despise yourself and me as well."

"What does it matter, provided you live?"

He put his hands on her half-bare shoulders. "Verity, I am not easily destroyed. I've faced four opponents on the dueling field, and lived." Somehow the frothy sleeves had slipped from her shoulders and he suddenly found his arms full of lithe Verity, her fingers twined in his black hair, her mouth on his, her kisses demanding that he carry her upstairs, strip off that wicked chemisette dress, and pin her moaning to his bed.

"Enough of this," he commanded her—and himself as well. Disengaging her arms from around his neck, he stepped back and shouted for his butler. "Robling, order the carriage round back. The lady is leaving. Now."

"Don't send me away, Alaric," she whispered, her body seeming to burn its way toward him through the white dress. "Don't send me away tonight when you could die tomorrow."

Silently he picked up her cloak and wrapped it around her. Then he picked her up as if she were a child and carried her through the kitchen and out to the stableyard. The kitchen staff watched but said nothing.

An expressionless postilion opened the carriage door. Through it went Verity, deposited unceremoniously on the carriage seat despite her pleas, the door closed forcefully behind her, rather as if his lordship was caging a dangerous lioness.

"Verity, go home," he ordered through the carriage window. "Go home and say your prayers and go to bed, and when you awaken tomorrow it will all be over.

"Drive on," he shouted to the coachman and watched as the carriage bore her away.

The scent of roses still lingered in the air reminding him of what he had foregone. On what was possibly the last night of his life, he had given up the thing he desired most in all the world. He had made a Noble Gesture. Earl Brat threw back his black head and laughed at himself.

The morning mist lay cold and grey on Hounslow Heath. Two figures stood back to back, dark silhouettes in the dawn light. One figure was tall and straight as a blade. The other figure limned against the lightening sky was shorter with decades of soft living showing in the barrel belly.

At the end of ten paces the duelists turned. The shorter man's pistol seemed to waver uncertainly, and the taller man's arm flew up before he fired. The shot exploded sharply among the morning bird song, the pistol ball loosing itself in the misty sky. A breath's space later, a second shot followed, tearing into the man who stood opposite, freezing him in an attitude of disbelieving shock before he fell. The physician and his Second ran to him. An instant later, a figure in a dress that matched the grey morning mist flew across the heath to the side of the fallen man.

Alaric floated back from oblivion with reluctance. He opened his eyes to an unfamiliar room. The last thing he remembered, he was standing in a damp field, making himself a target for one of the biggest jackasses in the English peerage.

Quick, light footsteps approached his bed. Verity's anxious

face floated into his line of vision, and a cool satin hand slid across his fevered forehead.

"You are better," she said softly. "We've been so worried."

Alaric looked up at her, the memory of that morning suddenly clear. "That fat fool shot me!" he said as indignantly as his weakened condition would allow. "He actually shot me."

"A not uncommon result when one engages in duels," Verity pointed out gently as she straightened his covers.

Alaric stirred restlessly on his pillow, still indignant. "His pistol was waving back and forth like a weathercock in a high wind. I didn't think he could put a pistol ball within a yard of me, so I fired up into the air. If he had deloped as well, we both could have left the field with honor intact. But no, the fat fool had to shoot me."

"Christa says he will be ostracized for failing to delope after you did," Verity told him soothingly. She folded her cool hands over his fevered ones. "I know you missed him for my sake, for if you had meant to kill him, he would certainly be dead. I shall never forgive myself that you were injured because of me." Her voice dropped. "I must confess that when I saw him shoot you, I had the most shocking urge to pick up your pistol and shoot Lord Pollard myself. I can only thank Providence that you had already expended your bullet, or I might have brought him to an untimely end after all."

Alaric grinned at her through a fog of pain. "We are a pair, aren't we?"

Verity summoned up a faint laugh, her first since that awful dawn three days before. There were shadows beneath her flower-colored eyes, caused by days and nights spent at his bedside.

"Am I at Thornrose House?" he asked. The room in which he lay was a combination of wealth and austerity that seemed to particularly characterize the Thornrose way of life. The furniture was of exceptional quality, but antique in style, and there were none of the currently popular Chinese and Egyptian knickknacks. It was apparent that the Thornrose ladies did not sway to every fashion in furnishings.

"Why did you bring me here, Verity? It will only cause more gossip."

"Do you think I care for that, Alaric? Do you think I would

countenance your being taken to your own residence with only paid servants to care for you? My aunts and I intend to nurse you ourselves. But no more talk, you need your rest." Silken fingers brushed across his burning lips and he surrendered obediently to healing slumber.

Over the next few weeks, the Thornrose family physician was kept excessively busy tending the recuperating Rafe, the fallen earl, and the failing Mrs. Sedgewick.

Alaric made steady progress in the care of the Thornrose ladies. He was petted and cossetted and bullied in a manner unlike anything he had hitherto experienced. Aunt Hope dosed him with apothecary potions and forbade his indulgence in spirituous liquors. Aunt Charity took his money at piquet, telling him cheerily she would donate it to the Artists Benevolent Fund. Aunt Faith read to him daily from high-minded books made by the bookbindery students at the Philanthropic Society's Reform House. On warm afternoons he was permitted to sit before an opened window, the sash cords of which had been woven by children at the School for the Indigent Blind.

It was Verity's company that Alaric waited for most eagerly. She would come to him in the morning after his valet finished his morning toilet, to see how he had passed the night. In the evening she would come again, to talk of her day or to read to him from the latest tract of her composing.

And once or twice, he awoke in the middle of a restless night to find Verity standing over him, candle in hand, her unbound hair flowing in black rivulets over the white bosom of her nightdress. She didn't bind up her hair at night in confining braids, and he promised himself that one day soon she would let down her hair and come to his bed as his wife and those rivulets of black silk would flow across his pillow . . .

He was content.

It did not take long for word to get around that the Earl of Brathmere, having defended Miss Thornrose's honor, was now recuperating at her aunts' establishment. Not unexpectedly, Octavian came to deliver himself of a thunderous protest. But Verity remained unmoved throughout his fulminations on backsliding, declension, hedonism, carnality, latitudinarianism, and reprobation. Though she had never been good at standing up to Octavian for herself, she found herself a tigress when it came to protecting Alaric, lying weak under her own roof.

Finally, the day came when Alaric had regained his strength and the doctor pronounced him fit to leave Thornrose House. He came into the Blue Salon to bid her farewell. Once again, he was the assured aristocrat in fine clothes, and suddenly Verity was shy of him.

"Well," she said in a too-bright voice, "I suppose this is farewell."

"Do you really think so?" he asked quietly.

She looked quickly away. "Alaric, please don't say anything that will—"

"On the contrary, Verity, I think I must have my say."

"V . . . very well."

"Verity, I know I'm thought to be the worst of rogues, and I'll own there's truth in it. If you could marry me anyway, I swear I'll do everything in my power to make you happy."

Verity suddenly found she had to sit down on the nearest sofa.

"As bad as that, eh?" he said sympathetically, sitting beside her. "Well, I can't say I blame you."

"It's just that there would be so very many difficulties," she said in a troubled voice. "My cousin Octavian will be violently opposed."

"Your cousin," said Alaric rather grimly, "is already violently opposed. I made the mistake of fencing with him at Angelo's. He tried to hack me to pieces."

Verity felt a chill. "How like him that sounds. He wishes to marry me himself."

Alaric smiled thinly. "I knew him for an enemy the moment I laid eyes on him, and now I know why. Does he persecute you?"

"Yes, only he doesn't realize that he is doing so. He believes we are predestined to marry and unite the two branches of the family."

"And is that what you want?"

"Oh, no! Marriage to Octavian would be repugnant to me. But still, it would be wrong for me to marry you simply because I wished to be rid of him."

"Well, you would be rid of him," said Alaric in a hard voice.

Then his voice softened to ruefulness. "Still, you mustn't marry me because you are looking for a safe harbor, for I don't suppose I could offer that."

She looked up at him, her eyes hungry and intent. "Oh, Alaric, are you certain that I'm not just a passing fancy and that you won't become bored with me?"

"Boring is one thing you could never be, Verity. You're the only woman I've ever encountered whose daily round I would care to hear about over my dinner table. And as for your being a mere passing fancy, I've had dozens of them, and what I felt for them is not to be compared to what I feel for you."

"Dozens?" said Verity with disquiet.

"I fear so, my love. I won't try to deceive you, my reputation is too well known."

"I . . . that is another thing," said Verity in a barely audible voice. "We Thornroses have never been . . . romantic or amorous. It may be that my nature is not passionate enough to satisfy a man who . . . who has had . . ." She looked at him helplessly, unable to finish.

The dark eyes met hers steadily. "Verity, I would never propose marriage to you if I wasn't sure I would be satisfied with you and you alone. And as for my heart . . . well, as black as it is, all of it belongs to you."

"I . . . see," said Verity, the blood leaping through her body in a most un-Thornroselike manner.

And then the Thornrose library was treated to a most un-Thornroselike exhibition: the daughter of the house sinking upon the couch beneath a rake's long deep kisses, sinking beneath the rake himself, her body breathing out the scent of roses and the promise of wild nights once they were wed.

"I believe," said Verity, looking up at him breathlessly, "I just said yes."

"And a good thing, too, I would think," said Alaric, smiling as he ran a finger along her lips, flushed from his kisses.

Recalled to her sense of place, Verity managed to squirm out from under him and into a more dignified position. "Well"—her voice was very demure, but the look in her violet eyes would have roused him had he been near dead—"they do say it's better to marry than to burn. Wouldn't you agree, my lord?"

My lord would.

Chapter Eighteen

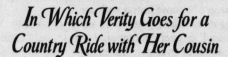

In Which Verity Goes for a
Country Ride with Her Cousin

*T*he announcement of the betrothal of Alaric Edward
William Tierney, eighth Earl of Brathmere, to Miss Verity
Valora Mercy Patience Thornrose caused sundry interesting
reactions.

From the Interested of London Society there came wise
nods and the assertion that they had known it all along.

From Sir Jasper Ramsey there came a pithy letter expressing the hope that Miss Thornrose would be the making of his
whelp of a nephew.

From Miss Drusilla Sedgewick came the request that she be
permitted to act as secretary and companion to the Thornrose
aunts upon the marriage of their niece.

From Octavian Smythe there was ominous silence.

From Lady Christabel Toddington there was ominous
flouncing. "I come near to wrecking my constitution dressing
and displaying Miss Dru in Society, and now she's to be a
companion, after all. In the meantime, Verity, what do you do
but fix your interest with the most unsuitable man possible, a
man I warned you against in no uncertain terms. Well, do not
come crying to me when he makes you entirely miserable as
he surely will." With this parting shot, Christabel stomped
daintily from the room.

"Oh, dear," murmured a shocked Drusilla. "How can your
friendship be mended after this?"

Verity was undismayed. "Christa will come around. I

promise you, next week she'll be back to take charge of my wedding clothes."

As for the Earl of Brathmere, now that he had found his countess, he suddenly remembered that he had three estates of which she would soon be mistress. Until now, he had taken no great interest in his manorial holdings in Hampshire. As long as the rent roll receipts came in on time, he was content to leave the management of his lands in the capable hands of the bailiffs his Uncle Ramsey had installed there. But now it behooved him to make an inspection tour of his properties, to be sure there were no conditions that needed reforming, for he intended that his bride should lavish all her beneficial exertions upon him. He took himself off to Hampshire, little realizing that he was leaving Verity with a noose around her neck.

At the same time, the Thornrose aunts, with Drusilla acting as their secretary, departed for a long-planned tour of midlands' orphanages, and the noose around Verity's neck tightened. Soon after, Christabel took herself and her wrecked constitution off to Bath to take the waters, and the noose got tighter.

"Mr. Octavian is without."

Verity rose resolutely to her feet. She'd known this encounter was coming, and she was determined not to be intimidated. As Octavian strode toward her, floorboards groaning beneath his feet, she took a deep breath and launched into her defense. "If you've come to protest my betrothal, Octavian, I must tell you at the outset that I have formed the deepest attachment to Lord Brathmere and nothing will serve to make me sever our connection."

"Nothing?" inquired Octavian direly. "Are you sure about that, Verity?"

Verity felt a prescient chill slide along her spine. "What are you saying, Octavian?"

"I'm saying, my poor foolish cousin, that while you sit here believing your betrothed to be inspecting his estates, he is in fact disporting himself with his mistress even as we speak."

Verity went white. "You are wrong, Octavian. He told me himself that he's had no more to do with Lady Sherbourne, nor will he ever again."

Octavian made an impatient gesture. "Not with that mistress. She was nothing but a diversion when he was in town. The mistress I speak of is the one he has had established for more than five years in a tidy little cottage in South Lopham."

Verity stared at him, staggered. "I don't believe you! And how would you know such a thing in any case?"

"As soon as I saw how things stood between you, I had my agents make inquiries of all his associations. There have been many women, true, but his devotion to this one has been ... singular. She is beautiful and low-born and quite unsuitable to marry an earl, but Brathmere has in his own wayward way been constant to her."

"No," said Verity. "I don't believe you." But she did a little, for one's worst nightmares were always believable.

"I made very certain of this intelligence, cousin. I went there myself, discreetly of course. She's very like you, Verity, or should I say you're very like her."

Verity spun away from him, wanting to shut out his words and the meaning that went beyond the words ... that she was a pale counterfeit of Alaric's true love. Sheer female jealousy shook her to the heart. She was very unlike the old Verity in that moment, but she had never been so completely in love before, and she had never experienced a torment remotely like this.

"And their son," Octavian went on remorselessly, "is very like his father."

"No," whispered Verity.

"I've seen the boy myself, Verity, watched him play in front of the cottage. The child has a great look of his father. You'll see for yourself if you accompany me now to South Lopham. You'll also see Brathmere's famous set of bays and his racing curricle in the stablehouse next to the cottage. Come with me, Verity."

"I could not," Verity managed through stiff lips. "It would be spying. And I don't believe you anyway."

"Indeed," rumbled Octavian, a note of triumph in his voice, "I think you believe me all too well, and you fear to find his lordship in the arms of another woman."

"I don't fear any such thing." Oh, but she did. She did.

"Then come with me, Verity, and prove me wrong."

Verity closed her eyes, all her old doubts about Alaric and

his rake's reputation haunting her. Whatever had made her think that she, prim little Verity Thornrose, could satisfy a man like Alaric Tierney? She had to know the truth.

"All right, Octavian." Her voice was barely a whisper. "I'll come with you."

Octavian had come prepared for the expedition to South Lopham. In addition to his coachman and two postilions, he was attended by two outriders. All were dressed in the sober black livery he provided for his town servants.

The atmosphere inside the coach was oppressively warm, for Octavian had ordered the curtains closed. His gaze was fixed upon Verity with a brooding intensity that would have made her profoundly uneasy had she not been immersed in thoughts of Alaric. As they traveled northward, Octavian's eyes bored into hers, trying to bend her to his will, and at last she closed her own eyes to be free of him.

When next she opened her eyes, she realized she had dozed off. They were well into Norfolk now, traveling through the marsh-covered, grey-green landscape that was the gateway to the fens. When she caught a glimpse of a signpost through the gap in the window curtains, she realized that something was amiss.

"Octavian, your coachman has lost his way. We're almost at Norwich."

Octavian suddenly seemed very massive in the seat across from her. "My coachman proceeds as he has been instructed, Verity. It is you who have lost your way in the thickets of wickedness and temptation, but I shall bring you back to the straight and narrow. Today I set your feet back on the proper path."

Verity's mouth went dry. "What have you done, Octavian? I demand that you take me home at once."

"I am taking you home, Verity. To our home, Crowhaven Hall."

"Your home will never be home to me, Octavian."

"I think once you and I are married you will grow accustomed to it over the years."

Over the years . . . The words echoed in Verity's mind like a prison sentence. Years with Octavian. All the dark unease he had always inspired in her rose up in her throat to choke her.

She fought to keep her voice steady. "Surely, you do not stoop to abduction, Octavian."

"This is not abduction, Verity. This is rescue." His eyes glowed. "Your demon lover will never possess you, Verity. You were meant for me."

Verity looked at her cousin Octavian Smythe, truly seeing him for the first time. She could almost pity him, for it was plain that he was in the grip of a terrible delusion. It was also clear that he had lied about Alaric—as she should have known from the start.

Forgive me, Alaric, she whispered in her soul, *I should have known you better.*

Relief over Alaric gave her new courage despite her dreadful predicament. "Octavian," she said as equably as she could, "I think you are not well to have done this. You must know that you cannot force me to marry you. No clergyman would celebrate the wedding of a bride as unwilling as I promise you I shall be."

Octavian smiled a slow menacing smile. "Again you underestimate me, cousin. I number among my acquaintances divines of many persuasions. Among them there is one who believes that Verity Thornrose's body, soul, and fortune are meant to be in my hands where they will do the world great good and not in the hands of that dissolute scoundrel who has caught your foolish fancy. This clergyman will marry you to me out of the respect he bears for the Thornrose name, and out of the pity that he feels for your foolish self. He will do it to save you from yourself, and he will swear that you came cheerfully and willingly to your wedding."

Verity shrank back in her seat, suddenly sick with terror. She had no doubt that Octavian had discovered a likeminded clergyman who would aid him in this plot.

She had one last hope. "My aunts will discover that I am with you and raise an alarm."

"No," said Octavian omnisciently, "I do not think they will do that since I have left them a letter saying that you have repented of your desire to be a countess, and you now mean to take your predestined place as my wife. By the time they return from their tour, you and I will have been married in a quiet ceremony in Crowhaven Hall."

His words impacted like blows in Verity's mind. Deluded or not, Octavian had closed every avenue of rescue. She cast a quick desperate glance out the window, wondering if she could somehow fling herself from the coach—

"I wouldn't," advised Octavian. "My outriders would pluck you up in a trice."

"I won't marry you, Octavian," she whispered. "I won't."

"I think in the end, Verity, you will be glad to marry me. And pray don't provoke me to an unseemly display of brute force. You will regret it, I promise you. Ah, we have arrived."

Crowhaven Hall sat stark and forbidding at the end of a willow-choked lane. To stray more than three feet off the rutted track that led to the house would place an unsuspecting traveler in the dank expanse of marshland that the locals called Darkwater Fen.

The manor itself was set inside a walled enclosure that looked remarkably warlike for peacetime. During the Civil War, Cromwell's forces had brought royalist captives here for interrogation and, sometimes, execution. Verity felt her hopes sinking with the setting sun. If cavalier soldiers could not escape from this place, what chance had she? After she was married to Octavian, there would be no escape. He would be the master of her fortune and of her.

The coach clattered into a walled courtyard, a spiked portcullis falling behind them with an echoing clang. Black-clad servitors came to await her descent from the coach. Their livery was even more severe and antiquated than that worn by Octavian's town servants. Though her legs would hardly support her, Verity managed to step down.

"Goody Tayside will see to your needs," said Octavian.

He beckoned to a harsh-faced woman clad in an old-style servant's garb. She came and curtsied very low before them.

Verity had not missed the archaic way that her cousin referred to Mrs. Tayside. The terms "Goody" and "Goodwife" had not been in general use since the Puritans had been chased to America. Apparently Octavian had decreed that time should stand still in his little fiefdom in the fens. And Goody Tayside's humble curtsey did not disarm her in the least. The woman had more of the look of a wardress than a lady's maid.

And wardress Goodwife Tayside proved herself to be.

Silently she conducted Verity into a tower bedroom whose sole adornment was a series of antique woodcuts depicting Reformationists being burned at the stake during the time of Bloody Mary. While Verity was staring uneasily at this evidence of her cousin's appalling taste in decorating, Goody Tayside slipped from the room and turned the key in the lock. She was a prisoner.

She was released for dinner. She had no appetite, but she walked to the dark-paneled dining hall anyway. Perhaps while she ate she would be able to observe some method of escape; perhaps some spark of sanity would flicker in her cousin. Neither of these things happened. By the end of the meal she was more oppressed then ever. She had kept careful count of the men who waited upon them, trying to gauge the strength of her cousin's forces. There were ten male servitors at least— grim, close-faced men with an air of conspiracy and cabal about them. They made her very much afraid . . . not for herself, but for Alaric when he came to Crowhaven Hall after her, as she knew he would.

Chapter Nineteen

In Which the Earl of Brathmere Gives Chase

*H*is first afternoon back in London, Alaric called upon his beloved, and found himself received instead by her three aunts. They came fluttering into the Blue Salon, exchanging stricken looks.

"Oh, dear," murmured Aunt Faith.

"Oh, dear, oh, dear, oh, dear," elucidated Aunt Hope.

"We're in a fine pickle now," concluded Aunt Charity.

Alaric began to feel uneasy. "Ladies, is something amiss with Verity?"

"It rather depends upon your point of view."

"Your point of view of Verity eloping with our cousin Octavian, that is."

"She left with him the day before yesterday, you see."

Alaric's face went slack with shock, then black with rage. "I don't believe it."

"We wouldn't have, either, but for this letter our cousin left for us, saying that Verity has come to her senses."

"That she realizes she was not meant to be a countess to you."

"That she is meant to be a sober goodwife to him—"

"Does your cousin write how this will be done?" interrupted Alaric, soft-voiced and dangerous.

"He says they are to be married privately at Crowhaven Hall, his estate in Norfolk."

"It's a very old dwelling in a rather isolated locale."

"It's a dreadful moldering pile in the middle of the fens, actually."

"A private wedding at his estate." Alaric was pacing. "Such things take time to arrange, so perhaps it's not too late. Perhaps there's still time. There must be time."

"If only," lamented one of the aunts, "we had been here to counter Octavian's persuasions . . ."

"A most dreadful twist of fate that we were not here to protect Verity from his blandishments . . ."

"It's all most puzzling, for we were certain she couldn't abide him . . ."

Alaric took a hasty leave of the lamenting ladies.

Verity awoke from a sleeping nightmare to a waking one. Octavian was standing over her bed, clad in a black velvet nightrobe. Only a headsman's mask was needed to make him the perfect image of a medieval executioner.

Verity gasped and shrieked, but of course no one came to her aid. Octavian seized her by the arms and lifted her bodily from the bed as if she were a rag doll.

"Your demon lover is knocking at my gate, cousin. I shall admit him presently. But first you and I shall come to an understanding." He wrenched her closer, so that the broad face filled up her vision, blotting out everything else. "Listen, little cousin, and listen well. I have twelve loyal men here. Cromwell had no better men than these, and either they or I will kill your cavalier before I let him take you from me. Yet, we need no more scandal. Better that Brathmere be jilted and alive, than dead by my hand. So I will give you one chance and one chance only to send him on his way with his whole skin. Do you understand me, cousin?"

"Yes, yes, anything," Verity heard herself babbling frantically, "only please don't kill him."

"Only if you contrive to send him on his way without challenging me, for I tell you this, Verity, my sword hungers for his blood. If he challenges me now, I will put him down."

Verity closed her eyes against the sight of him, but the awful truth of the words rang in her mind. She remembered Alaric's account of how Octavian had toyed with him at Angelo's. There was no way Alaric could win a battle within the precincts of Crowhaven Hall. Octavian stood too strong on his home ground. She must do what Octavian ordered if she wanted Alaric to be safe.

There was a sudden commotion in the courtyard below. She twisted from Octavian's grasp and ran to the small high window, straining for a view of the torchlit enclosure below.

Alaric rode through the iron gates on a lathered, heaving horse. He slid from his exhausted mount and bellowed up toward the lighted window in which she stood. "I know you're in there, Smythe. Come down and show yourself."

Verity felt her heart quicken with fear at the sight of him. He was still gaunt from his dueling wound and he had hours of hard riding behind him. Why had he come so recklessly and alone? It was folly, sheer folly!

Octavian grasped her arm and led her down the donjon stairs outside the tower. Alaric watched them come with their black robes flowing behind them and it seemed in that moment that they stood together, and with each other, both arrayed against him. Verity would not meet his eyes.

Verity was counting the men arrayed against Alaric: Two on the landing, blunderbusses in their hands; two more in the shadows at the bottom of the stairs, and surely several more on the wall. Alaric was hopelessly outnumbered, and if he got the slightest inkling of her terror and distress, he would be at Octavian regardless of the odds against him. She felt the numbness of despair seeping into her heart. Octavian would kill Alaric unless she contrived to save him.

Alaric watched them slowly descend the stairs, his eyes hot and hard, for it seemed to him that Octavian paraded Verity at his heel, and that all the Thornrose blood that bound the two of them together was roiled against him.

Octavian's voice boomed down through the fitful torchlight. "What do you mean by this unwarranted intrusion, Brathmere?"

"You know why I'm here, Smythe. I want Verity."

"You no longer have a fiancée, Brathmere. Your engagement is at an end."

Alaric's face hardened to stone. His eyes fixed on Verity. "Is that true, Verity?"

In the moment of her great trial, Verity was as steady as a blade. "Yes, it's true." She took a step toward him and was so close she could have smoothed back his hair and touched his face. But she did none of those things for it would mean his death. "I see now that my duty and my destiny lie with my cousin. One cannot escape one's predestined path, and I know now that my path cannot lie with you." She forced herself to look straightly and sincerely into the narrowed dark eyes. "You were a May fever, Alaric. But that was all you were, and now I am over you."

He drew back as if she had struck him, for these, her own words, he believed, as he had already half-believed them, along the grueling ride to Crowhaven Hall. His eyes went to Octavian, triumphant on the stairs, and back to Verity, so beautiful and upright as she cut out his rake's heart. The old cruel and mocking be-damned-to-you Earl Brat returned with a vengeance.

"All right, Smythe. You may have won the lady's hand, but you'll get a cold bed for all your trouble. It takes a rake to stir Verity's passions, as I have reason to know—"

Verity struck him across his handsome mocking mouth, struck him for his own good, but also a little out of hurt at his cruel words.

The blood drained from Alaric's face except for the mark where she had hit him, and his whiplash tongue lashed back. "Allow me to felicitate you upon your upcoming nuptials, Verity. You and Smythe are a matched pair after all."

And he turned and mounted his lathered horse and rode out of Crowhaven Hall leaving Verity to her fate.

A desperate triumph soared in Verity's heart as she watched him ride away. With Alaric safely out of this deathtrap, Octavian lost his strongest hold over her. Now she could fight her cousin. Even in his derangement, she understood the workings of his mind, for his madness was a terrible dark distortion of her own beliefs. When the time came, she would give him a compelling reason not to marry her. He might murder her, but he would never marry her. Consoled by this thought, she let herself be marched back to her tower room where she fell into a dreary sleep beneath the pictures of the roasting Reformationists.

The next day, breakfast and luncheon were brought to her room by Goody Tayside. Verity attempted bribery, hinting at the vast sums she would be prepared to pay to gain her freedom. But her keeper's gimlet face only took on a more gimlet cast, and Verity realized she would get no help from that quarter.

At dinner she was allowed to dine with the clergyman who was to marry her to Octavian. The clergyman's wife was to be a bridal attendant and an additional witness against the bride should she ever try to challenge the legality of the methods by which she was married. Verity came downstairs possessed of a morbid curiosity to see which of the many divines who traveled in Octavian's orbit would stoop so low as to officiate at this travesty of a wedding. When she saw who it was that was seated at Octavian's austerely appointed table, she felt she should have known it all along.

"The Reverend Mr. Mortlock—and Mrs. Mortlock." She made no effort to conceal her disdain. "It does not surprise me that you are part of this heinous plot."

She caught a flicker of unease in the Rev. Mr. Mortlock's eyes. He seemed to lack Octavian's steely armor of self-righteousness. Clearing his throat, he ventured ingratiatingly, "Your cousin assures me that this marriage was your late parents' greatest desire. In time, my dear, you will see the wisdom of what we do."

"What you do, sir, is infamous. I would sooner be married in the Fleet."

The Rev. Mortlock tut-tutted unctuously. "Come now, Miss Thornrose, let us have no more recriminations, but instead let us gather joyfully to partake of the bounty of your cousin's board."

But Verity, who had no appetite, was determined that no one else would enjoy their dinner either. She turned her gaze upon Mrs. Mortlock. "Can you not dissuade your husband from this madness? He will be ruined when the truth is revealed, as it surely will be."

But Mrs. Mortlock kept her eye steadfastly on her plate and said nothing.

"Verity," growled Octavian, "you will kindly cease these exhibitions of maidenly nerves and sit down and be quiet."

But Verity did not. Pale but composed she faced her cousin. "Before this marriage is performed there is something you should know. For many months a notorious rake has made me the object of his gallantries. Marry me if you will, Octavian, but Lord Brathmere has already claimed me. You'll get no virgin bride on your wedding night."

There was a crashing silence. The Reverend and Mrs. Mortlock swiveled appalled glances to Octavian, who seemed frozen in the grip of a horrified dread, for how often had he been tortured by visions of Verity in the arms of her virile and promiscuous lordling.

Sensing that for once in her life she had brought her cousin to a standstill, Verity went on, in triumph and defiance. "And know this, dear cousin, that I would rather be Brathmere's whore than wife to you. And if you force me into this marriage, I swear to you that all the children that bear your name will be some other man's bastards—"

Octavian emitted an animal roar, his fists crashing down on the table. "Jezebel! Harlot! I had thought your Thornrose blood would raise you above the rest of womankind. Always since you were the littlest child, I have watched over you, molding you to be worthy of me. But now I see that you are no better than a serpent. You are a viper clothed in shining skin, you are a comforter of demons, you are the sting of the scorpion's tail."

Verity stood unflinching before the barrage of Octavianisms. If Octavian would only decide to cast her unworthy person out of his house . . . But perhaps she had overdone it, for Octavian had started round the table, his great hands reaching out, giving every indication that he intended to throttle her.

Mrs. Mortlock shrieked and her husband clung to Octavian's arm. "Mr. Smythe, think what you are doing," he implored, obviously afraid murder would be committed before his eyes.

Octavian shook himself free, his pale eyes glowing upon Verity. "There is a demon in you, Verity, is there not?"

"No," whispered Verity, now truly frightened by the irrational fury she had roused in her cousin.

Octavian advanced upon her. "You must be purged, Verity, purged of the morbid carnality that has driven you to sin. You must be mortified until you repent of your lust for that man, until you cast him out of your heart altogether like the demon he is."

"Never," whispered Verity. "Never in this world."

"Never is a very long time, little cousin, a very long time, as you shall discover to your long and everlasting sorrow."

Verity turned to flee, but Octavian struck her to the floor like a felled sapling. He bundled her up, and with the Mortlocks scurrying after him like chaff, carried her out into the waterish darkness that surrounded Crowhaven Hall.

Chapter Twenty

In Which Verity Is Immured in a Most Peculiar Institution

*I*t was dark and Verity did not know to what sort of place she had been brought, except that there was a stout door that prevented her from escaping. Two hulking men had propelled her by feeble lantern light into a narrow nun's cell filled by a wooden pallet covered with straw ticking. She sat down on her prisoner's pallet to wait and see what the dawn would bring.

Only there would be no real dawn showing through the boarded-up window in her cell. Whatever light was to shine upon her in this place would be only at the pleasure of her gaolers . . . whoever they were.

She met them soon enough.

There was a rasp of unoiled hinges, but the door to her prison did not open, only a judas window that allowed her to stare blinkingly into the light at the figures of a man and a woman. The woman was large and slatternly, her hair straggling untidily from underneath her mob cap, key rings rattling from her apron strings. The man was more presentable in a smart bottle green coat, though it only served to accentuate his yellowing skin and stooped, spindly frame.

The man addressed her through the window in a loud voice, as if she were deaf or very far away, "OH, WE ARE NOT WELL, ARE WE? WE ARE A SAD CASE, INDEED."

Verity summoned up all the Thornrose starch at her command. "If you are the person in charge of this place, I must tell you that I protest in the strongest terms—"

It was as if she had not spoken. "Observe her closely, Mrs. Clow," said the man to the mob-capped woman. "It's not often one sees a true example of the Nymphatomic Femina condition. What a pity. And her born of such good stock, too."

Verity struggled for calm, not the easiest thing to do when one is locked in a cell being accused of a form of perversity. In the sanest, most reasonable voice she could achieve, she told her gaolers, "I have done nothing to warrant my confinement here, and I have devoted friends who will not rest until I am found."

"AH, OUR SAD CONDITION HAS MADE US MUDDLE-HEADED, HAS IT?" There was a gleam in the thin man's slippery black eyes. "BUT WE KNOW HOW TO CURE CONDITIONS, MISS THORNROSE, AND IN THE MOST ENLIGHTENED WAY POSSIBLE. WERE YOU IN YOUR RIGHT MIND, YOU WOULD CERTAINLY AP-PROVE OF US. BUT THEN YOU ARE NOT IN YOUR RIGHT MIND, ARE YOU, MISS THORNROSE?"

Verity fought to keep her voice steady. "You must release me at once, sir. I do not belong in this place."

"I WILL BE THE JUDGE OF THAT, MISS THORN-ROSE."

"At least tell me what place this is, and what town it is near." (The first step toward getting out, Verity reasoned, would be to find out where she was.)

But her gaoler had reasoned the same and he tsked-tsked disapprovingly. "WE MUST NOT MUDDLE OUR POOR HEADS WITH UNNECESSARY QUESTIONS, MISS THORNROSE. ALL YOU NEED KNOW IS THAT I AM DR. DAGGETT AND THAT YOU," and his eyes were on her like snake eyes on a broken-winged bird, "ARE NOW AN IN-MATE IN DR. DAGGETT'S REFORMATORY FOR WAY-WARD FEMALES WHO HAVE FALLEN FOR THE FIRST TIME."

He shut the judas window and left Verity staring at the closed portal, stunned by the awful irony of the situation. She, Verity Thornrose, Mistress Reform, was now herself a prisoner in, of all places, a reformatory.

After a morning meal of bread soaked in gruel—lunch and dinner would be the same, Verity was to discover—she took off her own dress and put on the faded long-sleeved linen smock that she found hanging on a hook in her narrow room. She did this because she was given to understand that donning the reformatory smock was the only way she would be permitted into the common ward to mingle with the other Females Who Had Fallen for the First Time.

And the first time was the charm, no doubt about that, thought Verity as she watched several dozen young women, all of them in an Interesting Condition, emerge from their darkened, narrow rooms, the doors to which were unlocked by Mrs. Clow. Two burly male warders named Bart and Harvey stood on guard at the main entrance to the ward, though it seemed to Verity that none of the cumbersome wayward females were in any condition to attempt a dash for freedom. Then she noticed that not all of the inmates were in a family way. Sitting on a bench against the wall was a thin woman with matted hair who sat unheeding of Mrs. Clow's braying demands that her *enceinte* charges stir their stumps and line up for their morning constitutional walk around the long ward.

The seated woman seemed in a world of her own until Verity put out a hand to touch her, whereupon the woman gave out a canine-sounding snarl and seized the flapping sleeve of Verity's smock between her teeth. Horrified, Verity tried to pull her sleeve free, but the woman held fast and seemed intent on getting her teeth into her arm as well. In the next instant, a wooden gruel bowl came hurtling to strike the woman solidly in the head. She let forth a surprised yelp and released Verity's sleeve. Verity quickly retreated, to stand by the inmate who had thrown the bowl—a woman much older than the poor unwed girls who were now shuffling dispiritedly about the ward.

"The Dog Woman don't like to be petted," Verity's bowl-tossing rescuer informed her. "She bites. She don't talk, neither. She just yowls once and a while. That's how come we call her the Dog Woman."

"I . . . see," said Verity shakily. It was apparent that if there were not sufficient numbers of wayward females available, Dr. Daggett did not scruple to take a lunatic or two into his keeping.

"Blasted loonies," the woman went on conversationally. "I hates them, I do. Especially that one there."

"I . . . beg your pardon," Verity ventured, "but are you not a . . ." She trailed off, realizing the question was very tactless. The woman, whose name was Lizzie Shaw, was apparently nursing similar doubts about her.

"You," said Lizzie Shaw with suspicion, "ain't one of the loonies, are you?"

"Certainly not," said Verity crisply. "I am not insane. I've never been insane, and as soon as that is confirmed, I will certainly be released. I've only been put here because my cousin is displeased with me."

"Har!" said Lizzie with a harsh laugh. "And how do you think I got here? 'Twas my loving husband who was displeased with me. He took a shine to a plump widow in Ipswich with her own linen draper's shop. He put me away here so he could have the widow and her shop all the easier. He's set up very cozy now, and I'm sure he don't begrudge the five pounds a year he pays Dr. Daggett to keep me here."

Verity stared at Lizzie Shaw, her heart freezing with fear at what this poor woman's fate portended for her own. If Dr. Daggett knowingly imprisoned perfectly sane people for pay, he would most likely keep her here for as long as Octavian could afford to pay him, and Octavian had a great deal of money.

The full impact of her situation struck her and she had to sit down on one of the splintery benches against the wall. She watched numbly as several obviously lunatic women engaged in a shrieking melee. Mrs. Clow advanced upon them with what looked like a child's Father Christmas stocking—a stocking, Verity realized from the odor that floated toward her, that had been stuffed with lumps of lye soap. How strange, she thought dazedly, that she should be in a place where soap, whose virtues she had so often preached to the tenement poor, should now be used as an instrument of punishment. She watched in growing despair as several of the unruly lunatic women were shackled in neck irons that had been set into the wall of the common ward.

And now Mrs. Clow was advancing upon her.

"'Ere, now, Miss Thornrose," said the burly matron. "No sittin' down unless you're reading the Good Book. It's read or march for you. Dr. Daggett's orders." From her voluminous and far-from-clean apron pocket she took out a battered chapbook New Testament and dropped it into Verity's lap.

Verity stared down at it sightlessly, for she knew this particular chapbook very well. She knew that upon the flyleaf she would see the words "Printed in London by the National School Society for the Education of the Poor in the Principles of the Established Church." Once upon a time, Miss Verity Thornrose of the National School Society had commissioned the printing of such chapbooks for the enlightenment of those poor misguided souls confined in institutions of incarceration and imprisonment.

Realizing that Mrs. Clow's baleful eyes were still upon her and that the soap-filled stocking was swinging meaningfully, Verity opened the chapbook with stiff fingers and forced her eyes to the words she saw there, even though she knew they would bring her no comfort.

At the other end of the ward, the Dog Woman raised her voice in a long mournful cry.

Black despair descended upon Verity.

The full horror and hopelessness of her situation was crushing. All her life she had struggled to escape the looming doom of Octavian Smythe, and she had thought that as Alaric's wife she would be safe. But neither she nor Alaric had been safe, she had sent Alaric away hating her, and her aunts would be no match for Octavian's demented cunning. She was in Octavian's power more terribly and completely than she had feared in her worst nightmares. She was buried alive, and she had no hopes for herself.

She could give no comfort to a perpetually sobbing young girl locked away here by her stern father until she could deliver herself of her shameful burden. She had no word of counsel for a serving maid got with child by the master's son, the babe to be fostered at birth, the low-born mother to be turned out into the streets. Mistress Reform could muster no sense of outrage against the parish beadles who committed pregnant girls here and then took an under-the-table percentage fee out of the parish monies paid to Dr. Daggett for the girls' food and board. And Miss Thornrose raised no word of protest at the harsh treatment of the hapless Dog Woman, who, if not the looniest among them, was certainly the most pathetic, with her predilection for howling and occasionally sinking her teeth into another inmate.

Miss Verity Thornrose no longer reeled off lists of eleemosynary institutions at the drop of a hat. She no longer spoke at all. It took too much effort to shape the words. She had nothing to say, and the company she found herself in was not conducive to small talk.

Lizzie Shaw, who plodded beside her on their thrice daily constitutionals about the ward, was philosophical about this development. "You're not the first one I've seen go mute from the shock of being here. 'Tis a sore disappointment to me, all the same. I was hoping for some better conversation than what I get out of the Dog Woman and the rest of them loonies." When Verity said nothing, only plodded along, Lizzie shrugged and continued, "Them little wayward gels got no conversation, either. All they do is blubber about the strong-backed villain who got their heels in the air. And they don't stay around long anyway. Once they drop their foals, they're gone. But you and me and the loonies, we'll be here forever . . ."

One night after Verity had been in Dr. Daggett and Mrs. Clow's keeping for what seemed a long time, she woke in the dark to screams. One of the wayward girls had gone into labor, and at length a newborn infant's wail sounded through the chamber cells of the reformatory. Verity tried not to think of the fate of this baby, born in this unkind, cheerless place, midwifed into the world by the repellent Dr. Daggett. She did not want to think of it—she would not think of it—yet she could not stop her ears against this new little life that cried out in the dark of this place for a champion, the kind of champion Verity Thornrose had once been before Octavian Smythe had broken her.

The old Verity awoke then and began to struggle out of the terrible black melancholia that had possessed her. Her Thornrose conscience found its voice and rebuked her. *All your safe, soft life, you have prated about helping the suffering of the world, but now that you are brought down among them, do you have the courage of your convictions? No, you do nothing but wallow in the Slough of Despond, repine in the Dungeon of Giant Despair, and behold the sufferings of others with Dull*

Indifference. Shame on you, Verity! You are a disgrace to the name of Thornrose.

Having given herself a swift allegorical kick in her Thornrose fundament, Verity began her struggle to light her one little candle in the gloom of Dr. Daggett's reformatory. Her former want of character appalled her, and at the next morning constitutional, she had her first opportunity to mend her ways when she saw Lizzie Shaw and several others making sport of the hapless Dog Woman.

"Stop," said Verity. Her voice felt rusty in her throat, her tongue unwieldy, and yet she found she had plenty to say. "We mustn't mistreat each other and make our situation worse. And we mustn't mistreat the Dog Woman just because she is the feeblest among us."

Lizzie Shaw stared at her for a long moment and then exclaimed in disgust, "Garn! Don't tell me you stopped being a dumb mute just so's you could jaw at us."

"I'm rather afraid," said Verity, summoning up a faint wry smile, "that that is the case. And another thing, Lizzie. We really must stop calling her Dog Woman."

"And what, pray," inquired Lizzie acidly, "should we be calling her? Nobody knows her real name and dog's the only word that gets through to her loony brain. You start calling her Wilhelmina or Francine and she won't know her head from her tail meaning no disrespect to the poor dear creature, I'm sure," she added witheringly.

Lizzie had a point, Verity had to admit. To deprive the Dog Woman of that one familiar syllable might only make things worse. "Nevertheless," she told Lizzie, with something of her old Thornrose starch, "from now on I insist that we call her Dog Lady instead."

Lizzie Shaw eyed her darkly. "I think I liked you better when you was a mute."

Mute, no longer, Verity began to reach out to her sister inmates in the reformatory. Listening to the sad stories of the wayward females, she remembered with chagrin how once upon a time in her old life she had visited a place like this one, only it was a true haven for unwed mothers instead of this purgatory. The clergymen's wives who oversaw the establishment had asked her to deliver an uplifting homily about Resisting the Temptations of the Flesh, a subject about which she had known absolutely nothing at the time . . . for that was before she had lain trembling with desire in the arms of Alaric Tierney, that was before she understood the wonder and wild delight of passionate love. Mistress Reform knew better now, and her discourse upon the subject with the wayward females of Dr. Daggett's reformatory was infinitely wiser and more compassionate than it had ever been.

When not lending a sympathetic ear to the unwed mothers, Verity also made friendly overtures to the various lunatics, for they were the most needful in this place. Of course, making friendly overtures to lunatics had its hazards as she discovered when she approached Alice Barnes, who begged her to get the purple serpents off her and tried to strangle her when she declined.

Overtures to the Dog Lady were more successful. Making a concerted effort to help the afflicted woman, Verity began to slip her extra portions of bread from her own ration, trying to win from her some syllable of speech or human gesture. In this she never succeeded, but little by little she did begin to win the Dog Lady's trust, to the extent that she would troop devotedly along behind her and Lizzie Shaw on their everlasting daily turns around the ward.

Lizzie Shaw provided a tart-tongued Greek chorus to all these efforts, predicting time and time again that nothing would come of all the crusading, and that it would only get her into trouble. Still Verity persisted. Whenever Mrs. Clow took to thumping on some poor inmate with her soap-filled stocking, Verity would begin to sing, "Oh, Those Who Suffer in Thy Holy Name," which seemed to cause Mrs. Clow to thump with less enthusiasm. Sometimes the other inmates would join in, and for a few seconds within the grey reformatory walls there would be a tiny flicker of insurrection against the misrule of Dr. Daggett and Mrs. Clow.

Mrs. Clow complained of it to Dr. Daggett. "She's gettin' 'em stirred up, she is. And she's making the crazy ones crazier than they already are."

"My dear Mrs. Clow, surely you exaggerate."

"She's causing trouble, I tell you. She's making 'em restless, thinking they've got hope."

Dr. Daggett frowned, on the horns of a dilemma. Hope was of course a very bad thing for lunatics and wayward females, and he wanted none of it in his reformatory. Yet, Verity Thornrose was by far his most profitable patient and he meant to hold onto her as long as possible.

"And that's not the worst of it," Mrs. Clow persisted grimly. "She's always whispering behind her hand to some o' them girls. She's plotting to get out of here. I can feel it in my bones."

Dr. Daggett sighed lugubriously. "Ah, how sad it is, Mrs. Clow, that Miss Thornrose has benefitted not at all from our excellent regimen. We must do more to help her purge herself of her unruly humors." He rubbed yellow, spidery hands together. "I shall write Mr. Smythe and inform him that, regrettably, his poor cousin makes no progress at all."

Verity never knew who betrayed her.

Perhaps she betrayed herself with some ill-timed hint, some indiscreet gesture, for she had indeed been whispering to the wayward girls, whispering promises of rich rewards to those who would help her win her freedom. Her hope was that, upon their release, someone among them might get word of her whereabouts to her aunts, who would surely not rest until she was rescued. Once she was rescued, she vowed, Dr. Daggett was going to rue the day he took Mistress Reform into his reformatory.

But the unexpected appearance of Dr. Daggett on the ward brought a sudden chill of fear to her heart—and to everyone else's. As he walked along the row of locked chamber doors, the reformatory inmates trembled as rabbits in their hutches tremble at the sound of the gamekeeper's coming tread. And as he came to her open judas window, Verity fought an ignoble impulse to hide under her pallet.

"I SEE, MISS THORNROSE, THAT REBELLION HAS RAISED ITS UGLY HEAD. THAT WE CANNOT HAVE. YOU WILL BE KEPT SOLITARY IN THIS ROOM UNTIL YOU HAVE PURGED YOURSELF OF YOUR REBEL-

LIOUS HUMORS. YOUR WINDOW WILL BE OPEN
ONLY AT FEEDING TIME."

He closed the judas window on Verity's suddenly blanched
face, for the freedom of the common ward and the company of
the other inmates was all she had left. Now there would be no
hope for herself and no chance to give hope to others. There
would only be darkness and tormenting memories of Alaric.

The Dog Lady howled mournfully and sat down outside
Miss Thornrose's door, patiently waiting.

Chapter Twenty-one

~✦~

The Aunts Take Charge

Alaric Tierney, eighth earl of Brathmere, was in his Albemarle Street townhouse recovering from the previous night's bout of solitary drinking. The appearance on his doorstep of three ladies dressed in sober grey and demanding to see him was met with stern repulse by his butler Robling. But Robling was unceremoniously thrust aside by the three ladies, who rustled upstairs to the earl's sitting room, the horrified butler dancing agitatedly behind them, begging them to halt, threatening to have them ejected by force if need be, all of which protestations the ladies heeded not at all.

Pressing onward and upward into the darkened master suite, the faint odor of spirituous liquors assailed their nostrils. There, in the curtained dimness, they beheld his lordship, unshaven, en dishabille in a rumpled dressing gown, his dark hair disordered. He was slumped in a chair in an attitude of slumber that did not seem benign. The cause of his torpor was readily apparent. An empty wine bottle sat on the table next to his chair. The aunts clucked disapprovingly.

"Ladies, please!" implored Robling. "His lordship will be incensed if you disturb him." His lordship had been incensed a lot lately.

But the ladies were undaunted. One of them hastened to open the drapes and let in the morning sunshine. Another shook Alaric vigorously by the shoulder, but was rewarded only with several incoherently mumbled expletives which the ladies affected not to hear. A third aunt picked up a charming Wedgwood vase filled with lilies and hefted it suggestively.

"Ought we?"

"Oh, yes!"

"Most definitely!"

Whereupon, the aunt removed the flowers and dashed the remaining contents on his lordship's lolling black head.

Alaric erupted from sleep and then winced as his aching head was simultaneously assaulted by shattering sunlight and the sound of his own outraged bellow: "What the bloody hell?"

"I'm sorry, my lord," said Robling distressfully, dabbing at his master with a shaving towel. "I did my utmost to stop them, but they would see you without delay."

"Ladies, what the devil do you want?" croaked Alaric. "Can't you see I'm . . . resting?"

"Ha! Resting, indeed!" harrumphed Aunt Faith.

"You were sleeping off a drunken debauch," accused Aunt Hope.

"Stern measures were required to bring you to your senses," Aunt Charity informed him.

Robling, noting the bellicose look kindling in his master's bloodshot eyes, hastened to intervene. "Ladies, please be so good as to state your business."

"It concerns our niece," they answered trebly.

Alaric groaned, for not only were hammers pounding in his head, but a hot knife was twisting in his heart at the memory of Verity. "I told you what happened," he grated out. "Your niece made it quite clear she prefers your oafish cousin."

"Ah," said Aunt Faith significantly, "but does she? Things may not be what they seem. In fact, we are very certain they are not!"

"We've written letter after letter to Octavian, demanding to see some lines writ in Verity's own hand. But we received nothing, not even an announcement of their wedding to give to the newspapers. And you would think that if they were married, Octavian would want it trumpeted about."

"It was only when we threatened to travel to Crowhaven Hall to see Verity in person that Octavian deigned to reply."

Alaric regarded them blearily. "Just what is it you are trying to say?"

"That you must stir yourself from this slough of insobriety and listen to Octavian's letter," commanded one aunt while another aunt waved a piece of writing paper under his nose and a third aunt added severely, "Rouse yourself this instant, my lord, or we shall be forced to use that vase of chrysanthemums in the hall upon you."

Alaric's muttered expletives were again ignored.

"This is the pertinent portion, my lord," said the aunt who had been waving the writing paper, "to wit: I beg leave to inform you of the dire consequences issuing from my cousin's ill-judged liaison with Lord Brathmere. Verity has become so greatly disturbed in her mind that it has been necessary to send her to a place of confinement and salutary regimen. As her trustee and her only living male relative, it falls to me to take such measures as I deem necessary for her own good. When she is herself again, she will write you of her progress."

Alaric rose unsteadily to his feet. "My God! Are you saying her bastard husband has had her shut up in a madhouse?" Then his tone altered as the whole sense of the letter came to his claret-fumed brain. "Your cousin speaks only of his rights as a relative and trustee, not as her husband. You think he's not married her, then?"

The aunts nodded in unison. "That is what we believe."

"Very astute of you, my lord."

"Your wits have made an excellent recovery considering that five minutes ago you were soused."

Alaric was indeed stone-cold sober. "My God, to put her in a madhouse." He remembered all too well having paid his shilling to tour Bedlam and stare at the wretched lunatics confined in their filthy cages. That Verity should be locked away in such a place! "How could Smythe do such a thing? He must be mad himself!"

The aunts nodded vigorously, pleased by his perspicacity.

"That's just the point, my lord. The wrong person has got shut away."

"It's not Verity who is mad. It's Octavian."

"We always suspected he was."

Alaric drew a deep soundless breath. "Ladies, I think you had better explain."

"Octavian has had a fascination for Verity since she was a

little girl. He thinks she's the only woman worthy of him since she's the last of the Thornrose line."

"He always wanted to have her under his thumb."

"He was forever playing the nastiest pranks on her . . ."

Alaric listened, his unshaven jaw slowly dropping.

"He burnt her marionettes at the stake so she would better understand the sufferings of the victims of the Spanish Inquisition."

"He tied her Punch and Judy to a tree and skewered them with darts so she would better understand the sufferings of the martyrs at the hands of their tormenters."

"He dropped her china doll in the starching kettle so she would better understand the sufferings of missionaries at the hands of cannibals."

Alaric remembered the desperate clinging embrace on the dark Soho stairs. "If you knew her cousin oppressed her," he demanded of the aunts, "why the devil didn't you keep him away from her?"

The ladies bridled at this implied criticism.

"We tried to protect her. We even sent her away to school though we missed her sorely."

"Octavian's bank controls our inheritance as well as Verity's. We never dared defy him openly."

"And now our dearest Verity is in a madhouse."

Alaric was on his feet. "That's easily remedied, ladies. I'll have her out of this madhouse."

But the ladies shook their heads, for things were not so easily remedied after all.

"That's all very well for you to say, my lord, but we don't know where she is."

"Anyone can set up an establishment for lunatics. For all we know, Verity could be locked in someone's attic or chained in a stable."

"We suspect, however, that Octavian may have her somewhere in Norfolk, near his estate."

"Then I'll make discreet inquiries," said Alaric. "But I warn you ladies that once she is rescued, it's not to Thornrose House I mean to bring her. It's Brathmere House for us, and your Mistress Reform will have to call herself Lady Reform instead."

*   *   *

Alaric went to Norfolk armed with that most potent of male disguises, a set of false calling cards. They were printed in a restrained, unexceptional style and bore the common and eminently forgettable name of John Brown, Esq.

Mr. Brown, who had a mad sister . . .

"I'm in need of a place to . . . lodge poor Ophelia. She's an odd sort, I regret to say. Very odd. To put the matter with no bark upon it, she needs looking after and locking up. She's always had queer fits and starts, and now she's taking to bursting in on my mother's dinner parties and scattering flowers about, not to mention trying to throw herself into the fish pond. There's nothing for it but to put her away . . ."

It was a spiel that Alaric had honed to perfection over the last few weeks as he made the rounds of provincial madhouses in the fens. He had seen terrible things in his journeyings. A more miserable collection of the troubled specimens of humanity could not be imagined, and the greedy persons who preyed upon them and their families disgusted him. At least, the place he was touring today was overseen by a doctor, so possibly conditions would be marginally better here.

The doctor was impressed by Mr. Brown's smart carriage and fine clothes. An acquisitive look gleamed in the doctor's moist eyes. Alaric had seen that look many times in the past few weeks. The look said: Ah, here's a wealthy one with a troublesome relation. How much will he pay to be rid of this inconvenient person?

"You must understand, Mr. Brown," expounded the doctor as he led Alaric through the front portion of his establishment, "that a regimen of circumambulating exercise and strict confinement under lock and key is beneficial to a wide variety of maladies, disorders, waywardnesses, and distempers." Swinging open the heavy door into the common ward, he announced in a suddenly loud voice, "LADIES, WE HAVE A VISITOR. YOU MUST BE ON YOUR BEST BEHAVIOR."

The women had apparently just been fed a meal of something Alaric was fairly certain he wouldn't care to know about. They were shuffling about the ward, herded onward by a beefy, hard-featured wardress, and surely, thought Alaric in a moment of grim reflection, the unhappy spectacle of so many seduced and abandoned females would cool the ardor of even the randiest rake.

When the pathetic parade of unwed and unhinged inmates was finished, once again Alaric knew bitter disappointment, and all he wanted to do at this point was to get himself out of this dismal place as quickly as possible.

Dr. Daggett cleared his throat expectantly, and Alaric recalled himself to the task at hand. "Thank you for your time, sir. My man of business will contact you if we decide this place is suitable for my sister." He bowed to the doctor and made for the door at an ignobly brisk pace.

A long shivering howl arose from the far end of the reformatory ward.

Alaric swung around. It was impossible to ignore such a sound. It came from a woman he hadn't noticed before who sat on a bench by the last of the chamber doors. And out of that chamber called a wavering voice, "It's all right, Lady. It's all right."

The voice was barely audible down the length of the ward, yet it sounded a clarion call in Alaric's mind. He stood transfixed for an instant, ignoring Dr. Daggett's chittering about Sad Cases and Incurable Dementias. He strode down the row of judas-windowed doors, torn between terrible doubt and terrible hope. A face appeared in the last judas window, a pale face, the color of winter ice, with violet eyes set deep in shadowed hollows.

"You're not real," she whispered to him, for how many times in the unrelieved darkness of her cell had she dreamed of Alaric coming for her.

"I am real," he said, reaching through the window to touch her face, carved down to ivory bone by the privations of this place.

"My dear sir," protested the hovering Dr. Daggett, "we don't permit—"

Alaric turned on him and seized him by the throat. Dr. Daggett, yellow eyeballs bulging, made inarticulate noises as long fingers tightened around his windpipe. Alaric slammed him against the wall and pinned him there with a vise-like grip on his throat. "I want her out of there, now!"

Through a series of strangulated syllables, Daggett gave

him to understand that he did not have the key. Alaric knocked him to the floor in disgust, suddenly realizing that Mrs. Clow was fleeing the ward, key rings jingling at her waist, cries of "Bart! Harvey!" emerging from her lips.

Alaric had no desire to meet either Bart or Harvey at this juncture, so he sped after Mrs. Clow, getting to the door a scant second before she did. Since she inspired very little chivalry in his breast, he swung her around and coldcocked her with a blow to the jaw. She went down like a sack of meal, and he tore away the key rings from her apron. There were four rings altogether, a dozen keys on each ring, and he realized to his chagrin that he hadn't the least notion of which of them opened Verity's chamber.

Daggett would undoubtedly know, however. Alaric grinned wolfishly as he beheld the good doctor sidling along the wall in the hope of escaping.

"Just the man I was looking for." He seized the cowering Daggett by the collar and frogmarched him through the crowd of bewildered inmates to Verity's door. "Now get that door open or I'll kill you with my bare hands."

Clearly terrified, Dr. Daggett began a fumbling search for the right key, while Verity held out a nearly transparent hand to Alaric as if to reassure herself that he was real.

"I struck you," she whispered, for it had been weighing on her mind that if she never saw him again, it would be his last memory of her. "Forgive me . . . those men in the shadows were waiting for you." A wild look came into her eye. "He was going to have you killed. He'll always come after me. He is coming after me now . . ."

No need to ask who.

"Hush, darling. He's nowhere near here."

"The hosts of the righteous are everywhere, Brathmere."

The words rolled down the row of reformatory cells and stopped the world.

Octavian Smythe filled the doorway, his Birmingham blade gleaming coldly in his hand.

Chapter Twenty-two

◆

In Which the Earl of Brathmere Wins the Battle But Not the War

*O*ctavian smiled ferociously. As he walked toward them, it could be seen that he had another sword girded to his waist.

Alaric knew the meaning of that second sword well enough, and he should have felt fear. But instead, something like exultation flooded through him. *At long last! A chance to finish him once and for all, for there'll be no peace for us in the world so long as he's in it.*

Octavian's sentiments ran similarly. "You've meddled in my affairs once too often, Brathmere. We'll finish this here, with no fencing master to interfere."

"Indeed, we shall," said Alaric, "and it will be my pleasure to skewer you like a roasted ox for what you've done to your cousin."

Octavian smiled grimly. "We'll see who skewers whom, Brathmere." His pale eyes flicked to Dr. Daggett, who stood frozen with shock, key ring dangling in his hand. "Daggett, stand away from that door. My cousin isn't going anywhere."

Verity had thought only for Alaric. "Alaric, don't fight him! Just get away from here . . ."

Alaric threw her a look over his shoulder, incredulous that she would even suggest such a thing. "Do you honestly think, my love, that I would leave you in this hellhole? Besides," he added grimly, "your cousin and I were fated to meet on the dueling field."

"But not here, not now," Verity tried to protest. "The sword is not your weapon, and he owns the creatures whose place this is, and he'll kill you and congratulate himself for it."

Alaric had already turned to face Octavian Smythe, who was stripping the riding coat from his heavy shoulders to reveal the abnormally developed sword arm bulging beneath the thin material of his white shirt.

"Tell me, Smythe," said Alaric, shrugging off his own coat and waistcoat, "if by some mischance you should manage to engineer my death in this encounter, how will you explain it to the authorities?"

"The truth will suffice, Brathmere." The granite eyes showed no flicker of uncertainty at the murder to come. "I come here to visit my poor ailing cousin, only to discover that once again you are trying to confound her with your lustful attractions. I discover you in the very act of spiriting her away and am justifiably enraged. We duel. You die. The good doctor witnesses all. And in the end, Brathmere, I don't think there will be overmany questions about your unfortunate demise, since it's generally assumed you were born to come to a bad end like your father before you."

"Very clever, Smythe," said Alaric with a grim little smile.

"Spare me your airs," snapped Octavian, "and look to your sword." And he tossed Alaric the spare rapier that he carried at his belt.

"How foresightful of you to carry this," observed Alaric, running his fingers along the blade, testing point and edge. "One would almost think you were expecting me."

"Your calling card mummery could not disguise you forever, Brathmere. Word of a gentleman seeking all the madhouses in the shire would inevitably be brought to my attention. I came at once to raise up my righteous sword in defense of my cousin."

"You had better," suggested Alaric gently, "look to the defense of your own neck first."

They wasted no more breath in parley or banter, nor did they bother with the ritual salute, but engaged at once, their blades running together with a venomous hiss.

Verity didn't want to watch, but she couldn't look away. She felt there could be but one outcome to this duel, that Octavian would win against Alaric as he had always won against her. If Alaric were to die, she would make herself watch. She would not spare herself the sight, for it was she who had brought him to this awful place.

Oh, Alaric, don't die. I love you so.

Fearfully she watched the two men circling, dodging, lunging, their blades crisscrossing and clanging as each searched for a breach in the other man's shifting wall of steel.

She watched as the blades swung together in great arcing strokes, each man after the other's lifeblood.

She watched as the famous Tierney temper got the better of Alaric and he lunged impetuously forward, aiming for his adversary's heart.

She watched as Octavian swept Alaric's sword aside and lunged forward himself to open up a long bloody slash in Alaric's upper arm.

"First blood!" roared Octavian triumphantly and smiled in the dark depths of his soul. "I'll rest you now, my prancing cavalier. See if I don't."

Though jolted with agony, his sword arm a welter of fresh blood, Alaric kept his sword in hand, parrying Octavian's thrusts. *Are you the man to lay Alaric Tierney in his grave? No, by God, no.*

The tide had turned against Alaric, though.

Octavian, with the tactical eye of a professional swordsman for his terrain, had noted the pitfalls of the reformatory ward. Now, with a storm of thrusts aimed at jugular, heart, and guts, he drove his wounded antagonist back toward the corner of the ward where the straw was scattered thickest. As purposefully, calculatingly, and pitilessly as he had drawn a net of fear around the little girl Verity, now he would draw a net of steel around her champion.

Parrying desperately, Alaric fell back, and as Octavian had hoped, slipped to one knee, his sword whipping reflexively to one side in his weakening hand. It was the opening for which Octavian was waiting. His heavy sword swung like the Grim Reaper's blade and broke Alaric's sword beneath his in a blow that struck blue sparks on the stone floor.

The eighth Earl of Brathmere was disarmed and on bended

knee before Octavian Smythe, with Smythe's Birmingham blade poised to let the blue blood out of his lordship's throat.

But Octavian being Octavian could not resist pontificating a little upon the occasion of his victory. "Tell your master in hell," he grated out in deep whistling breaths, "that he has a mighty enemy in Octavian Smythe."

Neither man had heard a faint urgent voice calling. "Sic him, Lady. Sic the bad man."

The Dog Lady sicced. She bounded across the space between them, and before the dumbfounded Octavian could react, she grasped hold of his arm and sank her teeth in it while Alaric, quick as a striking snake, slashed at Octavian's bulging thigh with his three inches of maimed sword. Roaring with pain and fury, hampered by ninety pounds of female lunatic gnawing on his arm, Octavian staggered to his knees. He switched his sword to his free hand, and Alaric knew in another second he would use that sword with deadly effectiveness on the crazed woman that hung on to him like a leech.

The Dog Lady had acquired some allies, however, for the blood and violence of the struggle spread like a contagion to the more violent of the lunatics. They set upon Octavian tooth and nail, like she-wolves upon a wounded bull. Octavian roared, struggling to shake them off, but Alaric, gritting his teeth against the pain in his arm, delivered his best taproom brawler's right to Octavian's jaw, then followed it up with another deadly left to the chin. Octavian's eyes rolled white and he fell to the floor with a crashing thud.

The Dog Lady rose up beside him with a triumphant howl.

Octavian Smythe was felled, but Alaric was under no illusions that he would stay down. In a few minutes Smythe would be up and charging again like a maddened bull. Fortunately, in Dr. Daggett's reformatory there were numerous instruments capable of restraining him.

Shooing away the triumphantly capering madwomen, he took hold of Octavian's booted feet. Panting with exertion, he dragged Octavian to the nearest shackle and closed it about his thick neck.

Now his reward—for Dr. Daggett, seeing how the fight had gone, had prudently found the key to Verity's cell—and she was winging to him, light and frail as a bird at the end of win-

er, to be held fast in his embrace, for he did not mean to let
her go again.

Then an imperative yelp broke into their charmed circle—
the Dog Lady tugging at Verity's sleeve, an eerie look of
Spaniel-like devotion on her face.

"We must take her with us," Verity told Alaric. "They will
punish her terribly if we leave her behind."

"We owe her that much, at least," Alaric agreed, though he
beheld the female lunatic with an inward shake of his head. He
suspected that she was but the first of a long line of odd and
distressed personages who would be coming into his care
thanks to his future wife.

Verity sighed against him, reveling in the vital strength and
life of him after having seen him come so close to death.
"Let's go away from here before Octavian wakes up. I never
want to see him again."

"In a moment, darling." Alaric's voice was light but very
menacing. He stooped to pick up Octavian's Birmingham
sword. "I very much desire to see your cousin once more."

He prodded the massive fallen figure with his boot. Octavian stirred, his face contorting into murderous fury when he
realized what had been done to him. Alaric stood above him,
sword in hand, frankly enjoying the sensation of placing the
point of it right where the heart beat in the barrel chest. He
pressed the sword point a little harder and smiled. It was not a
pretty smile.

"So," he told his antagonist, "you have a message for the
devil in hell, do you? Well, now you can tell him yourself."

"Alaric, no!" cried Verity, alarmed by the savage look on his
dark face. "You can't kill him."

"Can't I?" said Alaric silkily, for every instinct of self-
preservation told him that Octavian Smythe must die. *Kill
him!* howled the wild Tierney devils in his soul. *He's earned
his death a dozen times over for what he's done. Kill him now!*

"Go ahead and do it!" rasped Octavian. "Martyr me, if you
have the stomach for killing a chained man."

"No, Alaric, no!" Verity put her chilled hands on either side
of Alaric's sweat-drenched face and forced him to look away
from his fallen enemy and at her. "He can't hurt me anymore,
and did you not tell me that you would know how to guard

your own?" She looked down at Octavian, her childhood terror, almost pityingly. "I don't know how it has happened, bu
in him we Thornroses have bred a viper. But it's still my bloo
in his veins and I won't have it on your hands—and I won'
have another death on your soul."

Damping down the wild Tierney devils that clamored fo
vengeance, Alaric slowly took his sword from his enemy'
breast. "I hope we don't live to regret this," he said somberly.

"One can never regret showing mercy," said Verity wit
simple certainty.

Alaric was not so sure about that, in fact he was very certai
that Octavian Smythe would war on them again. Yet, he coul
not murder Verity's kinsman before her eyes, however much i
would have pleased the Tierney devils in his soul to do so, fo
his soul belonged to her now.

Chapter Twenty-three

~~~

In Which Sundry Interesting Entries Are Made in the Thornrose Book of Good Works

Miss Verity Thornrose has this day brought into our home an Unfortunate Creature afflicted with Canine Dementia. It is to be hoped that the application of kindness and upright example will effect a cure upon this poor woman, and in the meantime, she is fine company for Comfort and Prudence . . .

Miss Faith Thornrose has used her good offices among the clergy to procure a living for the Rev. Cyrus Mortlock on the Canadian Island of Labrador . . .

Miss Hope Thornrose has prevailed upon a Select Committee of the Royal College of Physicians and Surgeons to make a Critical Study of a Selected Private Reformatory in the Fens . . .

Miss Charity Thornrose has this day purchased passage to New South Wales for our faithful servant Raphael Bowen and his bride. We wish them Godspeed.

While the Thornrose ladies occupied themselves with sundry good deeds, the Earl of Brathmere occupied his time less benignly with private fencing lessons preparing for the day when he would issue Octavian Smythe another invitation to swords. Verity, learning of this, realized that her beloved was not as reformed as she had thought.

Meanwhile, the flash king White Willie scuttled like a pink eyed rat through the twisted tenement alleys of Seven Dials, cursing all his enemies; a certain fat merchant was totaling up the red figures in the column reserved for his India flesh trade and swearing that one day he would balance the books in his favor; and Octavian Smythe sat in his marble counting house, nursing his bitten arm and his bitter grudge, yet triumphant in the knowledge that the angels had protected him when he lay chained in iron with Brathmere's steel at his breast, and so would the angels protect him still when next he came up against the demon earl.

On a midsummer afternoon when the roses were at their highest bloom, Miss Verity Thornrose and Alaric Tierney, the Earl of Brathmere, were married at St. George's Church in Hanover Square. They made a striking pair, opined the wedding guests, with Miss Thornrose so virginally beautiful ("Ah, the wedding-night ravishment of such beauty," thought the gentlemen guests enviously) and the earl so handsome, his dark eyes glittering rakehellishly hot at the first sight of his lovely bride in the church aisle. ("Oh," sighed the lady guests longingly, "to be ravished by such a rake.")

That evening, after the happy couple had departed to the delights of the wedding night and the bliss of a country honeymoon, the following was inscribed in the *Thornrose Book of Good Works*:

On this day, Miss Verity Valora Mercy Patience Thornrose has wed the Right Honourable Earl of Brathmere and embarked upon a lifelong project of reform.

Historical Note

All the reform societies and charitable organizations mentioned in connection with the Thornrose family actually existed during the Regency period. As for the chimney sweep legislation that Verity Thornrose so passionately championed, it is unlikely that she lived to see it passed. It was not until the year 1874, in the thirty-eighth year of the reign of Queen Victoria, that a bill banning the use of climbing boys was passed by both houses of Parliament.

G. B.

About the Author

Geraldine Burrows *was born and raised in the Shenandoah Valley of Virginia and spent her earliest years living on the campus of a school for the deaf and blind, where her parents were teachers. Since completing her education, she has worked as a journalist, a community organizer, and a staff member of a legal aid office. She now lives in a seaport village in Rhode Island. She spends her non-writing time with her husband, two sons, a backyard garden, and a pair of calico cats.*

"This debut novel heralds the arrival
of a major new Regency writer."
—*Dallas Morning News*

THE SPINSTER AND
THE WASTREL
by
Louise Bergin

When Nigel Montfort dies, leaving his estate
to Miss Courtney, she establishes a school.
Left out of the will, the prodigal nephew
Gerald is outraged—until Courtney gives
him a lesson in love.

"Lively Regency...
A new voice to watch."
—Amanda McCabe

0-451-21012-3

S412